The Blue Suitcase

Marianne Wheelaghan

Marianne Wheelaghan

Published 2010 by Pilrig Press, Edinburgh, Scotland

Second printing 2011

ISBN 978-0-9566144-0-7

www.pilrigpress.co.uk

Printed in Great Britain by Imprint Digital

For Josée and Jack

If war should come, whichever side might claim the ultimate victory, nothing is more certain than this: that victor and vanquished alike would glean a gruesome harvest of human suffering and misery.

Prime Minister Neville Chamberlain,
July 31, 1939, to the House of Commons

Prologue

Mum was eighty-two when she died. I discovered the suitcase three months later. Her flat was to be sold. I was waiting for the estate agent to come and view it. Except for a feather duster forgotten in the airing cupboard, a kitchen chair and the big mahogany wardrobe, the place was empty.

Bored waiting for the agent, who was late, I took the feather duster and flicked here and there at dusty sills and skirting boards. I quickly found myself in Mum's bedroom, where she'd died. The big wardrobe was all that remained of her presence, somehow it had got left behind when the house had been cleared. It was chilly in the room. I checked to see if the window was closed. It was. A number fourteen bus rumbled past. The fourteen had been Mum's favourite bus. There was a stop in front of the flat and the bus took you to the centre of Edinburgh within fifteen minutes.

I glanced around outside. Still no sign of the agent. I turned and gave the top of the wardrobe a dandy birl with the duster. There was a plopping sound. The head of the duster disappeared inside its ornately carved top. I groaned. I didn't have a feather duster at home and I had taken a fancy to this one. I got the chair from the kitchen, sat it next to the wardrobe, hopped on, stretched up and blindly groped around for the duster head. I felt the hard surface of the case immediately. After a bit more groping I managed to manoeuvre it up and out and onto the ground.

It was almost small enough to be a child's suitcase and covered in gritty fluff. I wiped the muck off and immediately cursed myself – I had nothing to clean the mess off the floor with. The case was made from old-fashioned, blue hardboard and covered in scuff marks.

Three dog-eared travel stickers sat bunched in the bottom left corner: the first one was a yellow rectangle with a red edge. A small yellow and white flag dominated the one side of the sticker and a picture of a church the other. Between the two pictures bold red lettering said HIRSCHBERG IM RIESENGEBIRGE. This sticker overlapped a solid, grey square with a yellow border, which was filled with the orange silhouette of a palatial building. The words PALACE HOTEL shimmered across the top of the sticker and the word BERLIN glittered below. And then there was the last one, a black edged, brilliant yellow rectangle with a navy blue steam train in the middle of it and the word BRESLAU in blue bold letters across the bottom. Mum said she'd gone to school in a town called Hirschberg.

I'd not seen the case before but it had the feel of one of Mum's bargains about it. Once, at one of the many jumble sales Mum had dragged me to when I was wee, she'd wanted to buy a suitcase similar to this. It had been much bigger and had far more travel stickers on it. I was mortified when she'd started to haggle with the elderly spinster selling it, who still had her bunnet on even though it was summer and we were inside a church hall. In the end Mum had said that at 50 pence it was ridiculously *teur*.

As she'd marched me home, she said she'd liked the case because of the stickers. In the olden days it was hugely impressive to have such stickers on your luggage. However, what most travellers didn't know then was that the positioning of the sticker on a suitcase had a significance – it was the way porters in one hotel told porters in another hotel what kind of guest the traveller was: bad tipper or good tipper, rude or friendly etc. It never occurred to me to ask her how she knew this. Had she been a guest in one of those fancy hotels or had she worked in one? I knew nothing of Mum's life before she'd come to Scotland. No one did.

The little snib on the case was rusted but it clicked open easily, making a tinny echoing noise as it did so. As the lid fell back a warm smell of fried eggs, daffodils and stale cigarettes wafted into the room. The inside was crammed with greying tatty jotters, full of the smallest handwriting I had ever seen. There were newspaper cuttings, sepia postcards and dozens of letters. I thought I recognised Mum's spindly German script on one of the envelopes and gingerly picked it up. It was postmarked 1966, Argentina, and had Mum's name and address on the front. I turned it over, it was from her sister Hilde. She'd lived in Argentina until she died. She never married.

A second letter caught my eye. It had yellowed with age and had two blue stamps in the corner which had twin propeller planes on them. Both stamps had the words Deutsches Reich along the bottom edge and Feldpost along the top. It was postmarked 06.06.1941 and addressed to Mum. It was from her brother Hubert. Below his name were the letters FP followed by the number 45932 – all in the same spindly German script that Mum used.

I peeked inside the envelope. It seemed empty. I tilted it to check. A tiny, brittle flower – perhaps a forget-me-not – floated out and landed on the floor. I picked it up and it instantly disintegrated between my fingers. The feel of the fragile broken skeleton against my damp skin made me feel slightly sick. I wiped the crumpled flower off my sticky hand, put the debris back in the envelope, put the envelope back in the case and closed the lid.

For months I couldn't decide whether to read Mum's diaries and letters or not – I'd studied German at university, and thought I'd manage somehow. I worried that reading her personal correspondence would violate her privacy, Mum had been a very remote person. Not chatty or open like other mums. Finally, my curiosity got the better of me. I told myself finding the suitcase was my chance to get to know her, and if I came across anything of a delicate nature, I would not translate it.

It took me months to read the contents of the suitcase. I did not come across anything delicate. Instead, I discovered the story of a vital person, who endured a shocking history, and this is why I have translated everything and put it in book form here. Simply put, her story deserves to be told.

In translating everything I tried to be as accurate as I could. However, my German is rusty so there is a good chance I've made errors or used words and phrases that are inappropriate. This may be especially true in the early extracts when I was still getting the hang of what I was doing – and where I am especially conscious that some of the vocabulary I have used may seem too grown-up for a young person. Furthermore, many of the jotters and letters are in such bad condition that some of the entries are illegible. This means that from time to time I've had to make a guess at what Mum has written. Finally, some of the letters posted to Mum during the Siege of Breslau – or Battle of Breslau – were marked 'returned to sender' and not received by Mum until later. For convenience, however, I've presented these letters in the order they were sent rather than received.

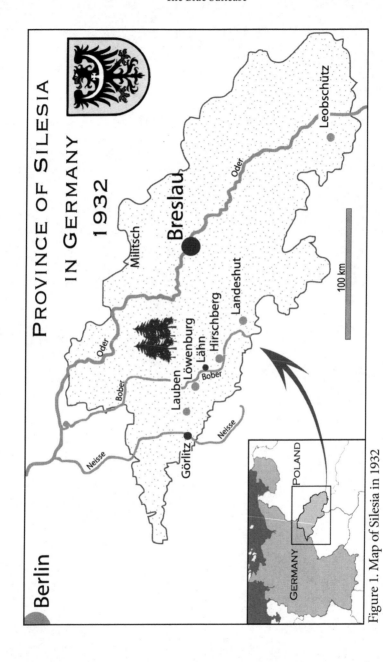

Figure 1. Map of Silesia in 1932

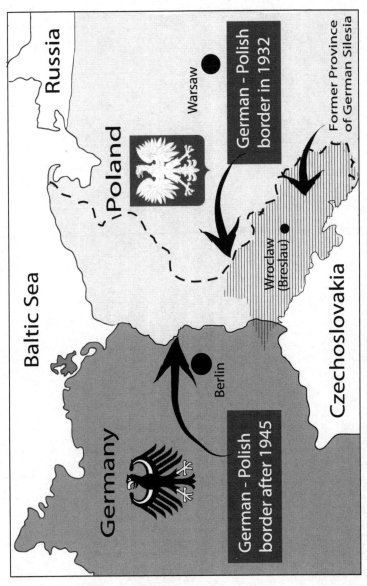

Figure 2. German-Polish border in 1932 and the border after 1945.

1932–1935

June 12th, 1932

I am Antonia Cecelia Nasiski. I am nearly twelve years old and I live in Kaiser Wilhelm Strasse, Breslau, Lower Silesia, Prussia, Germany, the World.

At school today my teacher, Sister Gertrude, said she hoped I would enter the school's Francis de Sales writing competition next year because, she said, I am very good with words. Every year since 1923, when Pope Pius XI proclaimed Francis de Sales the patron saint of writers and journalists because of the books he wrote, my school has held the big story writing competition

You can only enter if you are twelve or over. I am almost twelve and by next year I will be able to enter. When I told Mama what my teacher said she raised her eyebrows in a big questioning arch and said, 'Even Maria didn't win that competition.'

'Sister Gertrude must think I have a chance or she wouldn't have suggested it,' I said, trying not to feel cross.

'Maybe,' said Mama, sounding very unconvinced, 'but to be good at something, you usually need to practise it regularly. I've never seen you write anything.'

'But Sister Gertrude–'

'That's as may be,' she said interrupting me, 'but I'd rather you concentrated on passing your end of term exams than daydream about what might or might not happen next year.'

It's impossible to be good enough for Mama and Papa when it comes to schooling. Papa was very clever at school and could have gone to university but Opa made him leave school and get a job. And Mama is a doctor, which means she is very clever indeed.

I told Maria what Sister Gertrude had said and she was very excited for me. 'Excellent! Maybe one day you'll be as good as Thomas Mann and write another *Buddenbrooks*.' I hadn't heard of *Buddenbrooks*. She said *Buddenbrooks* was a famous story about a German family. So I have made a decision. I am going to write about my family and I will write every day – which will be my 'practice' – and by next year I will be so good at writing I will win the story prize and make Mama and Papa proud of me.

I'll miss Maria when she leaves. As soon as she's nineteen, which is only in half a year, Papa is sending her to a cloister in Holland where she is going to train to be a nun. Papa says this will be an excellent education for her. Holland is really far away. I don't want her to go but Maria says she has to go, that it's her "calling" to be a nun.

Hilde says she wants to be a nun too, but Papa says he can only afford to send one of his daughters away and that, of course, it must be the eldest one. Anyway, everyone knows Maria is much more intelligent than Hilde. Papa says Hilde can go to the local secretarial college if she does well enough at school.

When Papa and Mama aren't around Hilde says Maria is Mama's favourite and it's Mama who wants Maria to go to Holland. She says if it were just up to Papa she knows he would send her, his little St Therese, because he likes her best. That is, of course, nonsense! She is not his favourite, otherwise Papa's nickname for her wouldn't be 'little Therese'.

Sister Gertrude says St Therese was a very ordinary saint, who never performed any great works. 'She is a simple reminder to all of us that we can still help keep God's kingdom growing by doing little things when we can.' Papa would never favour anyone so ordinary. Of course, I don't say this to Hilde.

Whenever she blabs on about how Papa really favours her – his little flower, his little St Therese – I remind her that Papa calls Maria his little St Agnes. That shuts her up. Everyone knows that not only was St Agnes as pure as snow and hated sin more than death, she was so beautiful that every man who met her wanted to marry her. Hilde hates me saying this because she can't stand the thought that Maria is prettier than her, which she is. Anyway, Papa says Maria is the one who's going to be a nun, so that's that.

June 15th, 1932

School was awful. It's so unfair. I am not even twelve years old, so how am I supposed to know what a 'sufragen' bishop is! Sister Gertrude said I'd not done my homework. I thought I was going to get caned. But then she must have had a brainwave or something because instead of whacking me with her stick she sent Anna Dorothea – she always sits in the front – to get Hilde from the big ones' class. I thought my luck was in. But when big sister Hildegarde was asked if I had done my homework, she replied very loudly, 'No, Antonia did not do her homework last night!' For the rest of the day I had to sit in the corner with my back to the class – and I got an extra big whack across the back of the legs for telling lies.

I hate Hildegarde. I hate her! I hate her! I hate her!

June 18th, 1932

I was walking through the Old Town and a rascally boy came up to me and punched me right in the face. I ran all the way home and told Mama. All she did was frown and say, 'How many times have I told you not to go into the Old Town? Eh?' which made me feel a hundred times worse. 'But –' I wailed, 'I was just walking along, doing nothing!' 'I tell you what I think,' said Mama, 'you should go right back, find this lad and you punch him back. Don't let him get away with it.' Then she turned away and went back to reading her paper.

I couldn't believe it. Of course I wasn't going to go back there. What, so he could box my ears as well? I fled to my room and burst into tears. I hate Mama sometimes. I bet you no other mother would prefer to read the newspaper than help her daughter. That's all she does when she gets home from work now, read the paper and talk about the elections. This will be the fourth one in five months – blah, blah, blah. I don't know if I want to write about my family any more.

July 30th, 1932

It is my birthday. I am 12 years old. I deliberately came down late to breakfast. Maria, Hilde, Mama and Hubert were eating. No one said anything when I walked in. I sat down and smeared quark on some grey bread. Surely they hadn't forgotten it was my birthday? Papa had already gone out. Hansi was still in bed – since what Mama calls 'the cuts', his university course has been cancelled and now Hansi is never up before breakfast. Papa would be furious if he knew, but Hansi is Mama's favourite – never Maria, as Hilde says – and she lets him get away with anything.

Erna, our maid, was due at eight. I hate her. She's stupid and smells and talks funny. Mama says I have to be nice to her because her family are very poor. Hilde says Erna's Mama died in childbirth and her father was killed in the Bloody May riots of 1929. Erna lives with her Oma. I don't know what the Bloody May riots are, but it doesn't change the fact she smells. Then suddenly, just when I thought they really had forgotten Mama smiled and said 'Happy birthday' and the other three cheered and Mama took a book from out of the big pickling pot that sits on the iron shelf above the stove. *Emil and the Detectives*! It's all crisp and shiny and smelling of freshly cut grass. Maria gave me a tiny silver cross – she'd been hiding it on her lap – and 'from Hansi', she said, and gave me a special journal. Inside, on the very first page, Hansi has sketched a picture of me sitting at the kitchen table writing in a book. Mama said how much it looked like me and everyone agreed and I felt so happy because the girl looks so pretty and clever.

A new book to write in! Even Hilde gave me a present – a small flower press, which I'm sure I've seen before in her room, but anyway. Hubert gave me a magnifying glass just like the one the British detective Sherlock Holmes has. Then Mama had another surprise: we were all going to Kaufhaus Barasch on the Market Square am Ring for lunch, even Papa and Hansi would be coming. We all cheered! Kaufhaus Barasch is the absolutely fanciest and most expensive department store in all of Breslau. When I told my best friend Belen she said Kaufhaus Wertheim is much bigger and better than Haus Barasch – according to Belen, Kaufhaus Wertheim is the only department store in the whole of Silesia which has escalators, but I don't believe her. She also said if I was going to eat anywhere it has to be at the Monopol because that has the best food, and that's where Hitler stayed when he came in April. She's just jealous. I can't wait.

Evening of July 30th, 1932

The best day of my life has turned out to be the worst day of my life.

When we reached Haus Barasch Papa was there already and despite the heat he looked cool and smart in his stripy suit and brown felt hat (Hubert says it's called a Homburg hat). As soon as he saw us approach he lifted up his arm and made a great show of looking at his wrist watch – Papa loves his silver Cyma military watch. He's never done winding it up. His father gave it to him when Papa was an officer in the Big War. It's the only thing Papa has from Opa Nasiski, because at the end of the Big War Opa Nasiski lost everything and committed suicide, well that's what Hubert says. It's supposed to be a big secret but if Hubert knows, everyone must know.

Hubert says the watch is very expensive. It's much bigger and stronger than Mama's tiny little wristlet. It has a chunky brown leather strap and a handsome white porcelain enamel dial, which is protected by a solid silver cover with little round holes punched out of it to show where the numbers are. There's a further central hole, which shows the hands where they meet in the middle as they sweep round. Papa says that without this

Kaufhaus Barasch, Breslau

precision timepiece he could have never got to battles on time. For Papa, punctuality is everything.

When Papa looked up from the watch, he frowned as if to suggest we were late, which we weren't because the clock on the town hall opposite showed three minutes to one. He said, 'Hans Joachim?' When Papa is cross he calls everyone by their full name. I'm Antonia, never Toni, Hilde is Hildegarde and Maria is Eva Maria – Hubert is just Hubert, of course. Mama smiled and told Papa that Hansi was on his way and then they immediately began talking about the elections, again! He never even said, 'Happy birthday' to me, which wasn't very nice.

We all waited by the big display windows of Haus Barasch for Hansi. People rushed about all dressed in their brightest summer clothes, laughing and joking. It was as if the whole world was celebrating my birthday. Out of nowhere a cyclist whizzed passed us. He nearly knocked Mama over. 'Oye!' Papa yelled after him. The cyclist didn't even look back. Instead he darted across the square, just missing two clip-clopping horses pulling a wagon piled high with hay. The horses neighed and back-stepped on their hind legs. The sweet smelling hay wobbled dangerously. A big black car coming behind the cart had to swerve to avoid it and hooted angrily at the cart driver, who shouted at the cyclist, but the cyclist just grinned cheekily and dodged away. It was crazy!

Somewhere far away a hammer clattered against metal. Bubbles of chatter tumbled from the diners sitting at the street cafés next to the town hall opposite. Then a tram whooshed by and a swirl of dusty election leaflets flew up from the pavement and wafted into the air. Hubert grabbed one as it floated back down and stuffed it into his pocket. Hilde saw him and frowned.

Hilde is never happy unless she is frowning. Maria is the opposite, she's always smiling. Just then she was smiling at two Brownshirts standing at the advertising pillar on the corner. 'You'd better not let Papa see you making eyes at them,' tutted Hilde. Maria laughed. 'I'm not "making eyes" at them, I'm just nodding a hello to Georg,' she said. 'He's Hansi's friend from school.' At the mention of Hansi's name Papa turned round just in time to see two more Brownshirts appear, coming from the direction of the Mary Magdalene church. All four made the Heil Hitler salute to each other and that was all Papa needed to set him off.

'Will you look at that ridiculous salute!' he said.

'Are there really so few jobs that those poor boys have to join the SA Sturmabteilung to get some money?' said Mama.

'Hasn't the SA been banned?' said Hilde.

Papa said, 'Let them join the army if they want to wear a uniform. I've a good mind to call for a policeman!'

Maria took his arm and laughed, 'But they're doing nothing wrong, Papa.'

'Nothing wrong!' Papa's face turned dark red. 'They're lazy, good-for-nothing yobs, who can't be bothered to find real work. The private army of a jumped-up painter and decorator! They're behind all the trouble on the streets!'

Mama sighed and looked around. 'Everyone looks so happy today. It's almost impossible to believe there are millions of people unemployed and starving.'

Hilde nodded, 'Did you see that queue outside the unemployment office? It went all the way around the block and back. They say people wait for days on end on the off-chance of being given work. It must be awful to have no work.'

'What is going to become of our dear Germany?' said Mama all seriously. And then Papa said something about Kaiser Wilhelm and how things would have been different if only he had still been in charge and how the Weimar Republic was the ruin of all that was good in Germany. It was typical. They were turning my perfectly wonderful birthday into something all boring and serious.

We would have still been there listening to Papa's lecturing had Maria not said, 'Should we not wait for Hansi inside, Papa? They may think we're not coming otherwise and give our table away.' And Papa mumbled something that sounded like okay. Hurray! So one by one we followed Papa through the revolving door and into the department store. Hubert went round twice and that made us all laugh – even Hilde.

The first thing we saw was a group of male dummies lounging around a billiard table. They wore stripy summer blazers and cream slacks and straw hats, which Hubert said are called straw boaters. I don't know if he knows what he's talking about sometimes. Behind the dummies – Hubert says they're called mannequins, not dummies! – two parallel rows of mahogany counters stretched into a huge hall. Mama said the counters held rows of little wooden drawers packed full of exquisite clothes wrapped in the softest cream tissue.

On the first counter sat the top half of a dummy with no arms and a black shiny head with no features. The body of the dummy was smothered in fluffy white, feather boas. On the counter directly opposite stood a metal hatstand. Four metallic arms stretched out from its centre pole. Each skinny arm held a shiny black top hat – the top two hats were open full, all shimmering and velvety, while the bottom two hats were half-closed.

Our feet squeaked as we walked on the wooden floor and Hubert and me giggled. A cascade of shimmering chandeliers winked above our heads. The scent of lavender water and polish was overwhelming. A very tall man appeared, wearing a uniform. He looked like a general from the army. In a stiff voice he asked Papa if we needed help. Papa said we were going to eat. The man replied, 'The restaurant is upstairs. The lifts are by the staircase,' and pointed towards two wrought iron doors covered in golden swirls at the end of the hall. Papa nodded a thank you to the man but then muttered to Mama, 'How dare he wear such a uniform for shop work!' But before he could moan any further Maria had put her arm in Papa's arm and whisked him off. Mama and Hilde followed behind them, and Hubert and me came last.

It was exciting and scary at the same time. I wished I'd polished my sandals and my blouse had somehow wriggled its way free of the waist band of my dirndl skirt. I quickly tucked it back in. Maria looked gorgeous, of course. Her short blond, bobbed

Bubikopf is always perfect and sleek, and her blue dress was all fresh and flowing. Mama too looked beautiful in her red dress with the little daisy pattern on it and her white lacy cardigan over her shoulders. Her chestnut hair was tied up in a soft bun at the back – I like it like that. Hilde had on her long green pencil skirt and white blouse. Her short hair is more mousy brown than chestnut – even though she says it isn't – and she looked cross. She always looks cross. Hubert says it's because she's thinking pious thoughts, but I don't know if he means it, you can never tell with Hubert.

Papa always looks handsome. Mama says it's because he's a *Beamte* and has to wear his jacket and hat even when the weather is hot like it is today. Mama said he will never become unemployed because *Beamtes* are government officials or civil servants.

I was so proud of everyone, except maybe Hubert, who was in his shorts, of course, and looked as if he'd been kicked around a football pitch by a pack of Brownshirts. Papa says he'll never amount to anything if he doesn't buck up his ideas, which isn't fair, he is only thirteen.

The lift man wore white gloves, black shiny trousers and a gleaming white shirt under a stripy waistcoat. He didn't seem to see us, not even when Papa greeted him, which made Papa cross again – it doesn't take a lot to make Papa cross. As soon as we were all inside, the lift man slammed the iron gates shut and pressed a golden button on the side of the wall. There was a whooshing noise and the lift wobbled and then we surged upwards. I felt giddy. This was my first time in a lift. Could flying be like this? Within seconds it stopped again and we were there.

The restaurant sizzled with excitement. Some people waved their arms about while they ate, others whispered in huddles. Waiters and waitresses swooped to and from the kitchen and bar area, their arms laden with either bowls of steaming food or stacks of dirty plates. Black venetian blinds dressed six tall windows on the wall to the right. The early afternoon sun slipped through the slatted openings, sending gentle orange wedges of light dancing across the diners.

In the left corner of the room a skinny man in a light grey suit sat at a black grand piano. He played soft chirpy music while smoking a cigarette. A waitress, all in black except for a small frilly white apron and a tiny frilly maid's hat, led us to the nearest window table on the right. It was wonderful: all white tablecloths and napkins and triple sets of forks and knives and crystal cut water and wine glasses.

Papa took his hat off and held it out for the waitress to take from him, which she eventually did. I took the window seat. Mama sat down opposite me and immediately started fanning herself with the little Spanish fan she always keeps in her bag. I hoped the waitress would hurry back. The air was warm with the smell of fried onions and garlic and it made me feel hungry. I was so excited.

When our waitress returned I was ready to give her my order: hot potato salad and white sausage, followed by cheesecake. My favourites. But before I was even halfway through ordering, Papa held up his big hand and said, 'Stop! We are waiting for my son, Hans Joachim. Kindly come back when he has arrived.' The waitress shrugged and left. I was so cross. I wanted to shout, 'It's my birthday, not Hans Joachim's!' But you can't argue with Papa, not even on your birthday.

Mama began fanning herself a little bit more quickly. 'I'm sure he'll be here soon. It isn't like him. Maria, did he say anything to you about being late?' Maria shook her head, 'No, but isn't this just the most posh place you've ever seen?' And Mama said she'd been to much fancier restaurants and we all begged her to tell us one of her stories about her fancy life in Berlin before she met Papa. But before she could start Papa frowned and said to her, 'It's already ten past one.' And Mama said to Papa in her soft voice, 'I am sure there will be a perfectly logical explanation.' And then I began to get this nasty feeling in my stomach. Papa was getting a bee in his bonnet. And once that happens no amount of Mama's soft talking can help. Papa frowned and we waited while Mama fanned herself faster and faster.

Eventually the waitress was back asking for our orders again. Papa pointed to Hansi's empty place and said, 'Can you see my son?' The waitress looked confused. Papa said, 'We will order when he arrives.' The waitress went away again but returned almost immediately. She apologised then said there was a queue of people waiting to eat, if we didn't order soon we may have to vacate the table. Papa turned grey and said very loudly, 'Vacate the table?' Everyone turned to look. 'Vacate the table!' he said again, this time even more loudly than the first time. He stood up. 'Vacate the table it is then! My hat, please!' He strode across to the lifts. Pink-faced, the waitress scuttled off to get his hat.

Mama got up. 'I am going to go after your father,' she whispered. Her voice was all tight and anxious. 'But Mama,' I said, 'It's my birthday meal!' 'Can you think of no one but yourself, you selfish little girl!' she hissed. And then the worst thing in my whole life happened – with the whole restaurant looking, Mama slapped me across the face! Everyone gasped. I burst into tears and Mama marched away. Just then another waitress appeared with my potato salad, which had been ordered after all. An older waiter whispered something in her ear and she promptly turned and took it away. I'll never be able to smell sweet mayonnaise or fresh parsley again without thinking about that horrible moment. It was so awful. For a moment or two none of us knew what to do. Then the older waiter started to remove the water glasses and jug of water we had been drinking from. It was as if we were invisible. 'We have to go,' whispered Hilde, and in as dignified a manner as we could, we stood up and left.

All the way home I couldn't stop crying, even though Maria put her arm in mine and kept saying, 'Mama didn't mean it, she's worried about Papa and Hansi, that's all.' Hilde kept saying, 'How humiliating, how humiliating.' Only Hubert seemed not to be bothered, he just skipped along beside us, whistling silly tunes all the while with his hands in his pockets and kicking at the leaflets on the ground – Mama would have told him off for that.

And now my face still stings and no one knows where Hansi is and Mama and Papa have been called away somewhere. This is the worst birthday I have ever had.

I hate Papa and I hate Mama and I really, really, really hate Hansi, it's all his fault my meal was ruined.

31st July, 1932

Today when I got downstairs Erna was already in the kitchen slobbering down her breakfast. Hubert and Hilde were also there. Hilde said Mama and Papa had gone to vote, Maria had gone with them. I was about to ask if there was any news about Hansi, but she warned me with a frown to say nothing in front of Erna.

Erna took ages. Stuffing her face with our food. While we waited, Hilde reminded her to clean the hearth later. Hilde had to tell her three times before she nodded that she'd understood. She is so THICK! Finally, she finished. Hubert checked behind the door after she'd gone to make sure she wasn't hiding behind it trying to listen in because she does that.

Finally, Hilde said, 'Yesterday, when Hansi didn't turn up for the meal, it was because he was in jail.' I hadn't been expecting that.

Hubert slapped the table with his hand and laughed, 'Hansi, the brainbox, a criminal!'

Hilde told him to keep his voice down. 'He is not a criminal,' she said, 'it was all a big mistake. Some vandal painted a hammer and sickle on the town hall wall and because Hansi is a member of the Communist Party and happened to be seen nearby, the police hauled him in for questioning. Hansi, being Hansi, was not cooperative so they locked him up. Then, even though they found the real vandal, they refused to let Hansi go until Papa went to the station and vouched for him.'

Hubert looked bored. 'Is that it?'

Hilde scowled, 'I don't think it could have been a very pleasant experience for him, even if he did contribute to it by being antagonistic.'

'So,' I said, feeling a little bit more cheerful, 'if it was all a mistake, maybe Mama will say we can have my birthday meal now?'

Hilde looked uncomfortable, 'I'm sorry, Toni, I think you'll have to forget your birthday meal. You see,' she took a deep breath, 'Papa now knows Hansi is a member of the Communist Party and he's absolutely furious.'

Hubert groaned, 'We'll never hear the end of it.'

'It's not fair.'

'No, it's not,' said Hilde.

My birthday was ruined because of Hansi and now no second chance of a special meal at a posh restaurant just because he's in the *Kommunistische Partei Deutschlands*. Who cares if he is? We kids have known about it since January. Papa must have been the only one who didn't know. I'm sure even Mama did.

Hansi had been on a study trip in Berlin. It was late when he got back. He came to find us. We were in Maria and Hilde's room. Maria had lit a stubby candle on her dresser. The flame blinked and fluttered and threw wiggly shadows everywhere. She'd been telling us ghost stories and Hubert and me had snuggled under the covers we were so scared. Hansi burst into the room.

He was all excited, he wanted to know if we'd heard the old Walrus's speech on the radio – that's what Hansi calls President Hindenburg, the old pious Walrus. Papa would be furious if he knew. When we said we hadn't, he said he would repeat it as it was too good to miss.

So, still with his outdoor coat on, he cleared his throat and began to hobble between Maria and Hilde's beds. 'Let us face the coming days and their trials hand-in-hand,' he said in an old, decrepit voice. He's so good at impersonating people. 'Let us not waver ... The Lord has saved Germany from deep distress before. He will not forsake us now –' Then suddenly Hansi straightened himself right up and shouted, 'ATTENTION! The shadow of Communism is over Germany! PROLETARIANS UNITE!'

Hilde and Maria squealed. I screamed and Hubert got such a shock he fell out of Maria's bed. And Hansi, well, he just threw himself on to Hilde's bed, his whole body shaking with laughter. 'That's exactly what millions of Germans did, jumped right out of their chairs!' He laughed and laughed. 'You see, Hindenburg's speech was sent out "live" via the telephone line from Berlin to Königs-Wusterhausen radio station. One of my pals worked for the Berlin Telephone Company until he got laid off. He knew exactly where everything was. He sneakily prised open a manhole and taped a microphone to the telephone cable carrying Hindenburg's voice. At just the right moment during Hindenburg's speech he cut into the cable and interrupted the broadcast. It was so funny!'

'You idiot!' snapped Hilde, 'Mama and Papa will have heard you shouting!' We all scarpered back to our rooms. Just as I reached my bed I heard Mama asking Maria what all the noise was about and Maria say she'd had a nightmare.

Thinking about it, painting a hammer and sickle on the town hall is exactly the kind of daft thing Hansi could do.

Evening of July 31st, 1932

When Papa and Mama came back from voting they went straight to their rooms. Maria said they were upset because a terrorist had firebombed Breslau Radio Station the night before. Everyone was talking about it at the polling station. Some said it was the Red Front who'd hurled the firebomb, others said it was Brownshirts from the Sturmabteilung, but mostly they think the Red Front. Fortunately, the fire had been put out before anyone was hurt.

Election clashes leave seven dead!

July 31 1932

Berlin police said riots during the night left one person dead, hundreds injured and resulted in 287 arrests. The trouble started when opposing party men started to tear down each other's election posters. The fatality occurred when a Communist fired shots at the police.

There were similar sanguinary clashes throughout the German Reich, namely in Chemnitz, Essen, Lubeck, Krefeld, Itzehohe, Oppenheim, Magdeburg, Halle, Thiers, Hanover, Cologne, Dusseldorf and Breslau, which resulted in a further six fatalities.

A spokesman from the police said,"Individuals who take the law into their own hands will not be tolerated."

Breslau radio station fire-bombed!

An attempt was made to set fire to Breslau radio broadcasting station, but the fire was soon extinguished. The terrorists escaped after painting a hammer and sickle on the town wall.

Breslau and Bremen record highest voter turn-outs!

Heavy polling was reported for the fourth election in five months in Germany, with 75 per cent of voters turning out in Breslau and 80 per cent turning out in Bremen. After casting their vote many took advantage of the wonderful weather and headed to the countryside for a picnic... There were generally double the number of Nazi Brownshirts as other party supporters outside the polling stations. The police patrolled around the polling stations in twos with the main body of the force hidden down side streets at key points.

Maria said she didn't know what had made Papa more angry, the news of the firebombing or the fact that the polling stations were crawling with Hitler's Brownshirts, who way outnumbered the police, or the fact that lots of people had taken their picnic baskets with them to vote and were clearly going to take advantage of the nice weather, terrorist threat or no terrorist threat!

August 2nd, 1932

It is Mama's day off and she has gone to her allotment. Mama is a doctor and works at the hospital. On her day off she usually likes to go to her little Kleingarten where she grows blackberries and potatoes and parsley and kohlrabi. She calls going there her therapy. I went with her once, it was boring. She said I lacked patience and imagination.

August 3rd, 1932

Hubert showed me his picture of Adolf Hitler. Papa would belt him if he knew he had it. Papa hates Hitler almost as much as he hates the Reds. It was the old election leaflet Hubert had picked up when we were waiting for Hansi at the square on my birthday.

The picture was in black and white with a picture of an aeroplane in the middle on it. Hitler stood next to the plane, making his salute. Across the top of the leaflet it said *Hitler über Deutschland*. Hubert said Hitler had flown all over Germany in that plane, talking to crowds of people.

He was so excited talking about him. He said no German politician had ever before used an aeroplane in his election campaign. Sometimes Hitler went to four different towns in the same day. 'Can you imagine!' said Hubert. He wished he'd seen him when he'd come to Breslau earlier in the year. He said Hitler is the best thing to ever happen to Germany.

I hate politics but I do think Hitler looks quite handsome. I don't know why Papa hates him so much. Hubert said that since the elections Hitler's party is now the biggest party in the Reichstag and it won't be long before Hitler is in charge of Germany.

August 4th, 1932

Hubert took me to his gang hut today. You have to go to the main train station and then along to the goods depot. There's a gap in the fence by the bridge. It's not very far from Mama's allotment. You have to watch out for trams though. They swing round the corner without warning and then all the people on the tram see you. When we were sure no one was around, and there were no trams coming, we wriggled through the picket fence, nipped between the elderberry bushes and slid down the embankment into the railway sidings. And suddenly there it was, hidden behind bushes of scrambling brambles. It's a real hut, made from pieces of wooden crate with a slab of rusted corrugated iron for a roof. The door is made from rough planks nailed together.

He says there are seven of them in his gang and if I wasn't a girl he would have let me join, and to prove it he unlocked the padlock on the door and let me in. It was dark inside and it stank of stale boys' sweat and rotten eggs. The floor was flattened earth, littered with tiny, squashed cigarette stumps. A small stool in the middle of the hut had an empty brown beer bottle on it.

He's so lucky being a boy. I had to swear I wouldn't tell anyone where the gang hut was, not even Belen, my best friend, which is a shame because she's always telling me secrets and I never have any to tell her. Papa has absolutely forbidden us to tell anyone Hansi is a Bolshevik so I can't even tell her about him, even if I wanted to.

August 5th, 1932

I overheard Mama and Papa talking. Papa said he'd talked to

Archpriest Klose about it and he'd said yes. But then Mama said she didn't know if that was the right thing to do, to send him away. Papa got all cross and said how else was Hansi going to finish his education and get away from the influence of the Bolsheviks. Mama said nothing.

I'll have to ask Maria what it means.

August 6th, 1932

I agreed to meet Belen after school today at our secret hiding place in the willow tree between the Jewish cemetery and the Lutheran cemetery. The leaves of the bending branches of the tree create a curtain of green. Our secret den is invisible behind it. We found it by accident playing hide and seek.

Whoever gets there first lays out our blanket, which we keep folded on a stone at the base of the trunk – we use the stone like a table. Belen's mother gave her the blanket, she didn't even have to say what she wanted it for. Belen never has to explain why she wants things, she just asks and her mother gives. Not like Mama, who always wants to know every single thing I do and every single place I go. I was desperate to show Belen my *Emil and the Detectives* book. I'd hoped we could read it together.

Belen was already there when I arrived, half sitting, half lying on the rug. I flopped down beside her. It was only a little bit cooler inside. I brought out my book and put it on the stone table and asked if she wanted to read it with me. She smirked, 'I'd rather read my own book, thanks.' I should have known she would spoil it for me. Her book was *The Secret of The Old Clock, A Nancy Drew Mystery*. I couldn't believe it. How dare she have a Nancy Drew book? I was the one who told her about Nancy Drew! I was so jealous. I said, 'You can't even read English!'

'Yes, I can!'

'Since when?'

'You're just jealous!'

'No, I'm not! I could get a Nancy Drew book any time but Papa won't let me have American books in the house. He says they're trash. Not real literature.' Not that he'd ever said that, but it's the kind of thing he would say to me if I were ever lucky enough to be given a Nancy Drew book.

She handed me the book to look at. 'So, you don't want to read it with me?'

I opened the first page and read out loud, 'Nancy Drew, an attractive girl of eighteen, was driving home along a country road in her new, dark-blue convertible. She had just delivered some legal papers for her father...' It sounded so thrilling. 'Where did you get it?'

'It was a present from my aunt in Pittsburgh.'

'But your birthday's not till February!'

'It's not for my birthday, idiot, it's just because.'

I felt like pushing her glistening smelly face into her stinking rug. 'Oh, well, lucky you.' I handed it back to her and stood up. 'I have to go.'

For a second her face crumpled, 'You're really not going to read it with me?'

'No time,' I lied. 'I'm meeting the girls from the church group at Liebich Höhe. We're going to go rowing in the moat then for a swim in the river.'

Belen eyed me suspiciously, 'Well, if you gotta go, you gotta go! My parents won't let me swim in the river. Mama says it's not clean. The municipal baths are far more hygienic.'

'Well, Papa won't let me go to the baths in town, not now with all the trouble –'

'What trouble?' said Belen.

'Didn't you hear? Last week the Brownshirts and Red Front had a big street fight. They were throwing real hand grenades at each other! Papa says public places aren't safe any more and Mama says unless something is done it won't be long before someone is killed, just like that poor Hitler Youth boy, Norkus

Hurbert.'

Belen burst out laughing, 'He was called Herbert Norkus, you dimwit!'

I hate her so much sometimes. 'I know that, I just got muddled!'

'You are so ignorant!' she sniggered. 'Anyway, why would anyone want to lob a grenade into the municipal baths? That's just plain stupid.'

Sometimes I really, really hate Belen.

August 7th, 1932

Hubert sneaked into my room tonight. He wasn't even a tiny bit interested when I told him about Belen's book or Papa's talk about sending Hansi away. He only wanted to tell me his news. Two of the boys from his gang have joined the Hitler Youth. They go climbing and marching and if they pass all the tests they'll win a special knife with the words *Blut und Ehre* – Blood and Honour – engraved on it and a fancy scarf. Once they get the knife they get to do proper grown-up stuff. But the best thing, he said, is that the group are going on a special march to Potsdam in October to see Hitler!

He sounded so excited. I did point out that Potsdam is next to Berlin, where Oma lives, which is miles and miles away and the furthest Hubert has ever marched is down to the river. And, anyway, Papa would never let him go – Papa hates the Hitler Youth boys as much as he hates the Brownshirt stormtroopers and the Reds. But Hubert said he's joining no matter what Papa says because this could be his only chance to see Hitler. Just then a warm breeze drifted in through the open window, carrying the sweet scent of honeysuckle from Mrs Schwarzkopf's garden below – Mrs S lives on the ground floor, she's our concierge. I didn't believe Hubert. He always talks big but never does anything. Even if Papa were to let him go, which he wouldn't, Mama would never allow it, he's only 13.

August 8th, 1932

When Hansi isn't around, all Papa and Mama do is argue with each other about him. And then when he is around, all they do is argue with him about his being in the KPD. Hansi keeps saying to them, 'It's not illegal to be a member of a political party, so I don't know what your problem is.' And then Papa shouts, 'The Communists are immoral, that's my problem!' 'You're just an old fogey royalist, who can't move with the times!' Hansi says back. And then Mama says, 'Don't you talk to your father like that!' And on and on they go.

I don't even really know what a Communist is, except according to Papa they're supposed to be everywhere. It's all so rubbish! We've not been on a picnic for weeks and weeks – we haven't even been on a trip on the Flying Trebintzer train this summer and that's never happened before.

August 9th, 1932

I've fallen out with Belen. I don't even know why I was ever her friend. She said she had a secret to tell me and I had to meet her at the tree. It was urgent! When I got there she was pretending to read her Nancy Drew book. I know she's pretending because her English is so terrible she needs me to help her, but I won't so she's sunk – ha ha ha!

She sat on the rug, knees bent, her lovely checked skirt all smoothed out over them, all smug. She said she'd been to the cinema. 'Did I know *Emil and the Detectives* was on?' Oh, I hate her! Her Mama always gives her money to go to the cinema, but Mama will only give me money if it's a special treat – and just going to the cinema because you feel like watching a film isn't a good enough reason, even if it is *Emil and the Detectives*! 'Was it good?' I asked, despite myself.

'It was wonderful. I recognised Berlin immediately. You should really get your parents to take you. It's on at quite a few cinemas at the moment.'

'Is that what you wanted to tell me?'

'Of course not. You'll never guess who I saw on the way home.'

How was I supposed to know that? 'Marlene Dietrich?' She's always going about Marlene Dietrich.

'Ha ha, very funny! No,' she said, 'I saw Maria, your big sister.'

'That's it? That's your big secret?' I pretended not to be interested but she had that smirk across her face, the one she wears when she knows she has the upper hand.

'Won't your Papa be cross? It's a public place, after all, could be dangerous.'

'We're not actually forbidden to go out, we just have to be sensible. Anyway, it couldn't have been her because she's at her church group on a Saturday night.'

Belen chortled, she sounded like a horse neighing. 'I know what she looks like. She was in my house last week babysitting my little sister when Mum and Dad went to the theatre.'

I wanted her to just come out with what it was she had to say. I shrugged. 'So what. She can do what she wants, she is eighteen.'

'Yes, but the thing is, she was with someone...'

I got up on my feet. The smell of the rich warm earth was making me feel nauseous. I needed to leave. I shrugged again, 'She has lots of friends.'

'This was a young man. I don't know if you know him, he's called Georg,' she said.

'Of course I know Georg, we all know Georg,' I lied again. I was always lying to Belen. 'He was in Hansi's class at school. He's a family friend.' More lies, the first time I'd seen Georg was the other day outside Haus Barasch.

'Oh, he's more than a family friend. They were holding hands.'

'No way!' I said, shouting before I could stop myself. What cheek! 'Maria is going to be a nun. She's made a promise to God to never stain her purity.' I scrambled out under the branches. 'You're telling fibs!' I yelled back.

'I am not!' she shouted, 'because I did see her!'

'No you didn't!' I shouted back.

'I did so,' she screamed, 'and want to know something else, you English-reading show-off? They were kissing on the lips! Stuff that in your pipe and smoke it!'

'Absolutely no way!' I yelled. 'You fat liar! Jesus will be her only spouse!'

I hate Belen! I hate her! I hate her! I hate her!

August 10th, 1932

Today absolutely nothing happened.

August 11th, 1932

Life is so horrible. Late last night I heard yelling. I ran downstairs. Maria and Hilde were already in the hall, in their nighties and bare feet, clutching each other. Mama and Papa were in their fancy clothes kneeling on the ground. Hansi was sprawled on the floor by the front door. Hubert was behind the girls. He whispered to me that Mama and Papa had come back from the Thursday Theatre and found Hansi like that.

I thought at first maybe Hansi had been drinking alcohol. Belen says her brother had got drunk once and he fell down on the floor and couldn't get up. But then I saw the blackcurrant blood. It oozed from his head onto the parquet floor. Mama had a bandage and dressing in her hands and waited as Papa gently placed his folded jacket beneath Hansi's head.

At first I couldn't see Hansi's face, but as soon as Papa moved him, I got a good look. Hansi's left eye was all bloody and covered in little bits of stuff. Mama took the dressing and gently pressed it on top of Hansi's eye, then she carefully unravelled the bandage and wrapped it around Hansi's head to hold the dressing in place. All the while Hansi groaned and moaned. He didn't sound human.

Hilde went down to sit beside Papa, who was holding Hansi's hand, and Maria sat next to Mama. Then after what seemed a very long time a policeman and two ambulance men appeared at the front door with a stretcher. There was chaos for a few minutes as everyone tried to get Hansi safely on to the stretcher and down the apartment stairs and into the ambulance. But eventually he was in and they were gone, including Mama and Papa.

We went to the kitchen and Maria stoked the fire and made a huge pot of scrambled eggs for us and Hilde prepared some hot chocolate. I thought I wasn't hungry but then when I saw the steaming plate of creamy eggs, dripping in butter, I was suddenly starving. Hilde got a fresh loaf of Mama's grey bread from the larder – and some more butter. And for a while we all ate and said nothing. Then gradually, as if the food somehow triggered something in our mouths, we all started to speak.

Hubert thought a band of travelling gypsies had attacked Hansi. Hilde thought Hansi had tried to save someone from being attacked by an escaped murderer and in the process got beaten up himself. Maria said maybe he'd been attacked by an eastern worker – maybe? I didn't know what to think. It was sickening to see Hansi like that. Groaning. Blood all over him.

Mama didn't come home till the morning. We were all sitting back round the kitchen table. None of us knew what to say when she walked in, not even Maria. Mama's face was grey and her lovely chestnut hair was all straggly and poking out from beneath her scarf. Hilde was in Mama's usual place. She didn't even move away when Mama came in. Why is she like that, so disrespectful? Mama sat in Papa's seat. The fire hissed in the range behind us. Someone had put out the quark and jam on the table but no one had touched it. We had no appetite now.

Mama said, 'Last night, on his way home from one of his KPD meetings, Hansi was attacked by a group of Hitler's SA Brownshirts. They appeared to be waiting for him. They were drunk.' None of us said anything. Mama continued, 'You know Papa and I don't agree with Hansi being a member of the Communist Party, but being a Communist is no justification for an unprovoked attack. They chased him into a garden and into a small greenhouse. The Brownshirts then split up. Three of them followed him inside the greenhouse and trapped him in a corner. The two SA outside found some sharp sticks. While the ones inside kept Hansi in the corner, the two outside rammed their sticks through the glass panes of the greenhouse and stabbed him repeatedly. Eventually some people came and chased the SA brutes away but not before Hansi had been stabbed all over – including in the eye.'

I couldn't believe it. Our Hansi beaten like a dog. Hubert quietly put his arm round my shoulder. I hadn't realised but I was crying. Mama continued, 'The police have arrested the Brownshirt thugs who committed this atrocity. It wasn't difficult to find them, they were swaggering about town, bragging about what they had done to anyone who would listen. It's also no surprise the boys are known to the police. They live in the Old Town and have been in trouble many times before. They've been charged with causing grievous bodily harm. There will be a trial, of course, and these louts who call themselves Germans will then surely be sent to jail for a long time. But this doesn't help Hansi.'

August 12th, 1932

Everyone at school was talking about what had happened to Hansi. It was in all the newspapers. They said Hansi was a hero and the SA Brownshirts who attacked him should be locked up: *Lawless behaviour may be acceptable in Berlin but never in Breslau.*

August 13th, 1932

Something really, really, really terrible happened today, almost as bad as what happened to Hansi yesterday. Mama was nearly arrested! When Mama came home today, she was with Georg, the Brownshirt friend of Hansi's. He came into the house with Mama and they had a big talk with Maria. Mama was all white-faced and ill-looking. When Georg left Mama went to straight to her room. When I asked Maria later what had happened, she said when Mama was coming back from visiting Hansi she bumped into a Brownshirt. For some reason they argued. The Brownshirt accused Mama of being 'un-German' and Mama kicked him on the shin.

I couldn't believe it. Mama in a fight! Then the Brownshirt got really angry. He grabbed Mama and said she was going to jail. No matter how hard Mama tried to get free, he kept dragging her towards the police station, saying she would be arrested for sure. Luckily, Georg came by. He managed to persuade the other SA boy to let Mama go and forget about the incident. It's unbelievable.

August 14th, 1932

I am not going to write about my family any more as life is rubbish. Hansi is still in hospital. Mama spends all her free time running around after him and no one mentions what happened to her the other day. Now I'm not sure it really happened at all, but Maria never lies, so it must have.

August 24th, 1932

Well, I have to write in my diary today because I am so angry! Hubert joined the big Hitler Youth. He told them he was fourteen and they believed him. When Mama and Papa heard they were furious. Papa said, 'I absolutely forbid you to spend time with those delinquents! You have important exams coming up and you're already behind in your studies!'

Mama said, 'Going to the Catholic church group twice a week is quite enough, thank you very much! Those Hitler Youth yobs think of one thing and one thing alone, that is to cause trouble. It's bad enough one of my sons is a member of the KPD! I am certainly not allowing the other to join the Hitler Youth.'

Hubert said he didn't care what they said, he was still going to go – but that was just to me. He always talks big but in the end he never disobeys Papa. Then, and I don't know why, I told Hubert about what Belen had said about seeing Maria with Georg the other week. BIG MISTAKE! I just wanted someone else to say it was a lie and to be cross with me at Belen. But I shouldn't have told him, especially not the kissing bit. Later he went and blabbed to Hilde, who told Mama, who told Papa and Papa went berserk. Not only was his eldest daughter cavorting in the street with a boy, but with a boy who was a Brownshirt!

Maria said it was a deceitful lie. Yes, she said, she had bumped into Georg. Yes, she said, they'd been talking together. But never, ever, ever had she done anything improper. She didn't know why Belen would make up such a story or why I should have such a terrible friend.

So now I'm in trouble with everyone and no one will talk to me, especially not Maria. I'm never going to trust that conniving Hubert again. Of course, I know why he told on me. He was punishing me because he found out that two girls had turned up at his secret gang hut and he guessed it had to have been me and Belen. It was my own fault. I should have never, ever told Belen about the gang hut. But more than that I should never, ever have taken her there.

I hadn't meant to tell Belen about the gang hut but she kept going on about how wonderful her life is. If it's not how brilliant her Nancy Drew book is – her mother's reading it to her, she speaks English from all her visits to her sister in America – it's how great the cinema was the night before, or how delicious the food at the Monopol was when her mother took her there for lunch. And she kept on saying how sorry she was for me and my poor little dull life. 'It must be so awful not to be allowed to go to the cinema when you want.' So, just to shut her up, I told her my life wasn't dull at all, that I was a member of a secret boys' gang. Of course, she didn't believe me, so before I could stop myself I said I'd prove it. That's how I ended up taking her to Hubert's gang hut.

We'd got right up to the door of the hut before I heard the rumble of male voices inside. I never dreamed anyone would be there, it was the middle of the day! I grabbed Belen's arm, 'We have to go!'

She shook herself free. 'Of course we're not leaving.'

'Keep your voice down.' I pleaded.

'Maybe they'll let me join too.'

'I'm not allowed to bring anyone here.'

'I've always wanted to be in a gang!'

'It's against all the rules.' I tugged on her arm for a second time. 'I'll get into trouble!'

But Belen was having none of it. 'Don't be silly,' she laughed, barely able to contain her excitement, 'if you can be a member then so can I.'

'Belen, please!' I whispered as loudly as I could, but the more I tried to hush her up, the louder she spoke.

'Wait till I tell the others,' she blabbed at the top of her silly voice, 'they'll be so jealous! Fancy me being in a boy's gang –'

The door flew open. Two gaunt boys in shirt sleeves, dirty shorts and bare feet glowered at us. I froze. One of the initiation tests for gang membership was to skin a rabbit alive. Hubert had thrown up when he'd got home after attempting it.

The taller of the two boys spat at us. 'Who the hell are you?'

Belen's body went rigid.

The smaller boy said, 'This is private property and you're

trespassing!'

The taller boy spat again, his mouth hardly moved. 'How d'you find this place?'

I heard my voice tremble when I spoke, 'We just found it.'

'You couldn't have just found this place,' the small one said. 'Someone must have told you about it.'

'No, no one told us,' I gave Belen's hand a squeeze. I prayed she wouldn't mention Hubert.

'We were just out walking,' said Belen, her voice all on edge.

'Lying bitch!' said the tall one.

'No!' I said, 'Really, we just found it.' We started to inch backwards.

'We won't tell anyone –' Belen said.

'Bloody whores!' said the taller one and charged. We screamed and ran. They ran right after us. We ran faster and faster and faster. Brambles tore at my legs. Overgrown thistles whipped my arms. Their grunts grew louder. And louder. And louder. We ran faster. I couldn't breathe. My legs ached. And we ran faster. Then somehow the tall one was in front of us. Arms crossed. A mean smirk across his face. We turned back. The small one was there. Sniggering. A picket fence barred our way to the left. Thick brambles stopped us going to the right. We were trapped. We clung to each other. The boy in front wasn't much taller than me. 'You sluts made me run when I didn't want to run,' he said.

'Please,' I gasped, 'Just let us go and you won't see us again.' He wasn't that tall. I thought maybe I could push past him. Then. THUMP! Once. THUMP! Twice. He'd punched me. Right in my mouth. I crumpled to my knees. Belen stifled a sob.

'You're going to be sorry you came here. Really sorry,' the tall boy said, licking his colourless lips.

The boy behind giggled and began to whistle *Susie, dear Susie, what's rustling in the straw* and twisted and pulled at a stake of wood that had started to come away from the fencing.

The end of it was sharp and hard.

'We won't tell anyone, honestly we won't,' sobbed Belen, helping me to my feet, tears welling in her eyes.

'Shut up, cow!' the boy in front said. 'You've got a big mouth, do you know that? I don't like girls who have big mouths, and I especially don't like you.' Suddenly there was a dull snapping noise behind us. The whistling stopped. Above our heads the smaller boy handed the piece of broken fence to the tall boy in front of us. For a second or two he let the chunk of wood fall from one hand into the other as if he was trying to feel how heavy it was. Then he took the wood firmly in his right hand, as if it were a sword. He sliced the air at either side of our bodies. Swish! Swish! Swish! 'I hate bitches like you,' he said. 'You think boys like me are dumb –' Then from nowhere, a man's voice shouted, 'Oye, what do you kids think you're doing there?' 'Run!' screamed Belen. And we ran and ran and ran.

August 29th, 1932

Oma has arrived. Oma is Mama's mama and she reminds me of the witch in Hansel and Gretel. She has a mean mouth and a red wart on her nose that glows when she's angry and I hate her even more than I hate Erna.

Oma is to go in Hubert's room as it is closest to Mama and Papa's room. From now on Hubert and me have to share a room. It's so unfair.

August 30th, 1932

Hansi is coming out of hospital at last. Mama made us clean the house from top to bottom in preparation for his return. Mama has four big tidy-ups a year – spring, summer, autumn and winter – but this is an extra-special one. Apart from doing our own rooms, we girls have to do the boys' rooms. Mama does her and Papa's room and then we girls do the rest of the house with Erna. The clean-ups take ages, but Mama says, 'Cleanliness is next to Godliness'.

Erna moaned about the extra work but Maria said Mama will pay her double. Erna scrubbed all the floors while we girls opened all the windows and shook out the quilts. Then we collected and washed every bit of bed linen in the house and hung it out to dry. Then we took out the rugs and mats and beat them until there was no dust in them and left them in the sun. Mama says, 'Sunshine is the best disinfectant.' Then we wiped and waxed and tidied and eventually it all got done, all for Hansi! Lucky school still hasn't started!

September 1st, 1932

We were all desperate for Hansi to arrive but when Papa finally brought him in none of us knew what to say. A big black eye patch hid his left eye and the other eye stared at the floor. Maria moved first. She threw her arms around Hansi and gave him a big squeeze and that started Hilde off and then me. Even Hubert give him a sort of pat on the shoulder, which was something for Hubert. And then Mama appeared. As soon as she saw Hansi she shooed us all away and gently led him upstairs. All the while talking to him in her soft but firm voice. For a second I wished it had been me who'd been beaten up.

September 2nd, 1932

Oma is a witch and I hate her. At meal times we have to wait till she's finished eating before we can leave the table. This takes forever because she just sits and chews and chews and all the time she eats her mouth hangs open and as much food dribbles out as stays in. She only ever eats mashed bananas and quark. We wait in silence while she stares at us as if to dare us to comment, which, of course you can't. It's disgusting. Even Erna isn't as bad as Oma when it comes to eating. Sometimes Mama even asks us to help by taking a napkin and wiping away food that collects around Oma's mouth while she eats. Hilde says she doesn't mind at all. I bet she does mind.

September 6th, 1932

Papa announced over dinner that as Hansi's course at the university was definitely no longer running, he was sending Hansi to Leobschütz in Upper Silesia to train to be a priest. 'It's an excellent opportunity for him to finish his education,' he said. Mama looked very angry. Hansi looked as if he didn't care.

Hilde said, 'Oh!' and then made her 'hurt' face. No one knew what to say. Then just as a way of making conversation Hubert asked Maria where she'd go when she finished her training. She said she wanted to work in Papua New Guinea in a mission hospital. Hubert said Papua New Guinea was full of savages and she'd get eaten by cannibals if she did. Maria said she doubted that very much as there had been nuns there for over forty years and they were still very much alive.

September 7th, 1932

Oma doesn't come to breakfast anymore, instead we have to go to her room every morning and give her a kiss. We are only allowed in the room one at a time in case we tire her out. Usually the big velvet curtains are three-quarters drawn and all you can see of Oma is a ghostly shimmer hovering above the bed. No sooner are you in the room than her glassy eyes flicker open and she turns her tiny head towards you. She's supposed to be almost blind – there's this milky stuff floating across her eyes – but that doesn't stop those horrible hollow beads staring straight at you and staying on you until you've reached her side.

Her body is all crooked and propped up by half a dozen pillows. Mama's best silk navy-blue handmade quilt tucks her in and Mama's pretty lace cardigan drapes her hunched shoulders. Right beside the bed, at waist height, is Mama's oak bedside table. On it sits Oma's giant black Bible. It's always open as if she's just been reading it, which of course she can't have been. Mama suggested we read to her but Oma said no, not even the saintly Hilde, or wondrous Maria is good enough for Oma.

Only Mama is good enough to read to Oma. Oma's favourite story is the one about Sodom and Gomorrah, which is Mama's least favourite.

Up close Oma smells of carbolic soap and her skin clings to her bones like flakes of rancid pastry. Every morning I hope she's died in the night so I won't have to kiss her, but she never has. Her cheek tastes of salt and rancid milk and her hair – which Mama always parts right down the middle and ties in a pleated bun at either side of her head – is like white straw. As soon as you are within reach of her, she grips your arm and demands in a shrill squawk, 'Have you been good? Have you? Eh? God will always find you out if you've been wicked!' And I always say, 'Yes, I've been good, Oma, of course I have,' and hope God won't strike me down with a lightning bolt or turn me into a pillar of salt for wishing horrible things to happen to my Oma.

September 9th, 1932

When Mama isn't working in the hospital, she's either looking after Oma or running around after Hansi. She says Hansi is going nowhere until he has fully recovered and as she is now his doctor she will say when that is! If she's not taking him his meals on a tray or changing his dressing, she's running him a bath or bringing him a little present from the bookshop or Konditorei. She's even stopped going to church with us and now Hilde, little St Therese, sits in Mama's place next to Papa in the front pew. I don't like Hilde sitting in Mama's place.

September 10th, 1932

When I got back from school today no one was home – I don't count Oma as she sleeps all the time and is not a person but a witch – and Erna isn't a person but an idiot. When Erna let me in she actually asked me if I'd been to school. I was wearing my school uniform, so where else would I have been? She asked what school was like. What does that mean? 'School is school,' I said. She said she'd only ever been to the little ones' school. She was supposed to go to a special big school but her Oma wouldn't let her go as they didn't have any money. She had to find a job instead.

I hate it when she tries to talk to me. I normally ignore her but it's impossible when she's standing at the doorway not letting me pass. So, because she still wouldn't move I made conversation, and for want of anything better to ask, I asked her where she was from. She looked at me like I was the idiot and said Germany. I said, no, where are you really from and then she said Silesia, Germany, just like you. What rubbish. Everyone knows she's a Polak! Why else has she got that silly accent? She makes me so angry.

On the way to my room I noticed the door to Maria and Hilde's room was open. Usually it's locked. They started to lock it last year after Hubert and me put dandelion pee-the-beds and lots of tiny black frogs from Mrs S's pond in their beds. When they pulled back their quilts the frogs all hopped out, hundreds of them, and Maria and Hilde shrieked the place down. It was really funny. They must have forgotten to lock it.

The room looked just the same as before. Their dressing table was covered in Mama's old perfume bottles and face creams. Maria had a ball of knitting on her bedside table. Hilde's Bible was on her table next to a lace hanky Mama gave her on her last birthday. To the side of the hanky was a silk drawstring purse I'd not seen before. I decided to see what was inside it. I crept into the room and teased open the little cloth sack. There were five silvery-brown 50 Reichspfennig coins inside and two silver 2 Deutsch Mark coins. I snooped a bit more.

There was the usual stuff in the wardrobe and drawers. Then for some reason I peeked behind the wardrobe and there it was. A little notebook. Hidden down the back between the wall and the back of the wardrobe. I got a knitting needle from Maria's table and poked about until the book tumbled to the floor.

I don't know what I thought the book was – a diary? I was wrong. It was full of drawings. Of a young man. With no clothes on. UGH! Is that what a man's body looks like? Really? UGH! They were disgusting. I didn't want to keep looking but I couldn't stop. There were more and more wicked pictures. All of the same young man in different poses. Naked. I felt sick looking at them. Then I realised. It was Georg, the boy Belen said she'd seen Maria with. I really did want to throw up then.

I felt so confused. Maria has won the art prize twice. She is very good at drawing. But she's supposed to hate sin more than death. Jesus is supposed to be her only spouse! I wanted to cry. There was a noise downstairs. Someone was back. I chucked the sketch book back under the wardrobe and then, and I know I shouldn't have done this, as I left I slipped my hand into Hilde's purse and took one of her silver 2 Deutsch Mark coins.

September 11th, 1932

I can't look at Maria without thinking about the wicked pictures. I wish I'd never seen them.

September 29th, 1932

Big disaster! Hubert has actually gone on the Hitler Youth march to Potsdam. We didn't even know he was still going to the Hitler Youth meetings. Mrs Schwarzkopf saw him. He had a back pack with him and was wearing a brown shirt and was with a whole bunch of other Hitler Youth boys. They were marching towards Frankfurter Strasse and the airport – and everyone knows that's the way out of town to Berlin. I don't know what Mrs S was doing way over that side of town at seven o'clock in the morning, it's miles from Kaiser Wilhelm Strasse.

Mama was really worried. 'He's only thirteen,' she kept saying, 'Anything could happen to him!' But when Papa heard, he went berserk. He was all for going after him and dragging him back. In the end he didn't. Hansi said – on one of the rare times he chose to speak – that if Papa had dragged Hubert back everyone would have known he was against Hitler and the National Socialist Party, and as everyone in Silesia is Hitler and Nazi party mad these days, he said, maybe Papa would get into trouble.

Maria said Potsdam is something like 190 miles away. Hubert must really want to see Hitler.

October 7th, 1932

Hubert got back today. His boots and clothes were caked in mud and he smelled sweaty. Papa belted him really badly. Mama can never stop Papa belting Hubert the way she stopped him belting Hansi when he was in trouble. I hate it when Papa behaves like this.

Papa kept hitting Hubert over and over again, yelling, 'You will not disobey me! You will not!' But it didn't matter how hard Papa slapped Hubert with his belt, Hubert refused to cry. Eventually he let Hubert go, but not before telling him he was cancelling his allowance, that he wasn't giving him money just so he could waste it on the Hitler Youth fees. Hubert shouted he didn't care and that he'd get the money for the dues somehow. Papa started to chase him but Mama stopped him and this time she won.

Poor Hubert. I found him sitting on his bed. In between sobs he said he absolutely hated Papa. He said it didn't matter how many times Papa beat him, he would never ever give up the Hitler Youth. No sacrifice was too great for Germany and Hitler.

I helped him hobble to the bathroom and got some antiseptic wash from Mama's box for his feet. While his cracked soles and blistered heels soaked in the basin, he showed me his bronze badge: a sword with a little crooked cross in the middle of it. It was so smart. He said all the boys who went to the rally got one. The walk had been torture, his feet began to hurt almost as soon as they set off and his backpack was so heavy it dug into his shoulders and made his skin bleed. And he hadn't taken nearly enough food or water with him to last, so he was constantly thirsty and hungry. I asked why he hadn't just come back. He said he'd thought about it, especially at first when he started to lag behind all the others, but he was desperate to see Hitler.

'It was so embarrassing,' he said. 'I just couldn't keep up. Some of the bigger ones laughed at me. I was sure I'd be sent back home. But Ernst – he's our leader – he was great. Every now and then he would wait and walk with me. He'd tell me not to worry about the others laughing, that I was the youngest in the group and very brave. He said he would never let me be left behind. "We arrive together as one, or not at all." He even shared his water with me – and gave me a sip of beer one night!

'When we camped, he took the time to show me how to bandage my feet to stop the blisters getting worse. He also made everyone share their food, so those of us who hadn't any didn't go hungry. "The group comes before the individual." Every evening after we ate we sang songs and Ernst told us stories about the Teutonic Knights. Oh, Toni, I love being a Hitler Youth! And when at last we arrived you should have seen the flags and the banners and the young people! There were thousands of us, swarming all over the heath – even girl groups. You could have come!'

I laughed, 'Maybe you can walk 190 miles twice in a few days but I know I can't!'

'There were the SS Schutzstaffel and SA Brownshirt stormtroopers everywhere. They were putting up tents and a huge rostrum where the speeches were to be. And in the middle of it all I saw a post office – can you believe it, a post office!' He shook his head. 'Only a clever person like Hitler would have thought of that. I didn't have any money, otherwise I would have sent you a card. And you know how I was worried about being too young? Well, there were some kids much younger than me. In fact some were really too young because on that first night it was quite cold and they started to blubber for their mummies. Really, it was silly to have let them come. How could they understand?

'At first light we had breakfast, and again Ernst made everyone share their food. Some of the others started to complain, but Ernst said, "We are a holy fellowship, each dependent on each other. One day one of us gives more, the next day it is the turn of the other to help." The thing was, we could hardly eat we were so excited. Finally, we were told to assemble in our groups.

'It was a crisp morning. Towering posts held huge banners carrying either the Swastika or the SS lightning sign. The cloth material flapped in the wind. Then came the speeches and the cheers and more speeches. I can't remember now who said what but at some point there was a loud noise and everyone started to get agitated. Suddenly, Hitler was there. I saw him with my own eyes. He climbed up on to his rostrum. He was surrounded by a sea of the most handsome, smartly dressed officers you ever saw. I heard a roar, and another and then realised I was shouting. We all were! Sieg Heil! Sieg Heil! Sieg Heil!

'Finally, Hitler motioned for us to stop. A hush fell. He started speaking. I heard him with my own ears – these two ears, Toni. He's going to make Germany great! He said the old people had to make way for us young ones, that we young people were the custodians of the future. He said we stood at the dawn of 1000 years of National Socialist history. Together we would march into this new age. "A young army of self-sacrificing devotees." He said we would show the wishy-washy politicians that the time had come to stop discussing and start doing! "Fourteen years of driving Germany into the ground will soon be over!"

'Then Schirach spoke – he's the head of the Hitler Youth. He said we were a community of dedicated, self-sacrificing believers, who are prepared to exchange the "I" which has governed our people for the last 14 years, for the National Socialist "idea". Oh, Toni, it was magnificent. He said, "Let those old politicians think they can wear us down! Let them do what they will! They can terrorise us! They can ban us! They can tear down our posters! They can restrict our newspaper circulation! They can even kill us –" A huge cheer went up at that point. "– but we will never be beaten! Let us not forget Herbert Norkus!'" "Yes!" we roared back and chanted "Norkus! Norkus!" Schirach then shouted, "We will never surrender!" And we chanted, "No surrender! No surrender!" Over and over again.

'That night we couldn't speak because our voices were so hoarse from the shouting. Ernst said that when we returned to Breslau we'd have to start training to get strong and fit. "We German youth have to be tough as leather, swift as whippets and as hard as Krupp steel." This is it, Toni! This is it! Hitler is going to make Germany a proud nation again and we young people are going to help him do it!'

I left him with his feet in the basin looking at his badge. I wish I could have been there.

November 10th, 1932

Papa says Oma is getting sicker and so we don't have to go into her room any more. Yippee! Sorry, God, but she is horrible! It's the only good thing to have happened recently. Home life is awful! Mama and Papa are totally obsessed with politics.

The latest big worry is that the Communists are going to get into power. There was another election and this time the Communists increased their share of the vote. Because of that Papa and Mama are convinced Germany will become a state of the anti-Christian, anti-imperial, anti-democratic, Bolshevik Russia. Hansi says that would be a good thing. But Hubert said the Communists will never get a majority, not while Hitler is alive. Hubert said Hitler is the only person strong enough to kick the Communists out and restore law and order. As long as everyone votes for Hitler in the next election, Germany will be saved from Russia, he said.

Papa usually ignores Hubert when he says these things but this time Papa said Hubert had a point. Even though he disliked the National Socialists, Papa said they were preferable to the Communists because at least the National Socialists were Christians. Even Mama agreed. She said the violence on the streets had to stop. 'It's simply spiralling out of control!' Hansi said we shouldn't run for cover every time we get scared and that Hitler is not the answer. But Mama said, 'Who is then, Stalin?'

November 11th, 1932

Papa and Mama went out to the theatre this evening for the first time in ages. As soon as they had left, Hilde said she had something important to tell us and we couldn't eat until she had said it. I was starving, I hoped she'd get it over with quickly. Someone, she said, had stolen a silver 2 Reichsmark coin from her purse. I felt as if I'd just drunk some curdled yoghurt.

She said if the person didn't own up, she'd be forced to tell Mama and Papa – the only thing worse in our house than being a Red or a Hitler fan, but being a Hitler fan isn't even that bad any more, is being a thief. Maria asked her if she was sure it had been stolen. Hilde threw her a furious look and said, 'Of course!' Then Hans-Joachim asked if she was sure it wasn't just lost. She ignored him. I don't know how Mama persuaded Hansi to come to dinner. He usually stays in his room. None of us knows what he does in his room all day. He's supposed to leave for Leobschütz soon but he insists he's not going.

I said, 'What about Erna, she's poor, maybe she took the money?' I felt quite bad saying that but there was no way I was owning up. If I'd only taken a fifty penny coin she probably wouldn't have noticed.

Maria frowned, 'I don't think Erna would have taken it.'

'No, neither do I,' said Hilde. 'She's never stolen from us in ten years, why would she start now? No, I think I know who the real culprit is,' she said, staring right at me. I looked away – I don't know how I didn't blush. Then Hilde said, 'Right after dinner we will to go to Mama's writing room and swear the truth on the Bible. God will be our witness.'

I couldn't eat even though it was chicken noodle soup. After a few minutes and without looking at Hilde, I excused myself early, saying I had to go to the toilet. I hurried to my room. The incriminating coin was under my pillow. I grabbed it with the intention of sneaking it back into Hilde's room. Hopefully, she'd find it later and think it'd been there all along. But before I could make a move Maria called on me to come down. I was desperate. I needed to find a good hiding place quick.

Hubert's half of the room was a mess. Broken bits of toy railway and home-made wooden swords and daggers littered the floor. There were jars of marbles and jars of washers and pencils and paper drawings of bridges and war planes all over the bed. His duvet was on the floor too – Erna refuses to tidy our room while it is such a mess and Mama lets her get away with it!

I heard a rustle on the stairs, Maria was coming up. The wardrobe was open. Hubert's ice boots were at the very back where he'd thrown them when he'd been forced to share my room. I buried the coin inside the toe of one of his ice boots. I'd get it later. Sneak it back in Hilde's room later. Maria was at the door. 'Come on, Toni, let's humour her. At least then she won't bother Mama and Papa.'

The curtains were almost completely drawn so it was difficult to see in Mama's room. It was also hot and stuffy. Mama's piano had been pushed to one side, it usually sat in the middle of the room. Her writing desk was now in the middle. Three white church candles sat in a row on the top of the piano. They threw a flickering silver glow on to Oma's big Bible, which sat on top of the desk. I usually like Mama's room but not today.

Hilde pointed to the desk. She said we all had to kneel in front of it and silently pray. Hubert asked what we should pray for. Hilde threw him an ugly look and said, 'Forgiveness!' I quickly looked down. When I was sure she wasn't looking I peeked sideways: Hubert was simply staring at the candles on the piano, he looked bored. Maria was praying. Hansi looked as if he was snoozing – he doesn't even believe in God any more, at least that's what he keeps saying.

The candles made a hissing sound. Sweat trickled down my back. The wooden floorboards were uncomfortable to kneel on. Finally, Hilde stood up. She said each of us had to take it in turn to swear on Oma's Bible that we had not taken her money.

Maria went first, then Hansi. They were very calm and looked ever so slightly bored, then it was my turn. And suddenly I was scared. I would have to tell a lie. On Oma's Bible!

My mouth was all dry. My knees trembled. I couldn't stand up. Then Hubert suddenly upped and pushed me out the way.

Even in the half-light you could see he was smiling. He ran up to the desk, put his hand on the Bible and said very seriously, 'I did it, it was me.' Hilde gasped. I was stunned. 'Go on, God, strike me down! Now!' he cried. For a second I really thought something might happen. But nothing happened. Hubert laughed, 'No, God? Not today? So maybe you don't exist after all. Bye!' He skipped across to the piano, blew out the candles and ran out of the room.

Hilde flew after him, screeching at the top of her voice she would tell Mama and Papa, that he was a monster, that she would see him punished! Maria ran after her. Hansi simply opened the curtains and left. It took Hilde over an hour but she found the coin.

Hubert got the biggest beating ever. Both Mama and Maria begged Papa to stop, but Papa was as angry as I've ever seen him. Then Papa forbade us to talk to Hubert, but as he was in my room I couldn't avoid seeing him.

He was so pleased to see me. I felt terrible about him taking a beating because of me. If I had owned up I would have only got a telling-off, Papa never hits us girls, ever. Mama never hits us either, well, apart from that one time. Of course, Hubert had made it worse by actually saying on the Bible that he had taken the coin and that thing about God not existing, but he still didn't deserve that beating.

I wanted to say sorry to Hubert, tell him I hadn't meant this to happen, but I didn't know how to. In between sobs he said, 'You believe me, don't you, Toni?' Of course I did. 'You know what this means?' he sniffed. 'It means Hilde planted that coin and deliberately set me up.' I groaned silently. I'd only taken the coin so I could go to the cinema. 'She's an evil bitch,' he said, 'she's always had it in for me and I'll never forgive her.' Then he asked me if I would keep a secret and showed me a small blue suitcase. It was hidden under his bed. In it he had some clothes and a plate and knife and his Hitler badge from Potsdam, some sausage and bread. As soon as he got the chance, he said he was going to run away and join the SA. They'd put him up and feed him and he'd even get paid. He said, 'Hitler will look after me, which is more than Papa does.'

December 4th, 1932

No sign of the advent candles and no smell of baking – usually Mama's started her Christmas baking by now. She does it secretly at night, when we are in bed, or early morning before we wake up. When she's finished she hides everything. But you can always tell she's been baking because the house is smothered in the warm smell of cinnamon and cloves and super-sweet oranges and ginger and stewed apples. Every year Hubert and I try to find where she's hidden the ginger biscuits but we never find them, ever.

December 17th, 1932

Since Hansi's been home he stays mainly in his room. His eye patch is gone now but Mama says he is still not better. Maria says Hansi's suffering from something called 'depression' and he has fallen in a black hole and Mama's trying to help him climb back out because he can't do it by himself. I don't know what she's talking about.

December 20th, 1932

I was last down to breakfast today and as soon I walked into the kitchen I knew something was wrong. Firstly, no one was talking. Secondly, Maria had obviously been crying. As soon as I sat down, Papa stood up, cleared his throat and announced that Hilde and not Maria would be going to Holland to be a nun. Maria was going to the secretarial college now. At which point Maria burst into tears and ran out of the kitchen. Maria was always going to be a nun. I asked why she wasn't going to be a nun any more but no one would tell me.

Later, when everyone was out, I checked in Hilde and Maria's room for the book with the wicked pictures in it. It wasn't under the wardrobe any more, or anywhere else. I wish I could remember where exactly I left it. I have a horrible feeling about this.

December 21st, 1932

Mama still hasn't asked Papa to buy the goose for Christmas. We've always bought the goose by now. There's so much to be done to it. I like the goose fat the most. Mama always has little burnt bits in it, which just make it taste so yummy. When I spread it on my bread on Christmas day morning I know it's Christmas.

December 22nd, 1932

Hansi's Communist friends came round this afternoon. They ranted and raved at the door and demanded to see Hansi. Mama tried to send them away but Hansi kept asking for all four of them to be allowed in. All the while they were at the door they kept shouting, 'He's sent a letter! He's sent a letter!' Finally Mama yelled, 'Quiet!' When everyone shut up she said they could come into the kitchen for two minutes. No longer.

They followed her in and then when they were all sitting down, the red-headed one called Florian said, 'It's all in here!' He had a newspaper in his hand and waved it in the air. 'Here, look!' Mama grabbed the paper from his waving hand. Her face seemed to shrivel. 'It can't be true!' she gasped. Hansi took the paper from her and then everyone started shouting all over again.

I didn't understand what had happened until Maria explained. Hitler sent a letter to the judge who had sentenced the SA Brownshirts who had attacked Hansi. Hitler said he thought the Brownshirts should be pardoned because they had only been defending the country and its people against Bolshevik terrorists. He said no German should be condemned because of a Bolshevik. The letter was in all the papers. And Maria said it meant the Brownshirts would be released.

When Papa arrived from work and found Hansi's friends still talking in the kitchen, he went berserk and tried to throw them out. But Mama was having none of it. She said, 'Oh, be quiet, you silly man!' – she actually said that to Papa! 'Read this!' she said and stuffed the newspaper under his nose. Papa read it and exploded all over again. In the end Mama invited the boys to stay for supper and Papa couldn't do a thing about it.

December 23rd, 1932

Oma died last night. At last! But now we're not allowed to be cheerful. And because Mama has to prepare for Oma's funeral, Erna has been left in charge of the Christmas food preparations. How could Mama leave the food up to Erna?

December 24th, 1932

I had to kiss Oma's dead face. It was disgusting. Her hollow eyes seem to eat right into my soul and gobble it up.

January 4th, 1933

If it wasn't for Hansi's friends, life would be really, really dull. They're here all the time now. Papa storms off to his study if they're still here when he gets back from work but Mama says at least Hansi comes out of his room now. The 'boys' – that's what Mama calls them – sit in the kitchen, warming their hands and feet against the stove and talk and talk and talk. Maria says none of them studies any more because almost all the lecturers at the university have been sacked because of the cuts.

Hubert doesn't like Hansi's friends one little bit. He says they're the enemy. I like them though, especially Florian. He always says hello to me. When they joke and laugh Hansi is just like his old self – he even gave me a wink today. Erna hates them almost as much as Papa and Hubert do. I asked Maria if that was because she doesn't like Communists. Maria laughed and said no, it's because they make a mess of her precious kitchen.

Huh! It's not her kitchen.

January 6th, 1933

We got marzipan sweets for the Three Kings day today, the only thing that has made the holidays bearable.

January 9th, 1933

Sister Gertrude had promised to announce the title of this year's story competition today. I was so excited. I was sure I would be able to write something good enough to win whatever the subject was. Then she told us: *Write about an important event that took place in Germany in 1914.* How boring! What can I say about that? I'll never win.

January 11th, 1933

Hubert was in a fight after school today. His so-called friends called Hansi a Bolshi enemy of the state and Papa a wishy-washy Catholic. Then they kicked Hubert out of his own ganghut. The ganghut Hubert had helped build! They said they would get him kicked out of the Hitler Youth. He said let them try. He had a split lip and his face was all bloody. I sneaked him into the house and helped him tidy himself up.

Hubert said it was Hansi's fault and the sooner Hansi went to Leobschütz the better. I didn't tell him that I'd heard Mama and Papa having a big argument over Hansi: Papa said he was fed-up watching Hansi hanging about the house all day long doing nothing, that it was time for him to leave. But Mama insisted that Hansi was going nowhere until he was completely better. When Papa asked when that would be, she said only God knows that.

January 16th, 1933

I saw Hubert reading the newspaper today. I couldn't believe it. He's never read anything in his life before. He'd been given it by a friend. It was the Völkerscher Beobachter. He said he's reading a story by Karl Aloys. It's called Der Hitler Youth Quex. He says it's brilliant. There's a new instalment in every issue of the newspaper. It's all about the Hitler Youth boy Herbert Norkus, the one who was killed by the Communists. He said Quex is short for 'Quicksilver'. From now on he said he wanted me to call him 'Quex'. He said they're going make a film of the story and when it's out he's definitely going to go and see it.

I told him I was struggling to find something to write about for the story competition. He didn't know what the problem was, he said I just needed to write about the Great War. I am not writing about fighting!

January 30th, 1933

Hitler has been made Chancellor of Germany. Sister Gertrude made a special announcement at school. She had a big smile on her face and said, 'At last we have a chancellor who is prepared to do something!' Everyone was very excited. I rushed straight home after school. I wondered what Mama and Papa would say – I knew what Hansi and Hubert would. But when I got home I was locked out. It has never happened before. Ever. Someone is always in, even if it is only Erna. I had to ask Mrs Schwarzkopf for help as she has a spare key.

I don't like Mrs S one tiny bit. Ages ago when I was little I was down in her garden – well, it's not her garden, it's a communal garden, but you would think it was her garden the way she goes on about it. Anyway, I was in the garden and she'd left some bread crumbs out on the grass for the birds. I was only four and I felt hungry so I picked up a piece of bread and ate it. Mrs S went berserk. She actually ran all the way from her house to the garden to tell me off. 'That bread is for the little birds!' she yelled. 'It is not for greedy little girls like you!' Even when I started to cry she didn't stop yelling. I was only four years old.

One look at the scowl on Mrs S's face and you could tell she wasn't happy about me disturbing her. I asked for the spare key but under no circumstances would she give me it. She said she would come and 'let me in' herself.

I had to wait while she 'tidied' herself up. This involved her combing her long black straggly hair into a limp bun on top of her head, dabbing some orange powder on her droopy cheeks and pulling a sagging cardigan smelling of fried onions over her dirty house apron. Mama would have had something to say about that – for Mama appearances are everything.

As Mrs S closed her door she said she had better things to do than help lazy girls who had forgotten their keys. I tried to tell her I didn't actually have a key to forget but she wouldn't listen. She stomped ahead of me, saying she was going to have to have a word with Mama about this. And then she just stopped walking. I nearly bumped right into her. I thought she must have forgotten something and waited for her to turn back but she didn't budge.

She stood staring down the road in the direction of the post office. I followed her gaze. Two men in postal uniforms were mucking about on the post office roof. Between them they struggled with a huge rolled up piece of material. Carefully, they tried to fix the material to the flagpole on the roof. The men shoved and pulled and struggled and heaved but still the material stayed rolled up. Then from nowhere a gust of wind caught the material. In an instant it unfurled itself and flew open to its full length. It was a magnificent black swastika against a red background. It swirled and flapped in the wind.

Mrs Schwarzkopf suddenly turned and seized my face in her hands. Her eyes were all watery. She said in a voice all fluttery, 'What a day!' Tears started to run down her face. 'This is it! The beginning of a brand new era for Germany at last! The end of misery and poverty for ever! Justice will reign once more for all Germans everywhere! Oh, what a wonderful future awaits us! We are so lucky! So lucky!' And then she put her big rubbery wet lips on my mouth and kissed me! AGH! I couldn't wait to get away from her.

February 1st, 1933

Hitler was on the radio! I heard him speak, it was so exciting. Wait till I tell Hubert. We listened at school and Sister Gertrude made us write it down. All I could get was:

The new government will preserve and defend the basic principles on which our nation has been built up. They will regard Christianity as the foundation of our national morality and the family as the basis of our national life.

I showed it to Papa and Mama. Papa said, 'At least he's a Christian.'

Mama said, 'At least he recognises the importance of the family.'

Hansi scoffed, 'You're being fooled. According to Hitler you can be either a Christian or a German, but not both.'

Papa said, 'How dare you call me a fool!'

Hansi said, 'I said you're being fooled! Well, he won't get away with it! Every time that man speaks publicly, we'll be there! We'll demonstrate for as long as it takes!'

It probably was the wrong time to say it, but I chose that moment to tell them what the subject for the story competition was. Mama looked at me as if I was mad. She said, 'What has that got to do with what we are talking about?'

I felt about one centimetre tall.

February 2nd, 1933

Erna doesn't work for us any more. She sent a message via Mrs Schwarzkopf to say she had a new job and wouldn't be back. Just like that. Mama was furious. 'After all I've done for her! This is how she repays me! She doesn't even give us any notice! The selfish, ungrateful ingrate!'

According to Mrs S, Erna got a 'live-in' position in a big house on Kaiser Strasse. Mrs S said that Erna shares a room with another scullery maid and gets her own bed as well as three meals a day. She works seven days a week but can get time off to go to church and has every last Sunday of the month free to do what she wants. Finally, Mrs S said that Erna was really pleased with her new position because not only does she get better paid than she ever did from Mama – which I don't believe because Mama spoiled her – she doesn't have to share her bed with her old oma anymore. Mama wanted to know how Erna had heard about the job and Mrs S said she didn't know, but Mama reckons Mrs S had a hand in it. Mrs S used to clean for a judge in Kaiser Street.

Mama said we'll all simply have to do more around the house. I said I'd be happy to do more and Mama said that was good because I would have to, but she didn't sound as if she thought it was good.

Good riddance to bad rubbish is what I say!

February 4th, 1933

Sister Gertrude said Hitler has already started organising things. He's made a new rule for the 'protection of the German people', which allows the Nazis to forbid the meeting of any political groups. Hilde says this means Hansi and his friends won't be allowed to meet and chat in our kitchen any more. Oh, I hope not. I wish she'd hurry up and go to Holland!

February 15th, 1933

Hansi told Mama that some Jewish people were starting to leave Germany. When I asked him why, he said, 'Because Hitler hates the Jews almost as much as he hates the Communists – and Christians.' He raised his voice when he said 'Christians' and looked directly at Mama. She ignored him. 'But you're not leaving,' I said, 'are you? So why are they?' He shrugged, 'Maybe they have somewhere better to go to.' 'Are there many Jews in Breslau?' I asked. 'Of course,' he said, 'almost as many as Berlin.' 'What does a Jewish person look like?' I asked. He frowned and looked at me like I was stupid and left.

February 23rd, 1933

Mama found a copy of the Red Sailor in Hansi's room. She was furious with him but all Hansi said was, 'Hitler is evil! It's time to fight fire with fire.' Florian, his best friend – he's at the house all the time now – said, 'We must meet violence with violence!' Mama said, 'You'll both be lucky just to lose an eye if you don't stop this silly talk now!'

I asked Maria if she thought Hitler was evil, and she said no, that Hansi always exaggerates everything. She has already started going to the secretarial college and says she likes it. She still doesn't speak to Papa. They've never spoken since he announced Hilde would be going to Holland instead of Maria. I asked her again why Papa changed his mind about her going to Holland but she didn't answer.

February 28th, 1933

Papa came back from work all agitated and upset. He didn't even have his hat on. He burst into the kitchen and shouted, 'They've gone too far this time!'

Hubert hurried in behind him screaming, 'The Commies tried to blow up parliament! It's all over the papers. They actually tried to blow it up!'

'No one is safe in their beds!' said Papa, pacing up and down, 'What is Germany coming to!'

'The Communists have blown up parliament?' Mama said aghast. 'Are you sure?'

'They tried!' said Papa, 'Yesterday! They had a bloody good try!'

'But they failed, of course!' said Hubert, jubilant, 'They've got the Communist traitor who did it. The stormtroopers are helping the police look for his accomplices.'

'Can you imagine if they had got away with it!' Papa flopped on to his chair by the door.

'The Commies have had it now!' crowed Hubert

Papa pushed his hands through his hair, 'To come to this!'

'It's awful,' said Mama, sitting down next to Papa.

Hubert laughed, 'You know, Hansi had better lay low or he'll be arrested next!' Mama tried to give him a clip around the ear for that but Hubert just ducked and laughed again. He said, 'Hitler has vowed to stop the terrorism once and for all. He's got over 400,000 Brownshirts on orders to help the police round up every single Communist in Germany. Hitler says he will interrogate every one of them himself if he has to. He'll do whatever it takes to find the ones behind this attack against democracy! I tell you, Hansi had better lie low.'

'Will you shut up!' snapped Mama, 'You can't just round up someone because he's a Communist!'

'Hitler will find the guilty ones,' said Hubert, 'you wait and see!'

And then Mama said, 'Anyway, how will these Brownshirts know who to round up? Do they have a list or something?' Nobody heard her but me.

March 1st, 1933

Hansi and Papa had a huge row. Maria said it was all because Hindenburg has declared a state of emergency and there is a new decree for the 'Protection of the People and the State'. Hansi said this means no more free press and Papa said it was a small price to pay for stability and order. But Hansi called Papa a buffoon and said, 'It's not just the press he's muzzling, it's us! Don't you see? It's the end of freedom! The end of democracy! The end of liberty! The end of dignity! It's the beginning of the end of everything!' They argue all the time now.

March 2nd, 1933

Hansi didn't come home last night. Mama is distraught. She is convinced he's been taken by the Brownshirts but Papa says she's worrying about nothing, it's not as if it's the first time he's stayed over at someone's without telling them.

March 3rd, 1933

Hubert came home from the Hitler Youth with the full uniform – including the scarf! He said Hitler was coming to Breslau to make a speech in the Century Hall and his Hitler Youth group was going to be there! He looked really smart. Mama said he looked like a Brownshirt thug and told him to take the uniform off immediately. Hubert scowled, 'You should be proud. We Hitler Youth are the future. We are the custodians of the Third German Reich!' I thought Mama was going to explode. She called on Papa to talk to Hubert, but when Papa came he said that Hubert was right. I don't know if Mama will ever talk to Papa again.

Hansi still hasn't come home. Mama is really worried.

March 5th, 1933
Hansi still hasn't come home. Papa says he's probably staying away to avoid going to Leobschütz. Mama is furious with him for not taking his absence more seriously.

Still don't know what to write about for the story competition and the deadline is the end of March!

March 7th, 1933
I saw the blood stain yesterday lunchtime. I knew straight away what it meant. But there was no pain, nothing like the 'torture' Hilde talked about. That's why I was surprised. I went to see Mama, she was in her bedroom, she didn't go to work today. I gently knocked on her door and waited. Nothing. I slowly pushed the door open. The curtains were drawn. It was dark and stuffy but a chink of spring light sprinkled in and made things not quite so pitch black. I coughed. Mama didn't move.

Her body was all wrapped up in her quilt so just her brown hair was visible, all tousled and tumbling over her pillow. I coughed again. This time she half looked round. I told her it was me. She turned back to the pillow. Then I told her my periods had started. She didn't even look back. She said to the pillow, 'Go see Hilde.' I left the room and quietly closed the door behind me. I wanted to go to Maria but Mama had said Hilde. Why Hilde?

Hilde gave me this horrible belt thing with clips attached at either end and a blue box with a picture of a girl in the middle against a white halo. The box was half full of what Hilde called in a hushed tone 'sanitary towelettes'. I have to clip the towelette inside my underwear using the belt. Once the towelette is soiled I have to burn it in the kitchen stove – but only very last thing, after everyone else has gone to bed. I have never to burn it first thing because it can make a smell.

She also told me not to have a cold bath during my periods and that inside the box was a little slip of paper. It said *Please sell me a box of Camelia*. When I have only two towelettes left in the box I have to let Mama know. She will give me money to go to the pharmacist and buy more. I will need the little piece of paper from the box. I have to always ask for a women clerk. When she arrives I have to slip her the little sheet of paper. I don't know if I'll have the nerve to do that. I'll have to get Belen to help. I've to store them in my bedroom. Under no circumstances has Hubert to see them.

March 9th, 1933

When I told Belen about the 'curse' she laughed at Hilde's advice about not taking a cold bath. 'What rubbish. You've become a woman, not an invalid!' And she teased me all the way home but promised to come to the chemist when I needed to get some towelettes. She said she used Hartmann towelettes but that there was nothing wrong with the Camelia ones – of course, she would use a different one from me. Bet hers are more expensive.

I hate using the things. I had to take one with me to school and change there and carry a used one with me all day in my bag because the school incinerator wasn't working. It was horrible. I wrapped it and wrapped it in brown paper but I am sure everyone could smell it. Every time I ran I thought the one I was wearing would loosen itself from my underwear and fall to the ground. It seems so complicated and stupid. Why do we have to have periods and boys have nothing?

March 12th, 1933

Hansi is still not home. Mama is beside herself with worry. She even reported him missing to the police and she is getting angry with everyone for the slightest reason, even Hilde – Hilde said that while she was out shopping she saw some SA stormtroopers go into the Communist Party headquarters. They dragged KPD members out of their offices and flogged them in the market square in front of everyone. Mama shouted at her for hanging around places where she shouldn't have been. Hilde burst into tears and ran to her room.

March 13th, 1933

Belen said when her daddy went to work the SA had formed a sort of picket line outside the law courts and demanded everyone showed their papers. If anyone was Jewish they weren't allowed in, not even the judges. Anyone who complained got hauled away and beaten up. It wasn't very nice, she said. I asked her if her Papa got through and she was really angry with me for suggesting that he might not have. Her daddy is a judge or something like that.

I told Mama what Belen said had happened outside the law courts and Mama said that maybe if someone had rounded up all the SA Brownshirts Hansi would still be here! And then Papa said, 'He'll be found. Don't worry. He's probably just staying with friends keeping out of the way until everything calms down, which is very sensible.'

'For eleven days!' she yelled, 'Eleven days!'

Mama must be really worried, she never used to shout at Papa like that and now she shouts all the time. I hate it when they argue. When I'm married I'll never argue.

March 22nd, 1933

Hubert says the Nazis have arrested so many Communists and Socialists the jails are full and so they have started building special concentration camps to keep them in. When Mama heard him her face went all white and she left the kitchen without speaking another word. Maria gave Hubert such a look. Hubert just said, 'What?' but his face went red.

Hansi is still missing

I have got an idea for my story for the competition! Yes! Yes! Yes! I'm not going to tell anyone though, just in case they say it's a stupid idea.

March 24th, 1933

Sister Gertrude told us that President Hindenburg passed a new act called the Enabling Act. She said this means Herr Hitler will be able to look after the German nation without being hampered. She also said it's fitting that on this wonderful day Herr Hitler is opening the newly rebuilt parliament. But it doesn't feel like a wonderful day because when I told Mama what Sister Gertrude had said she replied, 'Yes, but did your precious Sister Gertrude say if she knew what Hitler had done with your brother? Did she, eh? Eh!'

March 25th, 1933

At last! Hansi has been found! He's alive and well! Thank goodness! Thank goodness! Thank goodness! Maybe Mama will stop worrying now. Maria said he'd been arrested for trying to break into a munitions plant near Orianenburg and is being held at Orianenburg concentration camp. Mama is so pleased to know he's alive but totally distraught he is in one of these concentration camp places.

Maria said the camps are supposed to be like prisons but not as bad. She said that Mama shouldn't worry. But telling Mama not to worry about Hansi is like telling the Pope not to believe in God.

As soon as Mama heard the news of Hansi's whereabouts

she rushed to see Papa at work. When she came back she was still upset. Apparently, when Papa had discreetly inquired about getting Hansi out of the camp on bail, he was told that 'enemies of the Reich' didn't get bail.

I didn't understand what that meant. Maria said it meant Hansi would have to stay locked up until his trial. When I asked when that would be, she said no one knew. Not even Papa or Mama. Hubert whispered to me, 'See, told you he was a terrorist!'

March 26th, 1933

Maria says Hansi is being transferred from Orianenburg to Breslau Kletschkau prison. It seems there is no room for all the prisoners at Orianenburg camp. Hansi will now be held there on remand until his case comes up in court.

I told Maria what Hubert said about Hansi being a terrorist. I thought she would laugh and say something like, 'Come on, Toni, it's Hansi! He's not a terrorist. He was probably at the wrong place at the wrong time.' But she didn't. She just said, 'Don't ever use that word again and don't talk about Hansi to anyone – and tell Hubert not to!'

Hubert says Hitler is now more powerful than any Kaiser in German history. Hitler can pass laws independent of the president, parliament or anyone else. And the first thing he's going to do, according to Hubert, is 'burst the fetters of the Versailles Treaty'. I asked him what that meant and he said that after the Great War it was forbidden for Germany to have a big army and defend herself. But no more! Hitler is going to create a huge strong army and Hubert says when he's bigger he's going to join it.

I like the idea of a big strong army that can defend Germany. Papa agreed. He said, 'At last we'll be able to hold our heads up high with our European neighbours.' But Mama said, 'Don't talk to me about Hitler. It's that man's fault Hansi is in jail.'

Mama is making Hansi a big parcel of food and clothes. She packed jam and bread and Würstchen and apples and clothes and even his sketch pad and pencils. Hilde says she doesn't know if she will be allowed to give it to him. Mama says she doesn't care, she's going to at least try.

March 28th, 1933

Papa told Mama that the church wants all its members to join the Nazi party. Mama says it's outrageous. Papa says he doesn't think it's such a bad idea. He thinks he will, finally, join the Nazi party. He says if he doesn't, people may think he is anti the National Socialists and that could make things tricky at work because all the jobs go to the Nazis now. Mama said she didn't care one way or another. All she wants is for Papa to find out when Hansi's trial is.

I handed in my story for the competition. Sister Gertrude said she hoped I'd do well.

April 1st, 1933

On the way home from school I saw some Brownshirts outside Haus Barasch. They barred the way to the revolving door and refused to let anyone in. Hubert said there's a nationwide boycott of Jewish businesses and lawyers and doctors. I said I didn't know Haus Barasch was owned by Jewish people. 'All Jews are subhuman scum,' he said. 'They've been robbing Germany blind for years.' I don't know what he means. I don't like talking to him sometimes.

April 2nd, 1933

Mama didn't come home from the hospital till the morning. She is a trained doctor and is very clever. She said it was one of the busiest nights they'd ever had. To make matters worse the SA Brownshirts wouldn't let the Jewish doctors into the hospital to work. The Brownshirts said it was part of a national boycott.

It didn't matter that it was bedlam inside and hundreds of people needed attended to. They absolutely refused to allow the Jewish doctors inside. That was why Mama stayed to help, she doesn't usually work nights.

She said she had never seen so many people who had been beaten up in the one place. When the people were asked what had happened to them, they said they had been attacked just because they were members of Communist or Socialist parties.

Some of the men were over sixty years old, she said. And one had all the fingers on his right hand broken. They didn't know how the SA knew what their political views were because they were just ordinary people, not fancy politicians. Someone said the church was giving out the names and addresses of all the Communists and Socialists in its congregations – only the church had that sort of information, other than the parties themselves. But a priest with a black eye disagreed, he said the church would never help Hitler. Two elderly businessmen had been so badly beaten they couldn't walk. A boy of fourteen had his arm broken.

Mama said it was atrocious. Most of the people who'd been beaten up have never seen a fight before in their life, never mind been in one. She said, to make matters even worse every now and then, whenever they felt like it basically, the Brownshirts stomped up and down the corridors checking on the doctors. If a doctor spent too long treating someone, he or she was accused of pampering the victim. If anyone said anything about the terrible state of the victims, they were accused of being anti-Nazi.

She said one of her colleagues was dragged away and severely beaten because he called the SA thugs. Then Papa said he hoped she'd not told anyone at her work that Hansi was in that camp. Oh, she was really angry at that. She said, 'You stupid man! We were overworked and understaffed. It was chaos. I had no time to discuss my family problems, even if I wanted to!' Papa looked a little sheepish then. 'I am just saying, it wouldn't do for too many people to know about where he is.' Mama gave him such a furious look. She said coldly, 'So much for Hitler the Christian!'

April 8th, 1933

Mama came back from work exhausted again. As always, the first thing she asked was if there was any news of Hansi. There wasn't. There isn't. She sighed. Papa asked her how work was. She said, 'Most of the Jewish doctors have returned. I thought maybe they'd stay away after that ridiculous boycott, but they've come back. Thank goodness. At least they're not scared by the Brownshirts!' I don't know what she meant by that. Is she trying to say that Papa is scared of them? That's so unfair.

April 10th, 1933

Hubert said Hansi was a traitor and refused to acknowledge Hansi as his brother. Papa threatened to beat Hubert if he ever said anything like that again. Papa said, 'Hitler himself talks about the sanctity of the family! It's at the centre of the National Socialist ideology!' But Hubert, who wears his Hitler Youth uniform all the time now, squared up to Papa. He said if Papa beat him, he would be attacking the German nation and it was a treasonable offence. For a second Papa looked as if he was going to give him a slap, but then he simply turned away and went to his study. Luckily Mama had gone to her room by then.

April 11th, 1933

We received our first letter from Hansi. It was addressed to Mama and not Papa. Papa was furious! He said that as the head of the family the letter should have been addressed to him. Mama paid no attention. She tore open the envelope and greedily read what Hansi had written. Then she read it out loud to us. Even Hubert hung about and listened. I don't believe he hates Hansi at all, he just hates the fact he's a communist.

Dearest Mama,

I have passed this letter to a comrade who is being released and promises to try to get this to you. By the time you get it I should have been moved to Kletschkau. I don't know why we are being moved. The old hands say it will be better there than here because Breslau jail is run by proper prison guards and they tend to be more decent than the Brownshirts who are deliberately malicious to us.

We are in an old paint factory. On arrival we were divided up into groups, but we all sleep together in the same place, on the old shop floor. There is no furniture at all, just some blankets on the concrete floor to indicate where we sleep. Some of the others are angry because they don't have a cell of their own, especially those comrades who believe themselves to be important functionaries. But I feel safer being with everyone else. There is a priest in my group and a few useless socialists, and a Jewish department store owner – he says the Reich demanded he sell his department store to them and when he refused he was arrested. There's also one mad man whose only crime seems to be to be mad and one Jehovah's Witness.

During the day we are marched out of town to a munitions factory about a kilometre away. There we are forced to carry out hard labour. It is a long back-breaking day. Dust fills our lungs and by the end of the day every single muscle in my body aches. But when we are out of the camp the SA are less likely to abuse us. As soon as we are back, however, it is a different matter – this even though the camp is slap bang in the centre of town, in full view of the townspeople.

Once there the officers continuously call us names and

wallop us with their blackjacks for no reason. We are refused privacy during our toilet and at night we are denied sleep. I have only been here 7 nights but on five separate occasions they have woken me up in the early hours of the morning and taken me to one of the smaller rooms. At first they tried to beat a confession out of me – though I am not sure what it is I am supposed to confess to. Treason, I think. But this I will never do. Neither will any of the others. We love our Germany. By day three, when they realised the violence wasn't working, they tried different tactics.

First, I was fed salty food at my evening meal and then denied water. It was unbearable. Then, when that also didn't work, they told me they would have my sisters arrested, that I would never be allowed to receive letters or parcels from you, that all my reading and relaxation time was going to be denied me until confessed. It was laughable! I know they cannot arrest the girls for no reason and I have no relaxation time to be denied me. Of course, I want to hear from you but if they withhold your correspondence I will still survive. I have my memories and they can't take them.

I am not alone in withstanding these tactics. My fellow comrades are equally resistant. And some of the more important comrades were treated far worse and didn't give in. They are so stupid, these Brownshirts. All their torture does is strengthen our resolve. We will never give in. I don't know when my trial will be and the not knowing makes me anxious, but my comrades here offer help and advice, which is reassuring.

Please send my love and good wishes to my sisters and brother and Papa, who I know will be disappointed in me, but I believe I am on the side of right. I hope that it will not be long

before I see you in my beloved hometown, Breslau.
Hansi

April 18th, 1933

Hubert is annoying just about everyone, even me and I do my best to be on his side but sometimes it's impossible to like him. His biggest newest hero is our Chief of Police and boss of the SA stormtroopers in Silesia, Edmund Heines. Mama says he is a horrible man. Maria says he used to be a member of the Fehme. Maria said the Fehme were a secret army and they used to kill people for the Black Reichswehr in the olden days. Even Papa says he is a villain, which is amazing as Papa is so for Hitler nowadays, especially as the Pope has said Hitler's treatment of the Communists is right. But Mama says that Bishop Josef Ferche is openly against Hitler and what higher authority is there in Breslau than the Bishop of Breslau? But Papa says if Her Brückner, our governor, openly supports Hitler, so should we.

As always, they're fighting over politics!

Dearest Mama,
It was wonderful to receive your letter and parcel, which found me at last here at Kletschkau. I'm not sure if all you sent reached me safely but what did arrive – the sausage and chocolate and socks and vest and writing paper and pens – are all very very welcome. How kind you are. All we possessed was what we had on us on arrival, which was the clothes we were wearing and a few pfennigs. We were given a piece of cloth as a towel and one tiny piece of soap to wash ourselves and our clothes. It has to last us a week but that at least is more than we had in Orianenburg.
    Food is noodle soup and grey bread and an occasional

piece of wurst. Anything else we want, we need to bargain for, which I am now in the lucky position of being able to do since receiving your parcel. I am also lucky because I was not sent to Durrgoy concentration camp which is also here in Breslau. They say it is very, very strict and the main camp in the area for us Communists. But they also say Durrgoy is only for the bigwig Communists and Socialists, not the small fry like me. So I am lucky I am not a bigwig politico and have been sent here.

That said, the conditions here are not wonderful. It is cold and miserable and there are eight of us crowded together in a cell meant for two people. I am confined with a murderer, three thieves, a gypsy traveller from Serbia, who has been accused of being a fortune teller and whom no one trusts, and two university lecturers. But while the conditions are not good, at least the nightly visits have stopped. To be able to get a few hours of sleep at night is such a luxury. However, what is becoming intolerable is the not knowing what is going on. From one day to the next we are told nothing. We don't know when our trial will be, or what exactly we are accused of. Of course, there are rumours about what has happened to other Communists but no one knows anything for sure. It is so frustrating and so unsettling to think that we could be incarcerated here indefinitely and that no one cares.

I have to stop. Please, please write again. I look forward to your news. Oh, and one last thing, has Florian been in touch? He seems to have disappeared completely. None of us has any idea what's happened to him. If you get any news of him, please let me know. And if you could send me a newspaper, any newspaper, that would be really helpful.

Your loving son, Hansi

April 22nd, 1933

Mama came back from hospital in a filthy mood. She said, 'They're at it again! It makes me so angry! They're saying Hitler is going to stop all 'non-Aryan' doctors, pharmacists and dental technicians from working in our state hospitals and health centres.'

Papa said, 'It's a crisis, my dear, and desperate times call for desperate measures.'

'What's having Aryan or non-Aryan staff got to do with anything? No sensible person is going to pay any attention to such nonsense!' said Mama.

'You can't just ignore the law!' said Papa, shocked.

'Of course, we can. We'll have no one left to run the hospital if we don't, especially now all the Communists and Socialists have been locked up!'

'You'll get into trouble!'

'Who's going to tell on us, eh? You?'

Papa got all blustery, 'Of course not! But Hitler must have his reasons.'

'Hansi is right, Herr Hitler is not a Christian. Cardinal Bertrand says he will never revise his opinion of the Nazis and as long as Hansi is locked up, neither will I.'

'Cardinal Bertrand is a renegade!' said Papa, 'Everyone knows that! All Hitler is trying to do is gain stability. If anyone can hold Germany together, he can.'

'What's gaining stability got to do with locking up my son and raiding bookshops?'

'What are you talking about now!' said Papa, growing angry.

'Don't you know what happened today? Don't you? The brave stormtroopers stormed into the big bookshops in town and removed all the books by Thomas Mann, Stefan Zweig and Emile Zola! They said they were "decadent". What has removing

these books got to do with gaining stability, eh? Eh!'
Papa didn't answer her.

I wish they would stop arguing!

Dear Mama,
They sent Papa's lawyer away, but you will know that by now.
Instead I have been given one by the State. This attorney seems
totally uninterested and completely incompetent. Please ask Papa
to see if he can do something to change him.

We are not sent to work here yet, so there is nothing to
do all day. We are woken at dawn and allowed fifteen minutes
of exercise then are bundled back into our cells, sometimes for
up to ten hours. If we are caught talking to our comrades we
are punished. This can be anything from being denied exercise
time to having no food or water. Of course, we still manage to
communicate – we make sure we are very quiet.

It is not as bad as in Orianenburg but the endless waiting
is becoming unbearable. Hopefully, though, I will be out soon.
Have you heard yet when my trial is to be?

Please write. Let me know your news. Still no word of
Florian? I am worried for his safety. And please, please remember
to send a newspaper, if you can. No matter if it is out of date. We
have no news at all. What are the German people saying about
all the illegal arrests?
Your loving Hansi

Leaders vow to crush Marxists!

Breslau, Silesia, April 29, 1933

The world looks on in horror as National Socialists in Breslau pledge to destroy Marxists and Jews with illegal floggings, imprisonment, social defamation and economic starvation. Chief of Police of Breslau and commander of the Silesian Nazi storm troopers, Edmund Heines, asserts in his defence, "We did not pass one death sentence as provided in the national decree, although some amply deserved it. But we will continue to use drastic measures to put the Jew in his place and crush Marxist organisations."

Helmuth Brueckner, Governor of Silesia, fully supports his Police Chief saying, 'Everybody who actively opposes the present regime must be wiped out. Did the world protest against the manhunt against the Brownshirts? It did not and today it should be ashamed."

As a consequence of these "excesses" the Marxists and Jews of Silesia are in constant fear of being beaten and imprisoned. It is estimated that among the victims 40 per cent are Jews and 60 per cent are Marxists. Many are still in hospital but doctors are afraid to attest to the beatings.

April 29th, 1933

I got a letter from Belen. She is in America. America! I can't believe it. She says her parents prefer it there. I didn't even know she had left, she just wasn't at school one day and no one knew where she was. There was never anyone home when I called. She could have at least told me she was leaving. She was supposed to be my best friend.

Dear Toni,
Sorry I didn't say cheerio. We had to leave quickly. Something to do with Daddy's job. My folks love it here. I hate it. It's cold and

horrible. The food is disgusting and there is only one cinema in this wretched little town. And everyone – and I mean absolutely everyone – goes to church. It's worse than in Breslau.

The school is hopeless – there's no uniform and the teachers don't even have Latin or literature classes. They are so ignorant! The only good thing is that there are boys in the school as well as girls. Can you imagine what Sister Gertrude would say to that? And, dear Toni, some of them are quite good looking, although nowhere near as handsome as German boys. And no one – and I mean absolutely no one – knows where Germany is, never mind Silesia.

I can't believe this is the country where Nancy Drew comes from. Utah has to be the least exciting town I have ever been to in my life. The only saving grace is the radio – there's a programme called The Shadow, it's wonderful.
Write back to me, pleeeeeeease!
Your best friend, Belen

May 2nd, 1933

Hubert is full of talk of the May Day rally. There are pictures of it in all the papers. Mama told us not to go but Hubert ignored her. He said there were huge crowds and flags everywhere. Hubert says he is so happy to be German. Me too. I know Hansi is in trouble but with Hitler things are going to get better. Anyway, they can't get worse.

Belen's mother sent us a cutting from a newspaper in America. It talks about Germany. She asked me to translate it for Mama and ask Mama to write back to her and tell her if it was true. Mama said, 'Some of us are too busy working to have time to write letters!'

Dearest Mama,
At last the trial is nearly here. I am so nervous. We ask and ask
but we are not allowed our own defenders, we must use the state
defender, who is acting more like a prosecutor. There are also
rumours that the Geheime Staatspolizei – the Gestapo – will
be involved, but no one knows if it's true. I don't know why the
Gestapo would be at the trial. My comrades say that I have not to
worry. That I have no case to answer. So I will be positive.
Your loving son, Hansi

May 10th, 1933

There was a huge fire in the middle of Schloss Platz today.
Everyone was looking. A group of very smart SS officers were
burning books. Hundreds and hundreds of books. The debris
spilled all over the square in random bundles. Someone said
they'd been collected from all the libraries in Silesia, even the
university libraries. There were all sorts of books – big ones,
small ones, thick ones, thin ones. I even saw a copy of
Buddenbrooks by Thomas Mann.

I rushed home to tell everyone but they already knew. Hilde
and Maria said I had to help them take Mama's books from the
shelves and hide them in the cupboard under the stairs. Papa
gave each of us a list of writers to find: I had all the books by
Bertolt Brecht, Heinrich Heine, Max Brod and Ernst Toller.
When I asked Maria why we were doing it, she said the SS have
decided that these books are 'decadent' and have to be destroyed
but Mama has forbidden Papa to destroy them. So for now we
are just hiding them. There are hardly any books left on the
shelf now. I wonder if Nancy Drew is considered decadent?

Dearest Mama,
Disaster! The June trial has been postponed and no one knows

when it will be. This means more sitting around in this damnable place, doing nothing, wasting away, while the rest of the world carries on without us.

I am sorry your parcel didn't get to me – sometimes the guards keep them. I suppose we should be grateful that these regular guards are not as mean or spiteful as the Brownshirt guards. And now at least we get out of the cell four times a day. We also have menial tasks to do – my job is to scrub the floors. This is very tedious employment – what man in their right mind would ever choose to do such a job for a living? But the work actually helps fill the time until relaxation time, which is when we get to read and write our letters.

You can't imagine how we all wait for this time of day. Even those who have no one to write to or to get letters from look forward to it because whoever gets a letter reads it out to us all. We are so starved of news that just hearing the minutiae of the daily life of ordinary families is reassuring. It reminds us that we are not alone, that there's a normal world full of normal people outside this dump and that one day soon we'll be part of it again. If only they would say when the trial is and then we would know how much longer we have to wait.

I've stopped sleeping at nights again. And now it seems we are only going to be allowed to write one letter every two months – and they are talking of censoring the letters. So, unfortunately, this is the last one from me for two months, Mama. But your visit in-between will make up for not being able to write. I am so looking forward to you coming, even if it is just for ten minutes. And if you come can you bring any books, but not the political ones, they don't allow that, or newspapers. Oh, and, Mama, can

you also bring my sketch book and charcoals.
Your loving son, Hansi

July 18th, 1933

I won the big story prize! I can't believe it. I won! I won! I won!

Sister Gertrude announced it at the end of the summer 'special' mass. I was presented with a Rothwell German-English pocket dictionary. It was handed to me in front of the whole school. Everyone clapped. It was wonderful. The cover is brown leather on the outside and creamy and marbly on the inside. It's lovely and it's all mine!

The title of my story was: *In 1914 a European monarch goes into a department store for the first time and my Mama was there*! It's about when Mama met Kaiser Wilhelm in the new Wertheim department store in Berlin. Mama used to tell us the story all the time and Papa would say it was his favourite story because it was about his two favourite people –Mama and Kaiser Wilhelm!

Kaiser Wilhelm was visiting the store when Mama happened to be there. A huge crowd had gathered to wait for him. When he arrived everyone got very excited. They started waving flags and cheering.

Mama was at the back of the crowd and couldn't see a thing. She was determined to get to see him so she could tell Papa. She pushed her way to the front. But just as she got close the crowd surged forward and Mama was squashed. Everything started to spin around her. Her legs started to buckle – she was pregnant at the time. And just when she thought she was going to fall over she heard a deep, rich, majestic, booming voice say, 'Make room there, that young lady is going to faint!' It was Kaiser Wilhelm himself! Everyone quickly made room around Mama. As she struggled to steady herself the Emperor came forward and gallantly propped his gloved hand in front of Mama's face.

She dutifully kissed it. 'There now,' he said and took his hand away.

Mama was so flustered she forgot to curtsey but by that time he was already striding into the store, waving majestically to the right and then to the left as he went.

Of course, I wrote more than that but that was the gist of the story. Sister Gertrude said it wasn't what she was expecting but she liked it. Then she actually said it was very accomplished writing. I ran all the way home to tell everyone but no one was in and I had to wait until later. I was so looking forward to seeing their faces when I told them.

When Mama did finally come home she arrived with Papa and they were having a huge argument. At first I couldn't make head nor tail of what it was about, but as they continued to shout at each other I began to understand what they were saying.

It seems Herr Hitler has passed this new law, which rules that some unhealthy people must have a kind of operation. After the operation the people won't be able to make a family. New Health Courts are to be set up around the country. They are to be attached to hospitals. One of these courts is going to be attached to the hospital where Mama works and she is one of the doctors chosen to sit on the Health Court panel.

The panel will decide which patients will be allowed to have children and which won't. Mama said the new law was unChristian and wholly unethical. Papa said it was 'eugenics'. Mama said 'eugenics' was ridiculous mumbo-jumbo. Papa said it was scientific fact, which is why you could study it at university. Mama said, 'Eugenics is applied bigotry.'

'It's improvement through exclusion!' said Papa.

'It is an outrage! One of my lofty colleagues thinks it's reasonable to consider an application for sterilisation for someone who has a harelip. A harelip!'

Papa said, 'You cannot deny it's a bad idea to taint the blood of healthy people with the blood of people who are unhealthy. I don't see anything wrong with it.'

'Another colleague says he has a female teenage patient in his care who suffers from schizophrenia and because he doesn't like her attitude, he's going to see to it that she is one of the first people to be sterilised!'

'German race hygiene and eugenics scholars have been producing the most advanced studies in favour of keeping races pure bred! We are ahead of all of Europe in this field, even America lags behind us now!'

'And what if our daughter, Johanna, had lived? Would you think it right that she be sterilised? She would have been 20 this year.'

When Mama said that Papa shut right up. Mama's first baby, our sister Johanna, died when she was three. She suffered from mongolism. It was about then that I decided to interrupt them and tell them my good news. I thought it'd maybe cheer them up a bit. But all Mama could say was, 'And how is writing a funny story going to help you get a job when you finish school, eh?' Papa at least muttered 'Well done'.

Later when I told Maria what Mama had said, she told me not to mind, that Mama's just worried about Hansi. When is she not worried about Hansi? I hate Hansi!

Dearest Mama,

It was wonderful to see you, Mama! And to get so much news! I've told everyone about Hilde going to Holland and Maria in the college. And how wonderful that Toni is becoming so grown-up and is so helpful. The photos are such a comfort, and every man who is not married or courting (and even some who are) has fallen in love with Maria.

Still no date for the trial.
Your loving Hansi

July 20th, 1933

All day Hubert has been making the Heil Hitler salute. It's driving us all crazy. If we bump into him in the hall, or the kitchen, or coming out of the bathroom, he screams Heil Hitler! or Sieg Heil! When we tell him to stop he says it's the official Nazi greeting now and he'll never stop.

Apparently, this is how Germans are supposed to greet each other from now on. I quite like doing it. Mama says she'll never use the Nazi salute. Ever. And she said she'd tan Hubert's hide herself if he didn't stop talking about the National Socialists, even if Papa wouldn't.

July 30th, 1933

It's my birthday. I am thirteen today. Only Maria remembered. She gave me a hanky.

August 3rd, 1933

Even though it was Mama's day off and we were on holiday from school, Mama decided to go into work. When she came home she said that Jewish doctors were now forbidden to work with Aryan doctors. She said it was ridiculous. If there were no Jewish doctors they'd have to close all the hospitals. Fortunately for the patients of the hospital, she said, no one was paying any attention to the ban.

August 9th, 1933

I went to the covered swimming baths in Zwinger Strasse with the girls from the church group today. There was a new skinny leisure attendant giving out the tickets. 'Any Polaks or Jews in your group?' she said before giving us our tickets, 'cause no Polaks or Yids are allowed in here.' We told her we were German

Catholics. She frowned, 'You'd better give me your names.' It was ridiculous. But she insisted. So one by one we said who we were. When she heard my name she laughed and said, 'Not Polish, eh? I think not! That's the most Polish name I've heard in a long time.' I was furious! How dare she! 'I am not a Pole!' I insisted. 'I'm German through and through!' The woman shrugged, 'Well, your name sure sounds Polish.'

All the girls defended me. They said I was the most German of all German girls they knew, that my father was even Prussian and you can't get any more German than Prussian. The ticket woman scowled, 'All I'm saying is that Nasiski sounds as Polish as Polish can be! I'll let you in this time but if it turns out you're from the East you're going to get me into trouble and I'll not be pleased, not one little bit!'

Stupid woman! It spoiled all my fun.

November 23rd, 1933

Hubert says I should join the Bund Deutscher Mädel or BDM – the German Hitler Youth for Girls. He thinks I would really like it. But Mama was furious with the suggestion. She said, 'It's bad enough that one of my children is indoctrinated by the National Socialists, I'll not have two of them brainwashed!'

Hubert laughed at her. He said he was proud to be in the Hitler Youth, proud to be a pure German and even prouder to follow a man like Hitler. 'A man who is going to create a pure and invincible Aryan race by sterilising all the duds and rejects in it!' Mama slapped him right across the face. Really hard. I thought he was going to cry. She told him to wash his mouth out with soap. 'Every human being is worthy of your respect, don't you ever refer to any person as a dud or reject' again!' He was furious with her. But not as furious as she was with him.

I think I would like the BDM but I don't want to upset Mama, she's upset enough. Maybe when Hansi gets out of that prison everything will get back to normal. Maybe I will then.

November 24th, 1933

Nothing to write about today. School is boring. Hubert is always out at his Hitler Youth group. Maria is either at work or with her boyfriend, Georg. Hilde is always at her church group or praying or something. My church group evenings are even more boring than school – all we do is sew little doilies and I hate sewing! And Mama and Papa never stop arguing about the Nazis. Papa said Hitler received 92% of the vote in the last election. Mama said, 'Well, of course he did, he's arrested all the opposition!'

Mama says Hansi is in jail because of Hitler and she'll never support the Nazis as long as Hansi is locked up unjustly. Papa just shakes his head. Mama says animals have more rights than some Germans. I think she's worried because we've not had a letter from Hansi in ages.

November 25th, 1933

Mama sent me to the haberdashery to get her sewing things. She usually goes herself but was too busy. She said if there were Brownshirts hanging about outside the shop to ignore them, that they wouldn't bother a child. That immediately made me worry.

I asked Hilde what a Brownshirt would be doing outside the haberdashery. She said the sewing shop was owned by a Jewish woman and Hitler didn't want us Germans to shop in Jewish shops any more. Every now and then he sends Brownshirts to hang about outside the Jewish shops to put people off shopping in them. 'It's not against the law to shop there though,' she said, 'so don't worry.' That just made me feel worse.

The closer I got to Mama's shop, the more nervous I became. And then for the first time I saw the posters plastered on the notice board and the shop windows: *Germans, shop no more in Jewish shops! Jews will not be served here! Whoever buys from a*

Jew is a traitor of the people! I felt even more nervous. What if a Brownshirt saw me go in the shop and decided I was a traitor? But luckily for me there were no SA hanging around when I got there. What a relief!

I pushed the door open and the little bell rang out to let the owner know she had a customer. I quickly got Mama's things and hurried home. I think I'll get my hair cut short. Everyone says it's very old-fashioned to have it long. All the Hitler Youth girls have short hair.

December 10th, 1933

Mama and Papa argue constantly. She says Papa isn't doing enough to get Hansi out of prison and Papa says there's nothing he can do, if he makes a fuss he'll be accused of criticising the system and it's forbidden to criticise the Nazis. The Nazi party and German state are one by law now, he said, doesn't she know that? Mama says all she knows is Hitler is a dictator just like Mussolini. Papa says he's a strong leader and we need a strong leader in these difficult times.

I hate Hansi. It's his fault Mama and Papa argue all the time. Mama still hasn't started the Christmas baking. No sign of a goose either. I asked Papa when he was getting the Christmas tree and he said when Mama said so. We usually go to the horse market and get it there. It smells so fresh and earthy. Once in the house we hang Mama's starshaped ginger biscuits from the branches. Then we put up the wax candles. The room looks so warm and inviting with the candles flickering away and the smell from the sweet ginger biscuits mingled with the tangy scent of the pine needles is delicious. It will be Hansi's fault if Christmas is ruined.

Dearest Mama,
It is clear now the guards were just teasing us when they said

we would be home for Xmas. I was so looking forward to your cooking and the lovely carol service at the Mary Magdalene church. I think people are spying on me. Have you heard anything of Florian?

We wear a sort of uniform now. It has a number on it. We still know nothing of the trial date. They tell us nothing. Please don't forget to visit – or to write.

Hansi

February 2nd, 1934

Mama is angry with the Nazis again. She said they've taken out all references to Jews in the Psalms of David. 'What's that all about, eh? Eh?' she said.

I wish she wouldn't go on and on criticising the Nazis. It's embarrassing.

February 8th, 1934

Mama's bible circle has been cancelled. The Gestapo have forbidden them. Mama insisted Papa do something about it. But he said if he were to file a complaint against the Gestapo, he would lose his job. 'A complaint against the Gestapo is an attack against the Nazi party!' He suggested that instead of complaining she should join one of the National Socialist women's groups that have sprung up everywhere. Mama was so furious with him when he said that, she stormed out of the kitchen and slammed the door behind her.

March 2nd, 1934

Mama keeps asking Papa when Hansi is coming home and he keeps saying he doesn't know. Sometimes he tries to ignore her but then she simply repeats her question seven or eight or nine times, and doesn't stop until he answers. I don't know why he can't see that ignoring her makes her worse.

March 10th, 1934

I went to the cinema to see Catherine The Great but it wasn't on. It had been banned because the actress Elizabeth Bergman is Jewish. I was so disappointed.

March 18th, 1934

Hilde finally left by train for Holland today. Hurray! I told Maria it should have been her but she said it didn't matter any more, that she was very happy because she'd finished her course at college, got a good job in the savings bank and she and Georg were engaged to be married. And, she said, with the National Socialist party in power they would get a marriage loan – and as long as they had four children, which of course they would, they wouldn't have to pay any of the loan back.

I still feel embarrassed when she mentions Georg's name and can't look her in the eyes.

Of course Mama and Papa are very pleased about Maria's engagement. Mama really likes Georg even though he is a Brownshirt. And it's so exciting to have a wedding to look forward to. Maria says as soon as she is married she will leave her job and do what she was born to do, what all women are born to do, which is to have a family.

March 21st, 1934

Hitler has waged war against the five million unemployed. Hubert says even Mama won't be able to find anything wrong with that idea! I bet she will though.

April 1st, 1934

Hubert says there is another mass boycott of Jewish shops by the SA stormtroopers and his Hitler Youth group are going to help them with the boycott. I'm glad I'm not going to get Mama's sewing stuff today.

April 13th, 1934

At last! Hansi has a date for his trial! Maria says too many people were complaining that the prisoners in jail and camps were being treated unfairly. The government had to do something about it. They're holding a mass trial for them all so they don't have to wait any longer. It's set for the 30th May. Mama is so pleased.

Mass trials of Bolsheviks!

May 30, Breslau, 1934

Mass trials begin of thousands of alleged communist offenders, who have been waiting for up to two years in German prisons and concentration camps to be tried. Over one hundred defendants will appear together before the Bar at the one time. Charges range from high treason to handling high explosives.

The State will try to show that the defendants were involved in a Communist plot to overthrow the government. One of the Nazis' main arguments in the campaign that brought them to power in early 1933 was the need to protect the People from a Communist uprising. They accused the attempted burning down of the Reichstag on the Communists and arrested thousands on the charge, some of whom were executed.

However, recently, the question as to who was responsible for the attack on the Reichstag has become international. The French and others insist the Communist involvement has not been proven and the Nazi stormtroops are part of Germany's military forces and this breaches the Treaty of Versailles. The National Socialist government insists the stormtroops are a safeguard from the internal threat of Communism.

Dear Mama

I have been declared an enemy of the state and convicted of treason. They are sending me to Dachau concentration camp, near Munich, along with virtually half of the staff of Breslau University, who have also been accused of equally ludicrous nonsense. I have been sentenced to eight years.

The Gestapo were all over the trial. They had a file on me. They knew everything about me. Even private things about me that I thought no one knew. My useless defence lawyer said I was guilty from the start but there were certain extenuating circumstances to account for my behaviour. He zipped through his arguments for my defence and before I know it I was pronounced guilty and sentenced. Effective immediately. It was a farce. I didn't stand a chance. No right of appeal.

I don't know if I am allowed visitors at Dachau. I will write as soon as I know. The others say it's not too bad, no worse than Orianenburg. And others say the Brownshirts are at least better than the SS Schutzstaffel, who some say are being trained to run the camps and take over from the SA Brownshirts. I will have no one there but I have resolve. At least I know what is happening to me now.

Hansi

June 6th, 1934

Papa and Mama were very serious today at dinner. Before we'd eaten Papa said because Hans Joachim was in jail for being an enemy of the state, the Gestapo could investigate Mama and Papa and charge them with being politically unreliable and both Hubert and me could be taken into care.

I couldn't believe it. I don't want to leave Mama and Papa!

Ever! And no matter how much Hubert says he likes Hitler, he'll always like Mama better.

Papa said it wasn't certain the Gestapo would investigate them, so it was especially important we didn't draw their attention by saying or doing anything that could be considered un-German or against the Reich. One black mark against us was bad enough, but two would mean Papa and Mama would be in trouble for sure.

Dear Mama from Dachau
The SS run this camp with help from the SA. It is not like Breslau jail. Or Orianenburg. It is very strict. They say we would have been better off in Durrgoy. But we are here. There are lots of rules. If we break any of them we are severely punished. I am going to do my best to work hard and not break any of the rules.
Hansi

June 13th, 1934

Every day when Mama gets back from work she cleans. She says she needs to get the house ready for when Hansi comes home. Maria keeps telling her he won't be back for another eight years but she doesn't seem to hear. Her fingers are red raw with the scrubbing.

Letter from Bezirksamt – Breslau City Council – to Frau Cecelia Nasiski:
June 15th
You are presently leasing Kleingarten two at the Burgunderweg near the Volkspark. Said allotment has not been managed since a long time, weeds have spread all over the whole parcel and have soared. The fence is not in order, and the whole allotment makes

an unaesthetic impression. We have to assume that you are no longer interested in leasing the parcel, and we will give it away to someone else, unless you object prior to the 25th of this month, and the allotment is put in order by that date.

Please take care of the removal of this nuisance, and give us further notice.

Bezirksamt Breslau

June 18th, 1934

Mama and Papa were arguing again today. It felt like the old days and it made me feel good – I never thought I'd feel good about Mama and Papa arguing! Mama said everyone at the hospital was talking about how Vice-Chancellor, Franz von Papen, had openly criticised Hitler and it would only be a matter of time before he took back control. Papa said Hitler was here to stay, and a good thing too. Then Mama said there was an infestation of little black bugs at the hospital, which no one seemed to be concerned about it except her. She said the hospital was getting dirty because they were short staffed and to top it all the Jewish doctors were talking about leaving for good – her colleague Dr Zimmermann, who's one of the longest serving members of staff, told her it was becoming harder and harder to make ends meet.

Dearest Mama,

We are allowed to write once a week every Sunday evening. The camp is an old munitions factory. We have to wear a blue and grey uniform or at least one part of it – either the shirt or the bottom. I prefer to wear the bottoms and my own shirt on top. I like having my shirt next to me because there is a patch on it, which you darned. I want that near to my heart.

On my trousers I have had to sew a patch with our prison number embroidered on it. We work every day but Sunday. I am not allowed to tell you what we do. In the middle of the parade area there is a ten man band. It plays cheerful music as we march back and forth to work or roll call.

We have also been given our own bowl for food, as well as a spoon, a slither of soap – one piece a week for clothes and our personal hygiene. It is very strict here. The SS officers punish us severely if we cause disruptions or don't follow the rules. One thing we have to be careful of are the crooks. The prison is full of them – petty criminals and thugs mostly. They have served their sentence in jail but have been sent here because the Reich feels that they are not safe to be released. We must watch our belongings at all times and they are always spoiling for a fight. I hate them.

Hansi

July 1st, 1934

Papa had the Völkisher Beobachter in his hand when he came in and wildly waved it about the room. He said the SA stormtroopers, headed by Hubert's hero of the day, Ernst Rhöm, had been caught red-handed planning a coup to overthrow Hitler. The report said Rhöm and many of his SA buddies had wanted to kill Herr Hitler and take over.

Hubert was horrified. His Brownshirt idols were traitors? No way! The paper said luckily Herr Hitler had found out what they were up to and suppressed the treacherous movement with a firm hand. The paper also said tens of SA leaders were killed in a big round up and thousands more were arrested. From now on the SA and the army were going to come under the direction of the SS, led by General Göring and Herr Himmler. It also suggested that the SA had been infiltrated by homosexuals. Hubert said he would never believe that any Brownshirt could be a homosexual. He also refused to believe the other story, which said the SA and not the Communists had been the ones who had tried to blow up parliament last year.

Then something odd happened, for the first time in ages Mama and Papa actually agreed on something – Mama said homosexuality was an abomination in the eyes of God and Papa said she was right. 'For people like them,' Mama said, 'no punishment is too severe!'

I asked Hubert what a homosexual was – I thought it meant men who like men and Hubert said it was. UGH! Disgusting! Hubert said the Gestapo had a special unit to hunt the sickos down.

For the whole evening Papa kept talking about the 'goings-on' and 'enemies within' and the 'Night of the Long Knives' and about how no one could trust anyone any more.

July 4th, 1934

At breakfast today Mama said she'd not been able to sleep the previous night because of the noise. When Maria asked her what noise, she said the noise of the mice scuttling about under the floorboards in her bedroom. Papa said he'd not heard a thing. Mama was cross with him. 'Of course you didn't because you're asleep as soon as your head hits the pillow.' Papa frowned. 'Okay,' he said, 'Get a cat.'

We've never had mice before. Ever. But a cat sounds like fun.

July 9th, 1934

We have a cat. Well, a kitten. She is so sweet. I call her Nancy and love playing with her.

Maria said that Georg has been banned from shopping in non-Aryan shops. Hubert asked why would he want to shop in such shops?

Dearest Mama,
There is a sign above the gate saying Arbeit Macht Frei – Work
Makes You Free – so I hope to be free soon.
Your loving son, Hansi

July 30th, 1934

I am fourteen today. No one remembered.

September 6th, 1934

We haven't heard from Hansi in over two months and it's all
Mama can talk about. 'Why haven't we heard from him? What's
he up to? What are they doing to him?'

October 12th, 1934

Mama didn't go into work today and it's not her day off. Instead
she stayed at home and scrubbed the house on her hands and
knees from top to bottom. We were not allowed to help her at
all. I could hear scrub, scrub, scrubbing long after I had gone to
bed. This was one of her biggest cleans yet.

I asked Maria why Mama hadn't gone into work. Maria said
that yesterday when Mama had been doing her ward rounds, a
Gestapo official had told Mama that the Reich didn't need
women doctors. He said her job was to look after the house and
her family. She told him she had good daughters who helped her
at home and that she was happy to continue to put her medical
training to the good use of the Reich. But then the Gestapo man
got nasty with her. He said it was because of women like her,
who didn't look after their home, that there were so many bad
Germans in jail. Mama was furious with him but she kept her
mouth closed because she didn't want to be accused of being
unhelpful and un-German. She'd pretended to agree to leave

but as soon as the Gestapo man left she just went back to work.

However, later in the day the director had called her to his office and sacked her. Mama asked if the Gestapo man had complained but the director said no, Herr Hitler has decreed that except in exceptional circumstances, women have to stop work and stay at home. So just like that she has no job. Poor Mama. She studied for years and years to be a doctor. It was all she ever wanted to do – that and have four children. I don't know what will happen now.

I thought Maria would lose her job too because she's a working woman. But Maria said, no, it's only married 'professional' women who have to stop work and secretaries aren't considered professional, and she's not married – yet.

I don't know why Mama tells Maria what's going on but tells me nothing. It's as if she doesn't trust me. I am 14 now.

Sterilisation operations a success!

November 11, 1934

A year ago to the month the Reich People's Hygiene court attached to Berlin Prison hospital sentenced its first male patient to undergo a sterilisation operation. A year later the hospital confirms over one hundred men have successfully undergone the sterilisation operation. A judge on the People's Hygiene panel attached to the hospital said, 'These men no longer pose a threat to the racial purity of the German people. We are on track to meet initial targets and anticipate a rise in the number of operations in the next year.'

Some of the scientific measures involved in assessing the success of the operation include taking photographs of the men before and after the operation, and the registration of the tone and volume of their voices on wax records.

December 18th, 1934

Mama keeps cleaning and scrubbing, it doesn't matter what it is, the floors and furniture, the windows, the stove. It goes on and on and on. Neither Maria nor Papa can stop her. And we've still had hardly any news from Hansi – only one small note in four months. Mama is sure something bad has happened to him and now she starts crying over the slightest thing. Christmas is going to be miserable again. There's no sign of any baking or of the tree or the goose.

January 9th, 1935

Erna called at the house today. She wanted to see Mama but Mama was out. Maria asked her to wait but Erna said she'd come back later. I think it's a right cheek turning up like that after walking out on us before.

February 2nd, 1935

Erna came to our door again today. That's the fourth time in as many days. I asked Maria why she keeps hounding Mama. Maria said Erna lost her job last year and since her old oma has died she has nowhere to stay. Mama feels sorry for her because she is all alone. Maria said Mama has agreed to help her find somewhere to stay and some work. I couldn't believe it. I asked Maria why Mama was helping Erna after the way she had walked out on us. Maria said Mama had told Maria not to tell me. That's just typical. I'm going to be fifteen this year and still Mama treats me like a baby.

March 3rd, 1935

Maria says Mama has found Erna a room in a hostel and we are paying for her rent until she can find Erna a job. Papa is also angry about the way Mama is helping Erna – he says we should make Erna work for us but Mama refuses to have her in the house.

March 16th, 1935

Papa said it was in the papers, compulsory military service has been brought back. Hitler said it was time to tear up the Versailles Treaty for good. Hubert said he's desperate to do his military service – he is 16, he has two years to wait. Papa says the army already has 300,000 in it, which is already 200,000 more than the Versailles Treaty allowed. Hitler wants there to be at least 500,000 in it by the end of the year. Mama's only comment was she was glad Hansi was in the camp, because at least he wouldn't be called up. Hubert was furious with her. 'No man doesn't want to do his duty!' Mama gave him one of her looks and walked away.

March 20th, 1934

Mama has found work for Erna. One of her old doctor friends is looking for a cleaner. Hopefully that will be the last we see of her. She's been coming round pestering Mama almost every day. I hate her!

June 24th, 1935

Hubert came back from a special Hitler Youth rally. He said that he, along with more than 10,000 other Hitler Youths, had taken a formal oath to 'eternally hate Jews'. Mama told him it was monstrous and they were behaving in a very unChristian way. Hubert laughed and said he didn't believe in God any more. He said from now on he swore allegiance only to Hitler and Horst Wessel and started to sing a song about hanging all the Jews and priests. Mama was furious. 'So much for Hitler the big Christian!' she said to Papa.

July 15th, 1935

Georg told Maria that all soldiers are banned from shopping in non-Aryan shops and all Hubert talks about is going to the Nuremberg Rally in September with his Hitler Youth group.

September 2nd, 1935

I got up early especially to wash my hair, nearly didn't. Glad I did though. When I got to school we were told to assemble in the hall by a very handsome young officer. All the nuns had disappeared. We girls were ridiculously excited. Instead of morning mass this extremely good looking SS man instructed us to swear allegiance to Hitler. We had to all recite, 'I give unconditional obedience to Adolf Hitler, leader of the German Reich and nation.' Some of the girls who go to the BDM already knew the oath. The officer said we were very lucky, we had new teachers at our school, who were young and well trained and going to give us the best education possible. He told us to study hard for Hitler. When we were allowed to go to our classes the first thing I noticed was that all the crucifixes and pictures of the Virgin Mary had been replaced with pictures of Hitler.

Our new teachers seem very nice. All the books are new too, they have the Reich stamp on them. After the SS officers left some of the girls cried. They said it wasn't fair that we hadn't been given time to say good-bye to the nuns. I would have liked to have said cheerio to Sister Gertrude, but that's all.

New Maths Homework
A mentally ill person kept in state care costs 4 Reichsmarks a day. There are 40,000 mentally ill people in state care in the State of Prussia. How much do these people cost the state each year? How many 1000 Reichsmarks marriage loans could be granted with this money?

A plane takes off carrying 12 bombs, each weighing 100 kilos. The aircraft makes for Warsaw, the centre of international Jewry. It drops all its bombs on the town. On take-off with all bombs on board and a fuel tank containing 1500 kilos of fuel the aircraft weighs 8 tonnes. It returns with 230 kilos of fuel left. What is the weight of the aircraft when empty?

Every year the State of Prussia invests 125 Reichsmarks on the education of a healthy German pupil, whereas 950 Reichsmarks are spent on a mentally ill child and 1500 on a child who is blind and deaf. How many healthy German pupils could be educated for the cost of educating 300 mentally ill children and 100 blind children?

September 15th, 1935

Hubert brought a picture of Hitler back from the Nuremberg Rally. He hung it up in the middle of the living room. Mama wanted to take the picture down immediately but Papa said he rather liked it. If looks could kill, Papa would be dead.

Hubert said the rally was wonderful. It was in all the papers. Hubert said the Swastika is now an official part of the German National flag. I think it looks excellent. Part of me wishes I'd gone to the rally but part of me feels very bad wishing that because of Mama. She hates Hitler and continues to blame him for Hansi's imprisonment and accuses him of being evil.

Later, when Mama had gone to bed, Hubert said that Hitler has decreed all Jewish civil servants be placed on leave, that German banks are forbidden from giving loans or credit to Jews, that extramarital intercourse with Jews is a crime and punishable by imprisonment and that the lottery cannot be won by Jews. He said from now on no Jew can work as a doctor or lawyer or journalist, and any Jew who hands in his passport will have it returned with a big fat "J" on it and will be allowed to leave but will never get back into Germany again. Finally he said, 'And you know what that means, don't you?'

I said, 'What?'

'It means your Hymie friend Belen won't be able to get back into Germany – ever!'

'Belen's not Jewish!' I was astounded. 'Are you mad! She

looks nothing like a Jew!'

'They don't all look like the posters!'

'I don't believe you.'

'I don't care what you believe. If she had still been here I would have had to report you for fraternising with a Jewish person!'

'I'm going to write to her right now and ask her. She wouldn't have kept something like that from me. I'm her best friend!' And that's what I've done, I've written her a letter.

October 5th, 1935

On my way home from school I ran right into Hansi's friend Florian. He was delighted to see me. He gave me a big playful hug and asked how I was. He even remembered that I had been doing the story competition all that time ago! I told him how I'd won and he said it was wonderful my getting the prize over girls who were much older than me. Then he said wasn't it bad about Hansi having to wear that pink triangle on his uniform and put up with so much shit in that camp. I couldn't believe my ears – he had heard from Hansi? I asked him when Hansi had last been in touch. He said his last letter was dated a few weeks ago. He gets one about once a month. All this time Mama's been worrying about Hansi and he's been writing to Florian! I invited Florian home. I said Mama would want to hear Hansi's news because we'd not heard from him for months. He said he would come round as soon as he could but for now he had to go. He sent regards to the family and then he was away. Just like that.

When I told Mama about seeing Florian and how Hansi had been writing to him, at first she didn't believe it. 'Why would he write to him and not to me, his own mother?'

'I think he's only allowed one letter a month?' I said

Mama said, ' I know what it is, he'll have written to Florian, expecting Florian to tell us his news. Well, he certainly took his time about it. What's Hansi's news then?'

'He just said Hansi had to put up with a lot.'

'That's it? He gets regular letters from Hansi and you didn't ask him what was in them?'

'Mama, calm down. He had to go. He said he'll come round soon!'

'When?' Mama was furious.

'Soon!'

'You go to wherever he stays and tell him he has to come and see us now. Wait, better still, give me his address and I'll go and visit him!'

'Mama, I don't have his address. Will you just calm down. He promised to visit. I am sure he will.'

'Well, I hope so. I hope so. And if you see him again, you make sure you get him to come round and see me, do you hear?

'Yes, Mama. Of course, I hear. Loud and clear.'

October 15th, 1935

Erna appeared again. Mama was furious with her. Erna said she'd left the job Mama had found for her at the doctor's. When Mama asked why, she said, 'Just because.' She wanted Mama to find her other work but Mama said she'd already found her work and she should have stayed in that job. Erna said she wanted to come back and work for us but Mama said no, under no circumstances. Then finally, Mama told Erna she would help her this one last time. But this really would be the last time she was going to help. After Erna left Mama locked herself in her room for the rest of the day.

I hate the way Mama runs around after Erna. Sometimes I think she is more bothered about what happens to Erna than to me. All she asks me about now is if I have seen Florian, as if it's my fault Hansi writes to him and not to her.

October 18th, 1935

Erna has started to hang around outside again. I see her talking to Mrs Schwarzkopf all the time. Mama says she is trying to find Erna work but it's not easy. In the meantime she says we have to be polite to Erna.

October 20th, 1935

Erna came to the door today and I answered it. She asked me for some food. I said we didn't have any. She said she was starving. I told her she was a lazy good-for-nothing parasite! I told her to leave Mama alone and never come back! Ever! She ran away sobbing. I didn't mean to shout but I was just so angry. Hopefully, she'll stay away now.

October 22nd, 1935

Still no sign of Erna. Good! I hope she's gone for ever. At least Mama won't have to worry about her now.

October 23rd, 1935

Something very bad has happened today. So bad I don't even want to write about it. But I will because otherwise I may start to believe it didn't happen. And it did.

I was in town and at last I saw Florian again. This time he didn't see me. I hurried after him. For Mama's sake I had to try to get him to come to the house. He was way ahead of me, going towards the university. He was walking quite fast and the town was busy with people so it was difficult to catch up. A couple of times I lost him but then I saw him again. No matter how fast I went his long legs gobbled up the pavement quicker than I could run. I was all for giving up but I knew it would make Mama so happy to see him so I carried on.

He bumped into a friend. I didn't recognise the young man. They walked and chatted. I paused to catch my breath and shouted Florian's name. He didn't hear. Their arms and hands waved up and down all over the place. It was just like Florian to be all excited about something. I hurried faster and faster. I had almost caught up with them when they turned down a narrow lane. We were at the edge of the Old Town now. I didn't want to go any further but I was so close. I looked down the lane. It stretched for about thirty yards and then turned at a right angle. The two of them approached the bend. I shouted after them again, but they disappeared. If I was really quick, I could finally catch them. I darted along the damp path. The lane walls were so tall they blocked out the sun. I decided, if when I got to the corner I couldn't see them I would definitely go back. I hated the Old Town and its dank smell of sewers and rancid grease and dirty washing. I turned the corner. There they were. Right in front of me. I nearly ran right into them. Florian had his back against the slime covered brick wall. His friend was standing in front of him. He had Florian's face cupped in both of his hands. He was kissing Florian on the lips and Florian was kissing him back.

I ran all the way home without looking back. As soon as I got in I threw up in the bathroom. I didn't know what to do about what I had seen. I couldn't think straight. In my mind's eye I kept seeing Florian kissing the other man. Their red, wet fleshy lips stuck together in that grotesque embrace. Then suddenly I knew. That sketch book I'd found in Maria's room. Ages ago. The one with the pictures of Georg naked. Hansi had drawn them. Of course. I realised now. Hansi is the best artist in the family. Hansi had made the wicked pictures. Hansi liked Georg. Hansi liked Florian. Florian likes boys. Hansi likes boys. I didn't want to believe it. But I knew it was true. Suddenly, Mama barged into the bathroom. Erna had been round and had told Mama how unkind I'd been to her.

"You selfish, spoiled girl!' she yelled. 'Do you never think of anyone else other than yourself? Does it not occur to you that we are the only help Erna has, eh? Eh?'

I burst into tears. 'I hate her. She's always snooping around here annoying you. I thought you'd be pleased if she stopped coming around!'

Mama grimaced, 'What did I do to have such an imbecile for a daughter!'

'I am not an imbecile,' I yelled. 'You like that lazy Polak better than you do me!'

'Maria and Hansi have brains, and even Hilde has some, but when it comes to you, I do not know what happened!'

'I hate her!' I screamed. 'You like her more than me. You like everyone more than me!'

Mama straightened up. She got all prim and proper. 'You can scream all you like but Erna is coming round to have dinner with us this evening and when she does you will apologise to her.'

'I will never ever apologise to her. Ever!'

'You will be confined to your room until you apologise. However long that takes!' She went to close the door behind her. 'You are the most selfish, stupid girl I have ever had anything to do with, and that includes all the poor imbeciles I've had to assess at the Hereditary Hygiene Court!'

'I saw Florian earlier,' I blurted. It was out before I could stop myself. I knew I shouldn't.

Mama stopped pulling the bathroom door shut. She did nothing for a few seconds but look at me. Then she frowned. 'Florian, really?' She pushed the door back open. 'Why didn't you say before? What did he tell you about Hansi – I assume you did ask him for news this time? And when is he coming round? You did invite him, didn't you? Please tell me you invited him round?'

'I didn't get a chance to ask him anything,' I said, 'because Florian was too busy kissing his new boyfriend. Seems like Florian likes men more than women. Poor Hansi, there he is writing to his boyfriend and his boyfriend is kissing someone else.'

Mama stared at me aghast. 'What did you just say?'

'What? You didn't know? Everyone else does. Your number one son, Hansi, is a homosexual. Hans Joachim kisses men.'

It was like a volcano erupting.

Mama threw open the door and charged at me. I put my arms up in front of me to defend myself but it was useless. She slapped me! And slapped me! And slapped me! 'Liar!' she shouted at the top of her voice. 'Liar! Liar!' I tried to hold off her blows. 'I'm sorry,' I yelled, 'but it's true! It's true! I saw Florian kissing a boy! He likes boys! Hansi likes boys! Hansi and Florian were lovers!' 'Liar!' She was hysterical now. 'Judas!' 'It's true –' Maria came rushing in and pulled Mama off me. 'Liar!' She kept screaming. 'Liar!' Maria dragged her away. 'It's true,' I sobbed, 'It's true!'

Maria came to find me later. She was very distressed. She said she'd never seen Mama so angry and upset. She wanted to know what was going on. I said the row was over Erna. I didn't tell her about Florian. About the kissing. About what I think about Hansi. About what Mama must think too. I wasn't going to tell anyone.

Mama stayed in her room for the rest of the day. I stayed in mine. If Erna came for dinner nobody told me.

October 30th, 1935

Every day Mama writes long, long letters to Hansi, which Maria says he will never get. He is only allowed to receive one letter a month and they are heavily censored so even if her letters get through, most of what she writes will be blacked out. It makes no difference to her. She keeps writing. She says she doesn't want him to think she has forgotten about him, because she has not. She will never believe the lies people say about him. When Maria asks what she means by that, Mama says nothing.

Mama still refuses to talk to at me.

November 1st, 1935

Papa had to apply for Reich identity papers for everyone, except for me because I don't need mine till I am sixteen – it's to do with the new Nuremberg laws. When the papers arrived they were yellow. YELLOW! Everyone knows yellow means you are not a Reich citizen but a 'foreign national', which means you could be anything, Czech, Pole or worse. Our cards should have been brown. Papa had a huge fight with the people at the Reich's office. They tried to say we were Polish! Were they mad? We are Aryan through and through. Anyway, it's all sorted now. Luckily Papa keeps everything and had all the important papers he needed to prove who we are. There are no Poles in our family. Not now, not ever!

November 3rd, 1935

As I was coming home from school I saw Mrs S and Erna skulking about together in Mrs S's garden. As I approached Erna ran off. When I got up close to Mrs S she muttered something about it being 'a disgrace.' Ever since Erna reappeared after leaving us that first time, Mrs S makes some snide remark under her breath when I pass. I'd had enough! It's bad enough that Mama ignores me because of that idiot Erna, I'm not putting up with Mrs S's snide comments too.

Instead of walking past Mrs S I turned and faced her. 'What's a disgrace?'

Mrs S huffed and puffed. 'What your Mama did to Erna, that's a disgrace!' she said.

'Erna walked out on us!' I was indignant. 'Despite that, Mama did what she could for her!'

Mrs S burst out laughing, 'Your Mama did for her all right. A while back Erna's case was sent to the Hereditary Hygiene Court for assessment and your Mama gave the authorisation for her to be sterilised.'

'That can't be right, Mama's always been against that sterilising stuff. And even if it was true, so what?'

'You selfish indulged brat! When Erna went to get her marriage licence she was refused, that's what!'

'She's getting married?' I couldn't believe it.

'Against all odds, Erna goes and meets this really nice young lad. They start courting – I was worried at first, thought maybe he was just wanting to take advantage of her cause she was simple, but they came round to me for their tea a couple of times and he was a right decent lad. They fall in love, they want to marry, but the church says if you can't have kids, you can't get married. Well, what boy's going to stay around if he can't get married or have kids? Poor dolt still doesn't understand why your Mama can't just reverse the operation.'

It was a blatant lie. 'Mama has principles. I don't believe you.'

Mrs S waved me away, as if I were a fly. 'Erna didn't deserve to be treated that way, not by anyone, but especially not by your mama!'

I tried to talk to Mama about what Mrs S said but she still refuses to speak to me. She acts as if I don't exist. It's not me she should be upset with, it's Hansi! I hate her. I hate her. I hate her. And I really hate Hansi!

I told Maria what Mrs S said about Mama authorising that operation for Erna and Maria said it was true. I was astounded. Maria said it happened a while back, when Mama was still at the hospital and obliged to sit on the Reich Hereditary Hygiene Court panel. Whenever it was her turn to sit she refused to judge the cases coming up before her as being so 'feeble' or 'disabled' as to warrant sterilisation. This made no difference to the fate of the patients because her other two colleagues would invariably disagree with her. She accused them of being in too much of a hurry to sterilise people just because they came from a working class background. However, her attitude brought her to the attention of the hospital director, who hauled her into his office and told her she was behaving in an 'Un-German' way. He said if she didn't authorise the sterilisation of the very next case that came before her, he would sack her and have her and her family investigated by the Gestapo for politically incorrect behaviour.

The next person's case to come up for consideration by the panel was Erna's. Mama felt she had no choice but to declare Erna 'very feeble-minded' and authorise her sterilisation operation to proceed immediately. Mama felt very bad about what she had done, but she said it was Erna's future children, or her own children. Straight after that the director threw her off the panel anyway and then, ironically, the majority of the women doctors in the hospital were 'let go' because of Hitler's new policy against professional women in the workplace. So, said Maria, when Erna came around and asked Mama for help, Mama felt obliged to do something.

I felt so confused. If only Mama had explained this to me before, I wouldn't have been so rude to Erna. Why am I always the last to know what's going on? Why doesn't Mama ever tell me anything?

November 13th, 1935

I have joined the BDM. I should have joined ages ago.

November 18th, 1935

Georg is an SS officer now. Maria says he was very lucky he wasn't one of the SA ones rounded up in June. She also announced the date for the wedding. But they can't get married in a church because SS members are forbidden to be part of religious gatherings. Papa and Mama weren't pleased when Maria told them this, especially Mama. But Papa said a wedding was a wedding and it was still very exciting. So we're all looking forward to that and then there's the Olympic Games in Berlin coming up too, everyone at school is talking about them and how well Germany will do. The school is organising groups to go and watch. It'll be such fun, especially going with all my friends from school.

November 23rd, 1935

When I got home from school I found Papa and Mama huddled at the kitchen table. Their heads were bent together in secrecy. Mama looked as if she had been crying. Papa said when Mama was in by herself the Gestapo had barged in – four of them in black suits and three policemen – and searched everywhere, tipping out drawers and emptying the contents of our wardrobes all over the floor. They were looking for 'politically incorrect' material. Mama was worried they'd find her books in the cellar but when they went down the books were gone. Papa had got rid of them ages ago – unbeknown to Mama. Just as well! The men left with a warning they could be back. When Maria told Georg, Georg said there was nothing he could do, even the mighty SS are powerless when it comes to the Gestapo.

December 1st, 1935

Papa says we are leaving Breslau! It is the worst news possible! He said he's been forced to retire early from the Civil Service. His boss made up some excuse but Papa said it was because he was a Christian. His unblemished service record means he got a pension but Papa said it is less than it should be although it's better than many others have got. He said he'd been expecting something like this and is prepared: he's bought a café in a small village called Lähn, near the Riesengebirge – the Giant Mountains. Papa said the café in Lähn will give us an income and there is a lovely house and garden attached.

The cowards are running away! They are running away! Well, I don't want to leave my beloved Breslau! Hubert says he won't go. Maria says she won't go, she will stay with Georg in Breslau.

They can get married in a day. This is all Mama's fault. We all know someone at the hospital must have reported Mama's un-German behaviour, which is why the Gestapo came to the house, which is why we have to run away and hide in some shitty village in the middle of nowhere.

1935–1941

Café Concordia, Lähn, Riesengebirge

December 15th, 1935

I hate Lähn. So what if we are in the foothills of the Giant Mountains? Lähn is a ridiculously small village with not so much as a cinema, theatre or ice rink. And it is so un-German! There is only one flag flying over the town hall and it is so, so pathetically small. You can't even get Breslau radio transmissions – how isolated do you have to be to not get transmissions from Breslau radio tower?

The house is a dump. It needs to be completely renovated. My bedroom is the size of a postage stamp. The hot water for the bathroom is heated by a wood fire that you stoke in the garden outside. As for the café, two elderly spinsters used to run it until they got too old to keep it up. It's basically the front room of the house with a couple of old formica tables in it. It's covered in dust and grime and looks as if it's not been used since the Great War. There is a floor-to-ceiling ceramic tile stove on the back wall. The tiles are a grotty green colour. It is so old-fashioned!

Papa said before the room was used as a café, it was the village dance hall and cinema, which doesn't seem possible. He also said that once the room was painted and cleaned it'd look lovely and we'd be able to open for business. He seems to think I will wait on the customers. I don't think so! I am never going to 'serve' strangers. The only person I'll serve is our Führer so they'd better get used to that idea. School is in a dump of a town called Hirschberg – 15 kilometres away. I have to actually get a train. I start after the Christmas break. It will be full of hicks and country bumpkins. I don't even think there is a BDM group here.

I told Papa I would never like being here and Mama said I had to pull myself together. How dare she talk to me like that. I had to give up my friends and the BDM, which I had only just joined, because of her. I will never, ever forgive her.

December 17th, 1935

I had another row with Mama. She says I'm being deliberately obstructive and unhelpful. I hate her. She says she will not tolerate my attitude. My attitude! She's the grumbler and moaner, always criticising the Nazis. It's her fault we had to move. Christmas will be awful as usual. I imagine my Christmas present will be some sappy book written by some decadent author, the kind Mama is so fond of. I hate her!

December 23rd, 1935

Walked round the village today, it was like a morgue. There are three churches – by far the biggest two are the Lutheran and Evangelical ones, the Catholic church is the smallest. There is one baker and one butcher, a post office-cum-grocery store, and a seamstress shop, as well as our soon-to-be-opened café, and a photographer's studio. It's all so pathetic and I hate it. Mama tried to get me to go to church on Sunday – I told her she could go and jump in the Bober river that winds through the village. All my friends in Breslau are going to the cinema and the theatre and enjoying the festive season and I am stuck in this dump.

December 28th, 1935

Christmas was rubbish. I should have known. Just the three of us, me, Mama and Papa. Hardly any decorations up because Mama and Papa are too busy getting the café ready to open in February. I got a pair of woollen stockings and a rubbishy notebook – as if I need another notebook! Of course, she prepared Hansi the biggest parcel you've ever seen, even though there's a good chance he won't even get it at that camp. Anyway, he's being punished. He shouldn't get it! She even sent Hubert a small parcel, and I bet you there was still more in it than a pair of decrepit woollen stockings and a ridiculously thin notebook, which is what I got! I assume the people in charge where he's doing his Hitler Youth service will let him have the parcel, but who knows? Hubert's been at his Hitler Youth service training camp for a month. He signed up almost as soon as Papa said we'd be leaving Breslau. I never thought Mama would let him go but she said there was no point in him coming to Lähn as only unemployment faced him here, and he wasn't doing well at school anyway, so why not? He'll be gone for a whole year. We've already had a postcard, he said he was doing all sorts of fitness and endurance training.

Of course, I have been absolutely forbidden to sign up for the Bund Deutscher Mädel annual service training. Mama said a year is far too much time for me to be away from proper school. She says all I would be doing is learning how to be a super mother, and I can do that here in Lähn. She just loves spoiling things for me.

January 13th, 1936

I've only been at school for one week and I hate it. The teachers treat me with disdain because I'm not a 'country girl' and the girls call me a snob and show-off, just because I told them I won the story prize at my old school and I am good at English. They're just thick! Well, they can keep their silly little bumpkin friends. I don't care. I don't want to be here and as soon as I am old enough to work I am going to leave this dump and go back to Breslau.

January 31st, 1936

On the way to catch the train I lagged behind the other girls. I didn't want to give them the opportunity to ignore me. While I hung about in the cold waiting for them to get ahead, I saw Liesl hiding down a little lane. Liesl also gets the train from Lähn. She lives with her Oma, who has a cottage just outside the village. She takes no nonsense from the other girls or the teachers. I think she must be poor because her clothes look very worn. She was smoking a cigarette. She saw me see her. I quickly looked away and hurried on. Then before I knew it she was beside me, all out of breath.

She begged me not to tell on her. Smoking was only something she did very occasionally and only when she was fed-up and wanted to feel better. She said if her Oma found out she'd get leathered. I could have told her how un-German it was to smoke, how she's damaging her body with drugs – at least that's what Herr Hitler says, he hates smoking. Instead I told her to forget it. It was nothing to do with me.

February 3rd, 1936

Liesl sat next to me on the train today. She told me she had been born in Königsberg but then her mama had died in a fire when she was eight. She had lots of aunties and thought one of them would take her in but none of them wanted her so she'd been sent to her Oma's – her papa was killed in an accident at the docks when she was two.

She'd never liked Lähn, with its small-minded people and small-minded attitude. While her Opa had been alive staying with her Oma had been okay. Since he'd died, though, the old boot – that's what she called her Oma – never missed a chance to slap her or call her names. Liesl said she didn't know why her Oma was so mean to her but as soon as she is old enough she is going to run away. She was so jealous of me having lived in Breslau for so long. I told her all about the city and the shops and the parks and the theatres and cinemas.

February 7th, 1936

My friend Liesl sits next to me every day now on the train. She's not in the same classes at school, which is a pity because I have no friends in my classes. I've told her all about how horrible Mama is to me and how much I hate my home. Today I asked her what it was like to smoke a cigarette. She said she'd show me. I said I wasn't sure I wanted to actually try one myself. She said I should think of it as a science experiment. I laughed. I told her how Mama was a doctor and how I didn't think she'd approve of that kind of experiment. Liesl said she thought I didn't care about what Mama approved of. I said I didn't.

February 11th, 1936

My friend Liesl and I didn't go to school yesterday. We pretended to go but when the train pulled into Hirschberg instead of going to school we sneaked around the back of the station and went into town and visited some stores.

Whenever someone asked why we weren't at school, Liesl smiled a big smile, flashed her blond eyelashes and said all innocently that we were on an errand for our chemistry teacher. Depending on who asked and where we were, she said we were looking for copper wire, bicarbonate of soda or soap flakes. In the afternoon Liesl invited me to have a hot chocolate in the posh café on the square with money she had stolen from her Oma's purse. Liesl said she had to steal money to buy food otherwise she would starve.

In the café she told the assistant we were twins and even though I am dark and she is fair, the assistant believed her! Liesl also said our Mama was dying of cancer and we'd been given permission to be off school to visit her in hospital. She said we were having a hot chocolate to cheer ourselves up. The waitress even gave us a little gingerbread biscuit each for free because she felt so sorry for us. And then while we sat there pretending to be fed-up, Liesl wrote out an absence letter to give to the teachers the next day. It was very good. She showed me how to do mine. She said she'd been writing herself sick notes since last year.

In my note she said my mother was ill and as there was no one else at home I'd had to stay off to look after her. When the waitress came up to clear our things away Liesl said we were writing a letter to our sick mother to tell her how much we loved her. I thought the girl was going to burst into tears. What a thicky! We laughed all the way to the train station. It was hysterical! Liesl says the trick about lying is to say it like you mean it, no hesitation or doubt.

February 14th, 1936

Liesl and I didn't go into school again today. We didn't even bother getting on the train this time. Instead, we hid at the far end of the station platform until the train had gone and slipped up the back path to the outskirts of the village. I followed Liesl to a set of crumbling stone steps, which took us up to a heap of rubble, perched on top of an exposed hill. Liesl said this was Lähn Castle.

The Giant Mountains sat in the distance and Lähn village stretched below us. We couldn't see a single person. The wind howled around us so we ducked behind what was left of the wall for shelter and waited for Liesl's friend, Rolf. He lives on a farm not far from her Oma's cottage. Liesl said that in the warmer months the fields are packed with people sowing and seeding and pruning and cutting. Then there's the harvesting after that, which is an ever busier time.

Rolf's family have peaches and plums and apples and pears and sugar beet and cabbages and turnips. In the winter there's less to do but they are still busy because Rolf's grandfather takes their wagon to the Bober river and cuts big chunks of ice out of it. He lugs the ice to the breweries. They use it in the beer cellars for keeping the beer cold while it's fermenting.

Rolf arrived after about ten minutes. He was wiry and not very tall, with mean-looking eyes. I reckoned he was no more than 17. He had short, thick black hair, which the wind was causing to wildly flip and flop in every direction, and a ruddy outdoor complexion. He wore a heavy winter coat and big leather boots, which were caked in mud.

He scowled as soon as he saw me and I immediately wished I'd gone into school. Liesl introduced me as her friend. He considered this for a moment or two then shouted above the wind, 'It's perishing up here, lets go to the snug,' and turned and left. Liesl hopped up and motioned for me to follow. I hurried after her.

Rolf led us back down the crumbling stairs and across a couple of fields to a huddle of outhouses and barns. They stood a quarter of a kilometre or so from a solid, ramshackle grey building, with smoke coming out of its big chimney. Various farm tools littered the yard in front of the building. Liesl said that's where Rolf lived with his brothers and sisters and mother and father and grandfather. She said she was jealous of his big family but Rolf had told her there was nothing to be jealous of – being so many of them just meant they were poor.

We followed him into a small wooden outhouse, furthest

from the main farm building. It was no bigger than my bedroom and lined with shelves, laden with rows of empty pickling jars. The floor was damp earth. In the far corner sat a small black pot-bellied wood burning stove, with a chimney that came out from its flat top and went up into the ceiling. A pile of logs sat next to it. Rolf immediately opened the door to the stove and mucked about with some kindling.

In what seemed like no time a small flame crackled and hissed from inside the iron tummy of the stove. After a few minutes Rolf chucked some of the damp logs into the body of the stove and we waited. Gradually, the wood started to hiss and sizzle and bit by bit the damp hut began to heat up. Rolf dug up a couple of empty jute sacks, shook the dust from them and laid them on the earth floor for me and Liesl to sit on. Liesl threw herself down on to the sack nearest her. I was far less keen to sit on the disgusting grot-riddled cloth but there was nowhere else and I didn't want them to think I was a snob.

Rolf sat straight down cross-legged on the earth. He said we were far away enough from the house not to be seen. But even if someone did see the smoke from the chimney, it didn't matter, no one would bother him anyway, it was his day off. Then he took a packet of tobacco from his pocket and some papers and started to roll a cigarette. He handed the first one to Liesl. Then made a second, which he handed to me. I took it – for some reason I didn't want him to think I couldn't smoke. He made a third one for himself.

While he concentrated on rolling the tobacco I learnt that he'd left school a couple of years back. All the time he'd been there the teachers had picked on him. They said he was a disruption, that he was slow and thick. All he knew was that he couldn't sit still. He'd left as soon as he was allowed.

When his cigarette was ready he tore a piece of sackcloth from Liesl's sack, opened the stove, let the end of the cloth fall into flames until it took, removed it and used the slow burning end of the cloth to light his cigarette. Immediately, he dragged on his cigarette and the end of it glowed and smoke spiralled upwards from its tip. He moved the rag over towards Liesl, who had her cigarette ready in her mouth.

I watched Liesl suck on the cigarette and pull the smoke into her mouth and swallow and then blow it out. Rolf dangled the burning rag at my face. I lifted up the skinny cigarette and put it in my mouth. Bits of tobacco fell between my teeth. I sucked in and the end of my cigarette started to burn. The chalky smoke made me feel wobbly. I coughed a little bit and tiny shreds of tobacco fell out of the end of my cigarette on to the floor but I kept going, careful to breathe in as deeply as I could, keeping an eye on Liesl and Rolf. When they removed their cigarettes from their mouths to talk, I did the same.

They talked about leaving Lähn and never coming back, about all the money they would make from all the different jobs they would do once away from Lähn. Then all of a sudden my hand began to shake. I felt sick. And I was sick. All over the jute sack. The puke narrowly missed Rolf. 'What the hell?' he yelled. Liesl laughed and laughed, 'She ain't never smoked before!' Rolf sighed, 'Stupid cow, why didn't you say?' He got a rag from somewhere and quickly wiped up the sick from the sack and chucked the mess into the fire. 'You want a drink of water or something?' he said with a gentleness that surprised me. I nodded. He grunted then disappeared out the door.

I didn't want to lie down but my whole body was buzzing and I needed to be straight. I lay on the disgusting floor, closed my eyes and didn't move. My heart banged in my chest so loudly it almost drowned Liesl's laughing, 'Your face was green! Hey, but you got Rolf to get you a drink, so it's not all bad, he ain't ever gone and got me a glass of water before, ever!'

March 3rd, 1936

When I got in today Mama said she could smell smoke on me. I

said I'd walked down to a farm after school with my friend
Liesl. I said they were burning stuff in the fields. It was only a
half lie. She didn't believe me. I know she didn't. She gave me
that look. Just let her say anything. I don't care what she thinks.
I hate this dump. Liesl and Rolf are the only people who make
being stuck here bearable.

March 7th, 1936

Had my first beer in the snug. It made me feel weird at first but
I made myself drink it then I felt quite good and we all had such
a laugh telling each other horror stories. I can smoke five
cigarettes now without feeling sick at all. Walked home at
midnight.

I thought Mama would have been in bed. No such luck. She
must have been listening out for me. Just as I was creeping into
my room, she appeared in her dressing gown. She was all
agitated. She forbade me to return to the house so late ever
again. Huh! I told her what I thought of that idea!

She said I was rude and disobedient, that she didn't know
what had happened to me to make me behave so badly! I just
shrugged and walked past her. She really went mad then. She
grabbed me and turned me round to face her. 'How dare you
ignore me!' I laughed and said, 'You've always ignored me, so
why shouldn't I ignore you?' I thought she was going to strike
me. Instead, she let me go and said I was 'a selfish, insolent
ingrate!' I shrugged again and said, 'Nothing new there, then.'
For a second she looked stunned, and then she looked as if she
was going to burst into tears.

Well, she needn't think tears will work. Not now. Not ever.

March 20th, 1936

Rolf, Liesl and I met up in Hirschberg for the afternoon. We
walked past a greengrocers and Rolf dared Liesl to steal an
apple from the display outside. And she did! She really did it!
She simply picked up one of the reddest apples from the top of

the heap and then she ran away as fast as she could. A man came out of the shop and shouted after her to stop, but she just kept on running. He began to chase after her but quickly had to give up because he was so fat and useless there was no way he could catch her. It was so funny.

When we met up with her she'd already chucked the apple. 'It's your turn, now,' she said when she saw me. I felt horrible when she said that but then I looked at Rolf and his eyes were all excited and smiling. Then I thought why not. If she can do it, I can. I'll show them.

We went into the haberdashery round the corner from the station. It was quite dark inside and smelled musty. Three women were busying themselves with two assistants, who were in the process of throwing a length of cream material from a bolt of cotton across the wide counter. In the cashier's box opposite them a feeble orange electric light bulb glowed above the head of the female cashier. She wore glasses and a frown and a pencil behind her ear.

A broad cupboard, full of drawers, stretched across the wall behind the assistants. One drawer was open. It contained tens of small square cards. Each card had a different number of buttons on it, some had six, some had four, some had twelve, depending on the size of the button. All the buttons in this drawer were made of blue glass. At the far end of the counter a third assistant rolled sheets of tracing paper into a tight huddle and tied it with some string.

Warm air belted out from a tile stove at the far end of the shop. The woman customer in front of me gathered her things, all wrapped in brown paper and string, and left. It was my turn. I told the assistant I was looking for rooster shaped, ivory buttons for my mother. I also wanted swatches of gold, red and cream cotton threads, some hemming thread and two yards of bias binding.

The assistant gathered all the items, including a card which held two rows of three tiny cream roosters – one of the girls at school had these buttons on her cardigan and had said they'd come from this shop. I told the assistant the buttons were perfect. She wrote out a bill and put everything in two little brown paper bags. I had to take the bill and the bags to the cashier's desk behind me. As I approached the desk I accidentally dropped the brown bags. The contents spilled everywhere. A different assistant helped me gather the things up. As we put everything back into the bags, I explained, with tears in my eyes, that I would have to return later to get the items as I seemed to have lost my purse. The assistant smiled kindly and said she hoped I wouldn't get into trouble. I gave her the paper bags and left.

Rolf and Liesl scowled at me when I came out of the shop, they'd been watching through the door window and thought I'd failed to steal something. I laughed at their sullen faces, glanced around to make sure no one was watching and produced the card from my pocket. 'Each of these tiny roosters is worth at least six apples,' I said triumphantly.

March 27th, 1936

Had another row with Mama today. She accused me of being a truant and letting the family down! I laughed and walked away – the best way to annoy her is to ignore her. She can't stand that. It worked. She stormed off, ranting and raving about my rudeness, and sent Papa to talk to me.

He asked me why I couldn't be civil to Mama. He said they were both worried about my school work, he said I never seemed to do any studying at home any more. In fact, he said, I was never at home any more. I said I was doing fine. I told him I studied at my friend's house. He said I wasn't going to amount to anything if I didn't knuckle down and start concentrating. What does he know?

I took three Reichsmarks from the café change drawer. Liesl

and Rolf wanted to go to the cinema in Hirschberg but didn't have any money. I told them I had money and I would pay for them. Why not? Anyway, there's so much money floating around in the café Mama won't notice.

April 12th, 1936

It's Easter Sunday and I had another big argument with Mama and Papa. Papa said there was money missing from the café takings. He said he knew I had taken it. Probably spent it, he said, with the degenerate people he'd seen me hanging around with in the market square. All this fuss over three lousy Marks. I denied it. Mama said I was liar. I shrugged. Let her prove it. Papa said he would not tolerate thieving in his house. He said I was forbidden to leave the house until I promised to mend my wicked ways. Well, let's see them try and keep me in.

April 15th, 1936

Everything has gone wrong, wrong, wrong.

Went to stay with Rolf and Liesl in the snug. Sneaked out after Mama and Papa had gone to bed. They'd locked the doors downstairs, as if that was going to stop me. What idiots. It was easy. Through the back bathroom window overlooking the oak tree, on to its broad branches, down into the garden and away. Earlier in the day I'd met Rolf at the gap in the hedge at the bottom of the garden and given him some money. If Mama and Papa had really wanted me not to take any more, why didn't they hide it? It's their fault.

Rolf had bought us six bottles of beer with the money I'd given him. He always drinks his beer in a special ceramic Stein he keeps hidden at the back of the stove. Liesl and me just drink our beer straight out of the brown bottles. I don't think he's ever washed the Stein – at least I've never seen him wash it, ugh!

We laughed and talked and had some smokes and I felt like

I never wanted to leave the snug. Ever. Then suddenly we had no beer left and Liesl had the idea of stealing some from one of the beer caves that Rolf's grandfather delivers ice to. Rolf wasn't sure, he thought the breweries locked the caves up. Liesl scoffed at his reluctance. She said he was a coward. I said we didn't need any more beer anyway. Liesl smirked at me. I said, 'Hey, don't give me that look. I'm the one who got the money!' Liesl laughed, 'Oh, yes, sure, it's very brave to take money that's just sitting there in a drawer.' Rolf told us to pack it in, he'd just remembered a small brewery with a cave cellar about four miles away on the Bober river. Liesl cheered with excitement, 'What are we waiting for?' Rolf looked at me. 'I'm in,' I said. I was in no hurry to go back home.

Rolf led us through some pine woods and explained how heat and light were beer's worst enemies. Beer needed to be kept in the dark at around five degrees centigrade. The ice his grandfather delivers keeps the caves cool all year round, even when it gets hot. Liesl said she was bored talking about beer so Rolf started to talk about his hunting trips .

He said he'd hunted wolves and lynxes and wildcats and deer and foxes. After that Liesl started to jump at every little sound of a twig snapping or owl hooting. She said he was giving her the heebie-jeebies talking about all the wild animals in the woods. So Rolf talked about the different birds he'd hunted: capercaillies, black grouse, white-tailed eagles and black storks. He even offered to take us hunting with him one day. I said I'd love to go but Liesl scowled. She wanted to know when we'd get there. She'd had enough of the woods and the dark and the creeping around in the cold. Rolf laughed and said she was a coward. She didn't like that one little bit.

When Rolf finally said we were there, it had got even colder. He pointed to the silhouette of a rambling barn. It sat twenty yards from a squat farmhouse. That was the brewery? I'd expected something bigger. Leafy stuff grew in rows in the fields to the left of the barn. Rolf said it was sugar beet. We could hear the river thrash and splash as it wound its way past the farmhouse and barn and beyond the field and away. An owl hooted and Rolf told us to be very quiet. 'If the dogs smell us they'll bark the house down then we'll be done for.' 'What dogs?' I said, alarmed. 'There are always dogs on farms,' said Liesl with exaggerated exasperation, as if I was really too thick. Rolf said, 'They'll be in the shed, locked up. We just have to keep quiet. Quick, follow me, we'll go along by the river. Less likely to be seen than if we follow the road.'

We sneaked after Rolf. The earth by the river was all muddy and damp and my feet sank into the soft soil. Rolf took us to a kind of wooden door in the side of the bank of the river. He tried the handle. Nothing. Then he shoved himself against it and it opened. We quickly glanced about to check no one had heard us. Apart from the cold splashing of the river as it raced along its course, it was silent. Rolf crept in first, then Liesl, then me. I didn't want to be last but I didn't have any choice. I left the door open a little to let the moonlight in so we could see. Inside it was even colder than outside. It smelled of dampness and earth and yeast and reminded me of Hubert's gang hut.

As we inched our way inside, I kept my hand firmly on Liesl's arm. As my eyes grew accustomed to the shadowy dark, I saw that on both sides of us there were shelves of fat upright glistening bottles of beer. The shelves went up to the top of the cave, which was only about one foot above our heads. Rolf took one of the bottles, unstoppered it and put it to his lips. 'Ugh!' he spat the liquid out. Liesl and I both jumped. 'Sh!' said Liesl, 'You'll wake someone up!' Rolf shook his head and said, 'Sour! Too young.' He inched further into the dark room.

Under the shelves, sitting on the earthen floor, I could see the blocks of ice, covered in layers of prickly straw. Rolf took another bottle from a different shelf further away. He licked his lips after tasting it. 'This is good,' he whispered and handed the bottle to Liesl. She took a swig and then passed it to me. It tasted thick and fruity. I quickly handed it back. 'Lets just take it and go, yes?' I whispered, 'It's freezing in here!'

'Sure,' said Rolf, 'but I'm thirsty and when I'm thirsty I drink. He drained some more of the beer and then handed it to Liesl. She did the same and then passed it to me again. I shook my head. I didn't want it.

She smirked, 'What? Too scared to have a drink?'

I snatched the bottle off her and took a long gulp.

Liesl sniggered, 'That's more like it.' She took the bottle back, drained it, put it down, took another off the shelf, unstoppered it and drank. 'This is so exciting!' she giggled. Rolf laughed. 'Shh!' I whispered angrily.

'Just shut up and have a slurp!' said Liesl, shoving the bottle into my hand.

I took it but I wasn't happy. 'I can hardly see, I'm freezing and this tastes awful. I'm going.'

Liesl smirked. 'You really can be pathetic at times.'

'Come on, Toni,' said Rolf, handing me a new bottle, 'where's your sense of adventure?' At that moment the cave flooded with light. I was blinded. A man's voice roared, 'You thieving bastards! Think you can steal from me!'

Liesl screamed. Rolf yelled. They charged past me towards the door. The man blocked their way. They smacked straight into him. His legs went flying. The lantern shot out of his hand. Everywhere went dark. I made a run for it. I didn't want to get left behind. The man hurled curses at the top of his voice. 'Toe-rags! Thieves!' Dogs started to bark somewhere far away. I was out the cave. 'Hurry!' Rolf's voice yelled. More dogs barked, closer this time. I stumbled. I scrambled back up on my feet. I could hardly breathe. Suddenly an iron hand gripped my wrist. Agh! I was stuck. I wriggled. I was still stuck. 'Let me go! Help!' The man held me fast. He smelled of sweat and potatoes. Rolf's voice screamed, 'Leave her alone!' The man shouted 'Think you can rob me!' He held me next to him. His cold spit splattered in my face. He laughed, 'Police'll sort you out!' He pulled me towards his house. 'Help!' Then there was a shuffling noise. A shadow darted towards us. The man snorted. And then there was a funny sound. Like all the air puffing out of a balloon in one go. His grip slackened. I was free. His body slumped to the ground. Rolf yelled, 'Run!'

After I don't know how long, we stopped by a pond in the pine wood. We'd been running for ages and ages. My legs were throbbing with pain. It was getting lighter – dawn was breaking. Liesl leaned against a tree trunk beside me. 'That was awful!' An owl hoot-hooted. We gasped for breath. I said, 'Do you think he saw our faces?'

Rolf sucked in huge breaths 'No, it was too dark.'

'You must have really thumped him,' I said between breaths, 'To make him let me go like that!'

'Yes, well, we weren't going to leave you behind,' said Rolf.

I kneeled down. I rested my hands on my hips. My hips felt wet. I looked down at my hands. They were covered in red stuff. 'Oh! Look! Look!' I showed them my blood covered hands. 'He's hurt me!'

Rolf said, 'No, you're fine. He's the one who got hurt.'

'What?'

Liesl inhaled long and deep, 'Show her, Rolf.'

Rolf took something out of his pocket and raised it up. In the cold early morning light I could see the glinting blade of the knife. It was about six inches long and smeared in blood. I gripped the tree for support. 'You stabbed him?'

'Had to. Wasn't anything else for it,' said Rolf.

'But –' my head ached 'I thought maybe you'd just punched him?'

'Did you see the size of that bastard?' said Liesl.

'Hey, what's wrong with you, you got free, didn't you?' said

Rolf.

'He was going to get the police, you heard him, yes?' said Liesl.

'But?' I couldn't think straight, 'What if he's really hurt?'

'That was the idea,' Rolf winked at Liesl and she laughed.

'We'll have to go back –'

'What is your problem?' demanded Rolf, 'You'd rather still be there, is that it?'

'No, of course not. But a knife?'

'Bitch!' said Rolf, walking away, 'This is the thanks I get for saving you?'

'Wait,' I ran after him. 'Wait! I'm tired. It's been a long night. And when that light flooded the cave I got such a fright!'

Rolf stared at me and then he laughed, 'Scheisse! What a night!'

Liesl ran up to us and giggled, 'I swear to God, that was awful!' and then we all burst out laughing and fell to the ground. I wanted to cry but instead I laughed and laughed. They left me outside Concordia at 6.30.

The kitchen door was open. Mum was waiting for me. Her thick woolly dressing gown was wrapped tightly around her body with a cord and it was buttoned right up to her neck. She had her outdoor shoes on but no socks. Her face was drained of all colour. Her hair was thin and ragged and tied in a loose heap at the back of her head. She took one look at me then turned to poke at the kitchen stove which had gone out overnight. She said without looking up, 'I've been worried sick. I even went to look for you. Where have you been?'

I said nothing.

She turned round and faced me. 'There's blood on your clothes? Are you hurt?'

I shrugged, 'It's fox blood. I was hunting with a friend. If I'd told you, you'd never have given me permission to go.

Her eyes narrowed, 'You're a liar.'

I shrugged again. 'I'm tired. I want to go to my room.'

She said, 'Where's the money?'

I said, 'What money?'

She looked at me one last time. There was no trace of emotion on her face at all. 'That's it. I give up. If you steal from us again I am going to report you to the police,' and then she left.

I stood there in the freezing cold kitchen for about five minutes and then I went up to my bed. As soon as I was in my room I began to cry and once I'd started I couldn't stop.

April 20th, 1936

Whenever I asked Rolf or Liesl if there was any news of the man Rolf had stabbed, they both got really angry. Liesl said, 'What do you care about him for?'

I said, 'Maybe we were lucky. Maybe he only had a small wound and recovered. Maybe he's forgotten all about it?'

Rolf said, 'What's he to you? Stop talking about that Dummkopf!'

April 23rd, 1936

Liesl keeps wanting me to skive school and go shoplifting with her like before but I don't want to. When I try to explain how I feel she refuses to listen and says if I'm not with her I'm against her. I was sure Rolf would be on my side but he was worse than Liesl. He said I was running out on them. I said it wasn't true, I just wanted a break from doing all the stuff we used to do. Of course, Liesl is pleased that Rolf is angry with me. Now she never misses a chance to stir things up between us.

May 1st, 1936

At school when no one is looking Liesl comes up behind me and whispers horrible things in my ear. If I ignore her she pushes and shoves me until I pay attention. Once I tried to push her back and she thumped me so hard in the stomach that my knees gave way and I ended up doubled over. She says I am a wishy-washy snob, who shits my pants at the slightest bit of trouble. She says I'm as bad as a looney 'useless eater' and a waste of space. She says if I tell anyone about her and Rolf she'll tell the whole school how I used to steal from my mother and that I stabbed a man.

I hate myself for not doing anything to stop her but I just can't. I'm too scared. After school it's even worse, especially if Rolf is with Liesl. They lie in wait for me and then block my way. Time and time again I miss my train – and the next one, and the next one. Yesterday I had to walk all the back to Lähn. It took three hours. I missed dinner. Mama just gave me a disgusted look when I came in. She doesn't ask where I've been any more. In fact she doesn't ask me anything any more.

If no one is around Liesl and Rolf shove and push me until I stumble and fall to the ground. Once Rolf kicked me. They call me the worst names and threaten to do the most horrible things if they ever catch me completely alone. If I try to resist it's even worse. So I concentrate on trying not to react. Eventually they get bored or someone comes and they have to let me pass. Each assault is a little bit worse than the last one though. I hate myself for letting them do this.

May 4th, 1936

I refused to get out of bed today. I told Mama I had a bad headache. Short of physically dragging me from under the covers and dressing me and walking me to the train station, she could do nothing. I stayed there all day and I am never going back to school.

May 6th, 1936

I offered to help Mama in the café but she said she didn't want my help because she couldn't trust me. I pleaded with her. I said I was bored. Eventually she agreed to let me do something if I promised to think about going back to school. She's always trying to get me to go back. Papa is furious that I won't go. He said I was being very un-German and throwing my life away.

I promised Mama I would go back after the summer, but I'll never go back. She said I could help serve and clean and cook but I was absolutely forbidden from going anywhere near the money drawer – she treats me as if I'm some kind of criminal. At least it keeps me occupied.

May 13th, 1936

Yesterday Mama was out shopping and Papa was working in the garden at the back. I'd actually been left in charge of the café – Mama said it was my absolute last chance ever. If I betrayed her trust this time that would be it. I hate the way she goes on but at least I am doing something.

Whenever we have a customer a little bell tinkles in our kitchen. Mama hadn't been gone five minutes when the bell gave a little jerky jangle. I went to the front and there she was, Liesl, standing as bold as anything, at the counter, in my café, in my house, wearing her horrible school smock with her hair all braided on the top of her head in a sort of halo shape. She stood there that way she does, sort of all lopsided. I didn't want to believe it.

'The man. He's in hospital,' she said, casually looking around the café. 'He's critical. Rolf found out. Rolf thought you should know seeing as you were so concerned.'

I couldn't speak.

'We miss you.'

I could hear my blood rush through my heart, whoosh, whoosh, whoosh.

'It's prettier than I imagined but five tables don't seem very many. By the way, Rolf needs a new Stein and he has no money.' She stared directly at me. 'He says you've to give him some.'

My mouth was so dry I could hardly speak. 'I haven't got any money.'

'You have. Right under the counter, in that drawer that's hidden there.' She nodded to where the money drawer was. 'You told us about it often enough.'

I moved my body in front of the drawer and leaned my stomach against it. 'It's locked. Mama doesn't trust me. I don't have the key.'

'It would be good if you could find the key because Rolf really wants to buy a new Stein.'

I shook my head. I didn't speak, I didn't trust myself to keep the fear out of my voice any longer.

She smiled. 'Rolf said I should tell you that he feels guilty about that man. He said to tell you he's thinking of going to the police and telling them what happened. He says he thinks me and him should testify to the truth, say how it was your idea to go to the cave, say how it was you who stabbed the man.'

Tears began to form in the corner of my eyes. I tried desperately to hold them back. 'I'm not giving you any money.'

She just laughed. 'It's up to you. But Rolf won't be happy. Not one little bit. It wouldn't surprise me if he decided to come and just take the money anyway. You always were an ungrateful bitch.'

There was a noise. It was Papa coming round the front of the house with his wheelbarrow. Liesl gave me one last look and left. Later Papa asked me who she was. I said she was just someone looking for work. I hoped he didn't notice how badly I was shaking.

June 12th, 1936

Maria got a shock when I turned up at her door. I'd simply taken Hubert's blue suitcase, which I'd found discarded in the back of his room, packed a few things, walked to the train station and got the train to Hirschberg and then a train to Breslau. I had to take money from the drawer for the tickets. I had no choice.

Maria said I had to go straight back, but I refused. Eventually she agreed to let me stay, but just for a couple of nights, until everything got sorted.

July 28th, 1936

Papa has written three letters to Maria demanding that she send me back. She's not pleased with Papa for suggesting that somehow my coming to Breslau had been something to do with her. I said if he had really wanted me to return he would have written to me directly. She said I was being unfair. Papa's letters are full of Mama's dismay, disappointment, distress, confusion, anger and hurt at my behaviour. But she hasn't written either. He said I was letting everyone down by running off. He said I had a choice, come back to Lähn and finish school, or stay in Breslau and throw away all the years already spent at school – and for what?

Maria says Papa is right, that I should finish my schooling. But more importantly she says Mama needs me. But I can't go back. When I think of Lähn I feel sick.

August 5th, 1936

Papa has written again. He says Mama can't sleep at night. She can't understand why I left the way I did. He doesn't understand either. He asks Maria to make me write to them – as if somehow Maria has any power over me. He says he knows Mama and I have had our ups and downs, but Mama needs me. I was the last child at home. Now I have gone, she feels lost. She feels bereft. Papa says he won't send Maria money for my upkeep. He says if I stay any longer he will wash his hands of me.

I tell Maria I am never going back. She says she doesn't understand. I shrug. She says if I don't go home she will throw me out. I tell her to throw me out. I'd rather sleep on the streets than go back. She keeps asking why. I keep saying just because. Eventually Maria gives up. Exasperated, she says I can stay in the baby's room until it arrives. But as she is still not pregnant that's a minimum of nine months. She says I have to at least promise to write them a letter. I promise but I won't. She says I'll have to find work. Her and Georg don't have enough money to send me to school, and I just can't do nothing all day. I am sixteen. I am sure I'll find work.

August 20th, 1936

Papa's last letter to Maria said that Hilde had returned from Holland. The National Socialists said they would cut his pension – meagre as it was – if he continued to support Hilde's religious education in Holland. He had to bring her back. I'm glad. Mama won't feel so 'bereft' now.

Maria asks me all the time if I've written to them. I say I am about to. She says I promised. She threatens to throw me out if I don't but I know she won't. She likes my being here. Georg is away a lot and when he is in Breslau he often doesn't get home until very late. Georg doesn't like me being here though. I know he doesn't. I don't know why. For some reason I thought he would be pleased to see me. How foolish was that? Whenever he sees me he looks sort of surprised and says 'Are you still here?' in a way that suggests he wishes I wasn't.

Maria tells him I'm going soon. Georg says they can't afford to keep me (not even on an SS salary! I never took him for a mean person!). Maria tells him I'm looking for work, and then Georg says, 'But I thought she was going back?'

Well, now I have work. The job is at the Monopol hotel. Chambermaid. I am to get training. Starting tomorrow morning at seven.

October 21st, 1936

I hate being a chambermaid. I have to wear silly overalls when I clean – I have two sets and must keep both of them spotless at all times, even though I have to wear one to clean in. There are two sets of stairs in the hotel – one for the staff and one for the guests. We must never, ever use the guest stairs. Ideally, the guests should never ever see us. If they do, we must bow or curtsey and look away until they have gone.

I have to clean thirteen suites every day. I must draw the curtains, open the windows, strip and remake the big double beds and puff up the pillows, tidy the cushions on the chaise lounge and dust and polish and sweep and wipe and wash and dry every inch of the room thoroughly, including the bathroom. I can't believe the number of things they want us to do.

Finally, when I am finished, the head housekeeper checks the rooms. She always complains something is wrong. Today she said I left a 'speck of shit' in the toilet bowl in one of the bathrooms. I had to go back and scrub the toilet bowl with the toilet brush until the shit was gone. It was so small a speck I couldn't even see it. She's a bitch. She never smiles and says I am lazy and slack. I keep looking for another job but no one wants to employ me as I don't have my school leaving certificate and have no skills and no experience. After I give money to Maria for food and board, I have nothing left. I had hoped I would earn enough money to pay the dues for the BDM Women's group but that will have to wait.

Lähn, November 3rd, 1936
Dear Maria and Toni,
I hope this letter finds you both well. As you know I was very disappointed to have to give up my training before it had finished. However, now I am back it is clear to me why our Lord God has done this: Papa needs help to look after Mama.

Papa says she has been tired ever since before they left Breslau. He says she is suffering from fatigue and just needs rest but I am not so sure. She's often distracted and very absent-

minded. Why did neither of you tell me? Her mind was so sharp before. But I will do my very best to help Mama and, our Lord God willing, hopefully it won't be long before Mama returns to her normal self.

There is little else to write about. No more news from Hansi in that awful camp. A postcard came from Hubert saying he is very happy doing his Hitler Youth Service. The café is busy. Papa works on his garden, preparing it for the winter.

Finally, I pray to our Heavenly Father that you become pregnant very soon, Maria, and I suggest you don't mention Toni's chambermaid work in any future letters home. Although I believe it to be admirable that you, Toni, at only sixteen years of age, have found work, Papa is clearly disappointed with you. You know what he thinks about people who do 'menial work'. Why exactly did you leave, Toni? And why won't you write? Papa says he doesn't want to hear from you, that you are no longer a daughter of his, but that's just posturing. It would make him and Mama very happy to get a letter from you. Is that too much to ask?

I will pray for you both – and for Georg – and for Herr Hitler. Do you know that man has forbidden women from attending jury service? He says we are too illogical and ruled by our emotions. Does he not know this is 1936 and not 1836? Your loving sister, Hildegarde

November 15th, 1936

I hear them arguing almost every night. He's not even bothered I can hear him. He says she should send me back home. He says it's not right that I just walked out like that. He says she's never in when he gets home because I'm taking her out 'galavanting'. I don't know how he makes that out. We've been to the cinema once – to see Erb Krank – The Hereditary Defect. Everyone was talking about it. It wasn't even that good. It was just a series of clips about a bunch of loonies. There wasn't even a story. Maria says she won't be able to cope if her baby is a mongol like our sister Johanna. She has to be pregnant first!

Georg tells her it's embarrassing to have a sister-in-law who is a cleaner. Does he think I like working at the Monopol? The head housekeeper is so rude and horrible to me. I'm going to hit her one day. I know I will. All the other girls are afraid of her. I'm not. There was an announcement on the radio the other day, saying Hitler wanted good English speakers to help the Reich. I thought this was my chance to leave the hotel, but when I inquired at the Town Hall they said as I haven't got my school certificate I couldn't be of help. So, that's that.

Lähn, December 15th, 1936
Dear Maria and Toni,
I am so sorry to hear you are still not pregnant, Maria. That's one year now. I will pray to our Lord God to help you conceive. As for Mama, she still keeps forgetting things and cries at the slightest thing. I think we should get advice from Dr Albers but Papa is adamant that she just needs rest. I pray to our Lord God that he is correct.

The café is busy. It seems our waffles are becoming quite the thing to have on a Sunday afternoon. Keep well and I will pray for your health and happiness.
Love Hilde

August 1st, 1937

Hitler came to Breslau to attend the Singing Festival and he stayed at the Monopol. I so hoped I would see him but they kept us plebs as far away as possible from the bigwigs and now he is gone. The night staff said in the evening scores of people had lined the streets with torches to light his way from the Century Hall, where the singing competition was taking place, to the hotel. It must have been a magnificent sight. Then there was a huge banquet in the ballroom. There had been fountains of champagne and oysters and truffles and music and lots and lots of dancing. Of course, I knew they were exaggerating, Hitler has renounced all luxury and forgone all pleasure. He would never be so hedonistic. I was on an early shift so missed it all. I wish I had seen him.

Maria met up with me after work today. She is still not pregnant. She is very fed-up. She took me to a little weinstube off the Ring. It was dark inside and smoky. We sat at a little round table by the window and had a small glass of sweet wine each. She said Georg used to bring her here before they'd got married. Now he has no time to do such things. We both agreed that the next time Hitler came to Breslau we were going to see him.

Lähn, August 18th, 1937

Dear Maria and Toni,

Hansi has been released from the camp. Our Lord God be praised! We are so pleased. Especially Mama, as you can imagine. Of course, it is wonderful to have him home and I am sure he must be happy to be back although he is not his usual self. Sometimes he stays in his dressing gown for the whole day and does nothing but play his gramophone records full blast. He's even taken to smoking cigars, but worst of all he refuses point blank to speak to Mama. This has had a very negative effect on Mama's condition, she's become even more distracted than ever and spends most of her day hanging outside Hansi's room, repeatedly calling his name, which he just ignores.

It's such a pity he can't give her just a little bit of attention. I imagine it will take a few weeks or even months for him to adjust to having his freedom, I hope so.

Of course, it must have been absolutely horrid in that camp. I did ask him what it was like but he said he had nothing to say about it. When I pressed him he said that the only reason he wasn't still in there was because they wanted the camps for the Jews – and because they wanted to free up all the able-bodied men for the predicted war. I asked him what war? But that was as much as I could get out of him. He really can be very trying but I pray he will be back to his old self soon enough.

Meanwhile, I am glad all is well in Breslau and I am still praying, Maria, for you to become pregnant. And, Toni, I can hardly believe you have already been promoted to a housekeeper. At the age of seventeen. Imagine! I think even Papa is secretly pleased with your rapid promotion.

You know, it would be so wonderful if you could see it in your heart, Toni, to write a little note to Mama and Papa. Hansi's return and his 'odd' behaviour has put a strain on everyone and some good news – and a letter from you would certainly be deemed as good news. It really would help to brighten everyone's spirits.

Your loving Hilde

Lähn, April 4th, 1938
Dear Maria and Toni,
It is with a heavy heart I tell you our latest news. The other night I was jolted out of my sleep by such a terrible hysterical wailing I thought someone was being murdered in our very home.

I rushed into the hall and found Mama crouched by the stairs, trembling all over, crying out, 'Don't let him see me! Don't let him see me!' Papa was on his knees beside her. He was clearly distraught to see Mama in such a state. 'Don't let who see you?' he cried. She just kept yelling, 'Hide me! Hide me!' Papa said, 'From who? Don't let who see you?' Then Mama screamed, 'There he is! Look!' Papa said, 'Who is there? Who?' And finally Mama said, 'The Devil! He's calling my name. I don't want to go! I don't want to go!'

The more we tried to convince her there was no one there, the more she insisted he was. On and on she yelled, 'Hide me! Hide me!' Only after Papa promised she would never have to go in her room again, did she eventually calm down and there and then we moved all Mama and Papa's things into Hubert's room. Poor Mama. I have never seen her like this before.

The next day she was still very agitated so we called Dr Albers. He said she has a 'psychosis' and sedated her so heavily that she fell asleep immediately. Then he insisted – despite Papa's protests – on committing her, saying she could be a danger to herself or others if she didn't get 'proper' treatment.

So, she was taken in her comatose state to the public psychiatric care unit in Hirschberg and is still there. Papa wanted to put her into private care but we simply can't afford it, which is such a pity as the public psychiatric unit is so unkempt and dirty.

*Of course we will keep you informed of her progress and
God willing she will be home soon.*
Your loving sister, Hilde

July 30th, 1938

The Sports and Games Festival has been on all week and Führer
Hitler was here to preside over the events. It's been so thrilling.
Breslau was a riot of colour and excitement and celebration. All
the city's best sports venues were used to host the events.
Everyone in the city was kept up to date with the results through
the fantastic new loudhailing system – before the festival started
one thousand loudhailers were set up throughout the streets of
Breslau, even in the outer suburbs. Maria and I both had Sunday
off and managed to get tickets for the games happening at the
Hermann Göring Sports Centre. And we saw Hitler. He is
absolutely wonderful.

We spent most of the morning gathering in the sports stadium
waiting for our Führer to arrive. It was a beautiful, sun-crisp
summer's day. A forty-piece band played rousing marching
music. We were all so excited. Hundreds of flags and banners
flapped and waved around the arena, including a wonderful
new red flag, which was dominated by a huge eagle with a
swastika in the middle.

The stadium was packed. Everyone was so happy and so
excited. And then the most wondrous thing happened. Above
all the clamour and the music there was another noise. It came
from outside the stadium. A thunderous noise. It grew louder
and louder. Like a huge wave, crashing forwards. Louder and
louder. STOMP! STOMP! STOMP! STOMP! A column of
giants exploded into the stadium. Row upon row of shiny black
leather coats. STOMP! STOMP! STOMP! STOMP! Row upon
row of glinting black helmets. STOMP! STOMP! STOMP!
STOMP! Human machines. Smooth as quicksilver. The column

parted. Then came all the important generals. And then at last he arrived. Our Führer!

The giants fanned out and created a ring of protection around the rostrum and our leader walked up the steps of the rostrum. He turned to look at us. He smiled and saluted us. As one, we cried, 'Sieg Heil!' He motioned for us to be quiet. Then a new noise erupted from the streets, more stomping and thumping, and our Austrian brothers and sisters, all dressed in their Lederhosen and fancy dark green felt hats with little feathers in them, marched into the stadium. Behind them came our Sudeten brothers and sisters in their local costumes. So much colour and fanfare. We all cheered again and again. Then came the flagbearers, rows of magnificent men in white vests, white shorts and white plimsols, carrying giant white flags, waving in the wind. Behind them came rows and rows of girls dressed in white shorts and T shirts, carrying wondrous giant red flags. Then row by row the gymnasts and athletes from all over Germany and the world entered the stadium, waving to us all in such a happy way. Some had come from as far away as the South African and the Argentine territories. They marched past Hitler and he saluted every single one of them. In one roaring voice we sang over and over again until I felt I would burst, 'Ein Volk! Ein Reich! Ein Führer!' – 'One people! One state! One leader!'

The group filled up the arena, a sea of shimmering white and red. And when everyone was assembled a gradual hush descended and at last our leader began to speak, quietly at first. I don't even remember what he said, something to do with our brothers and sisters from around the world. His voice grew louder and louder. He became more and more excited. So did we. And then the chanting started up all over again. 'Sieg Heil! Sieg Heil!' Suddenly BDM girls at the front surged forward. They swept the SS officers aside. 'One people! One state! One leader!' They were at the foot of the rostrum. The very front.

'One people! One state! One leader!'Our Führer leaned forward over the barrier. The girls stretched their arms up. He touched the hand of whoever was close to him. Then he was gone. Followed by his body guards and the other dignitaries. They were off on a tour of the city, all of them in a huge procession.

We wanted to follow but we also wanted to watch the events. Oh, he is such a wonderful, unselfish man! He wants nothing for himself! He only wants what is best for the German people. 'One people! One state! One leader!'

For the rest of the day we watched healthy German people compete in so many wonderful events. There was the football, and the shot put, and handball and the athletics. By dusk the mood of the crowd was ecstatic.

The last show was a display of athletic dancing and choreographed exercises. The all-in-white gymnasts glimmered in dynamic rows, hundreds upon hundreds of them. Then, as if by magic, as the very last acrobatic display came to an end, there was an explosion of light and six massive beams of silver erupted from around the sports ground. The giant shimmering rays soared upwards into the sky. The bright white slices powered upwards through the blackness and met together in a magnificent star above all our heads. It was unbelievable. Everyone cheered and cheered as the gigantic cathedral of light illuminated the sky. When at last it was over neither Maria nor I wanted to leave.

Later someone said that they'd used anti-aircraft searchlights for the big beams. The girls at work will be so jealous.

Lähn, September 3rd, 1938
Dear Maria and Toni,
More distressing news from the psychiatric institute. It seems
when Mama's sedation wore off and she realised she was in the

psychiatric hospital, she was horrified. She couldn't remember why she had been taken there. As far as she was concerned she'd gone to bed at home and woke up in the hospital. She wanted to go home immediately. The staff, of course, refused to let Mama leave. This made Mama so angry she went on hunger strike. Over the next couple of days, no matter what the nurses did, they couldn't make her eat – you know how single-minded Mama can be, her 'psychosis' hasn't changed that.

To stop her becoming too dehydrated, and from starving, the nurses gave her a saline drip. But as soon as they attached it, Mama ripped it from her arm. That's when they called me and Papa in. They said she was being deliberately obstructive and called her a troublemaker. They said if we couldn't make her see sense they'd sedate her so heavily that she'd be permanently unconscious. Eventually Mama agreed to 'behave' as long as we promised to do all we could to get her back home. However, the doctors in charge said her erratic behaviour was proof of how great her need was for psychiatric care. They won't release her, not yet anyway. Poor Papa. He blames himself. He says he should never have let Dr Albers take her away. All we can hope for is that Mama gets better by herself.

I will pray for us all,
Hildegarde

Lähn, September 30th, 1938
Dear Toni and Maria,
Every time we visit Mama she pleads with us to bring her home. Just yesterday she said the doctors took her into a dark room

with a chair in the middle of it. She was invited to sit down on the chair and only when she did so did they switch the light on. She was on a small stage, facing a room of sombre-looking men, wearing dark suits, not even white coats.

She wanted to leave but the doctors said it was part of her treatment and the sooner they finished the treatment, the sooner she would be able to go home. So she agreed to stay. They then attached lots of little metallic electrodes to her head and sent searing electrical impulses to her brain, which immediately sent her body into convulsions. As she shuddered uncontrollably the officials in the room looked on in silence. She said she felt like an animal in a zoo.

We speak to her doctor continuously and he says she will be allowed home when she is more cooperative. We ask him to explain what he means by this but he refuses. Poor Mama! The thing is, the longer she is in there, the worse she seems to become. We don't know if it's the new medication she's on or the strain of being there that is having this detrimental effect on her.

As for that place, it is an absolute disgrace! Those who have no relatives to visit them wander about unwashed and half undressed. Some occasionally soil themselves, which is particularly unpleasant. I don't know how Mama survives it. Some of the poor souls are so thin they look as if they are being starved. We need to get her home.

Very sadly, Hansi still refuses to visit Mama. It would make her so happy to see him – just as a letter from you, Toni, would make her happy. Really, don't you think that it is time to call a halt to your silent sulking? As for Hansi, he has no excuse. Apart from his periodic visits to Sommerfeld garrison in

Brandenburg for his military training, he does nothing but lounge around in his house coat and paint the occasional landscape. Goodness knows what Papa thinks of his behaviour.

You do know military service has been brought back, don't you? All men over eighteen have to do one year. It seems the year doesn't have to be carried out in twelve consecutive months so Hansi is only away for a few weeks at a time. And you do know, don't you, that Hubert has signed up permanently? Papa wasn't particularly pleased about that, but he says at least it's a job. And God be willing, Mama will receive a letter from you shortly. Toni.

Your loving Hilde

September 1st, 1939

As from today we are at war with Poland. Everyone is in a flap about it. All able men are being called to arms. Hilde says Papa can't go because he is too old.

September 3rd, 1939

Hubert visited us here in Breslau before he left. He looked very smart. He couldn't tell us much about where he was going but we know he is in the 18th Infantry Division. He promised to write. Hansi is in the 8th Infantry Division. He is so lucky Lähn is such an out of the way place. Most of the villagers don't care about his un-German behaviour. Like Mama, they seem to think his bohemian attitude is acceptable because he is an artist – he painted a picture of the square and now he can do no wrong. But what can you expect from a village with only one flag flying above the town hall? One flag is so unenthusiastically German! Breslau is adorned with flags and the SS and Wehrmacht are everywhere. It's wonderful. Everyone knows the Poles will capitulate under Führer Hitler's Blitzkrieg.

September 4th, 1939

We have all been issued with a gas mask. Nursing mothers have been given special ones with hoods – Hilde says in the countryside even horses have been given masks. That seems unbelievable but sensible. And now we have a wartime blackout at night time. If we let even a smidgen of light sneak into the street we can be fined or even jailed. The wardens check all the time. Maria and I immediately rushed out and bought blackout paper to cover the windows. There's already a sign in the street with a skeleton flying on top of a bomber saying *Der Feind sieht Dein Licht! Verdunkeln! – The enemy sees your light! Blackout!*

Well, I hope we women are asked to do something soon. Anything has to be better than working in this hotel, pampering the rich and idle – although I don't suppose it will take long for our boys to sort out the Poles.

September 19th, 1939

Poland has been defeated! In only eighteen days! Herr Göbbels says, 'In achtzehn Tagen hat sie der Herr geschlagen' – 'In 18 days He vanquished them!' Everyone is talking about how our Führer is the greatest field marshal of all time. Most of Poland is now under German rule.

Of course, we can't put the gas masks away or take down the blackout paper, because England and France declared war on Germany on the 3rd. If only I could do something. I am nineteen now. It is so frustrating not being able to do anything for the war. Hitler says that a woman's place is in the kitchen, looking after her children. And that's fine for women who have children – I am sure Maria will become pregnant soon and I know when I'm married I'll have six or seven children because there is no way that my beloved Germany is ever going to become Volkstot – people-dead – but right now I'm not married, so what about us women who have no children?

November 3rd, 1939

Maria and Georg have moved to Berlin. Something to do with Georg's work. So I am back in Lähn. I had nowhere else to go – Georg was never going to let me go with them and I couldn't afford to stay alone as I'd lost my job. The manager at the hotel said, 'The emergency situation requires all of us to make sacrifices.' That's all very well but I don't see how sacking me helps the war effort. I would rather be anywhere but here.

Hilde insisted the very first thing I do on my return was visit Mama in the psychiatric unit. Hilde said she'd already told Mama to expect a special visitor and so if I didn't go it would be a double disappointment. Eventually, she persuaded me.

The hospital was worse than Hilde described: the floors were spattered in grey grime and pastry-coloured paint flaked off the corridor walls in sheets, damp bubbled from black patches on the ward ceilings and the putrid smell was indescribable.

I didn't recognise Mama at first. She sat upright against the back of a metal-framed hospital bed, on top of a shabby sheet. She was much thinner and her hair was completely white, although long enough to be tied into a tidy bun. She looked older than forty-nine and wore her red woollen skirt and cream jumper with the crocheted lace neck. Her legs were bare despite the cold and there was a food stain on the front of the jumper, something she would never have usually tolerated.

Her hands sat on her lap and she stared straight ahead. Hilde ran up to her and I steeled myself for the meeting. Mama's face burst into smile as Hilde told her the special guest had arrived, but then when Mama's eyes fixed on me her smile collapsed and her eyes darted away in anxious search.

On our way back Hilde said she was sorry, she'd clearly made a mistake in not telling Mama who her special visitor was going to be. Mama had expected to see Hansi. Finding me standing there where he should have been had been very disappointing for her. Hilde seemed to think Mama's reaction bothered me. It didn't. As far as I'm concerned Mama's just like a character in the Erb Krank film I saw with Maria.

Berlin, December 4th, 1939
Dearest Toni,
It was so difficult to leave Breslau but Georg has to go where he is sent and we have a lovely flat near the Tiergarten. Berlin is so full of life and colour and so safe. In the hugely unlikely event of an enemy attack the Reich has already started to build air raid shelters. They are so safe and so clean and can house hundreds of people. You really have to see some of them to believe how big and modern they are!

And to answer your last question, the doctor says there is no reason why I shouldn't fall pregnant, but I still continue not to do so. And although it was very un-German of me to suggest so, I did asked Georg if he would get a check up. It's not unheard of for a man to be the one with the problem. But he refuses to acknowledge that possibility. So we are back at square one. I won't be defeated though. I am sure it will happen soon. We have just been unlucky.

I am considering going to a herbalist. There are stories of her having worked wonders with others, but I've not told Georg, just in case it is considered an un-German thing to do.
Maria

June 16th, 1940
Our troops took Paris on the 14th. The war will be over soon. I wish I could do more to help, other than serve coffee and cake to greedy businessmen avoiding their responsibility to Hitler.

They now call the area in the centre of Poland the 'German General Government', lots of Germans are moving there. I don't know where the Poles who used to live there have gone.

Mama is still in the psychiatric hospital.

July 28th, 1940

Hubert is here. He brought silk stockings and chocolate and coffee from France. He says the war will be over soon. He went to visit Mama. I was surprised, I thought he wouldn't want to. But he said it never occurred to him not to visit her. I asked him if she knew who he was and he said she seemed to.

Berlin, September 3rd, 1940
Dear Toni,
We have been bombed by the British. No one can believe it. Georg said it couldn't happen. Göring said it couldn't happen. Hitler said it couldn't happen. They arrived on the 23rd of August in the middle of the night and came back again and again. To add insult to injury, each of their bloody planes somehow escaped our anti-aircraft fire! Of course we have our shelters and there's not much damage to the buildings or even that many casualties, but they said it couldn't happen and it has! It has! And a day doesn't pass without someone talking of a loved one who has died in combat. Still no news from Hansi or Hubert? I hope no news is good news.

Sadly, no, the medicine I got from the herbalist hasn't worked. Georg says it is becoming embarrassing the way I refuse to get pregnant. It's not as if I am wilfully refusing to! Yes, I'll look out for suspenders for Hilde. You can get most things here on the black market, which is just as well as our rations have become rather mean and although Georg's position affords us privileges the average Berliner is refused, the shops are virtually empty.

I've been looking for a cot for the baby, for when it eventually arrives which I am sure it will, but it's simply impossible to find one. Nor, it seems, is there a carpenter left in the whole of Berlin who could build one. I may have to use a drawer. How ridiculous is that?
Maria

November 12th, 1940

Hilde and Papa are so pleased. We received a letter from the General Foundation for Welfare and Institutional Care concerning Mama's condition. It said that because of the severity of her illness she had been especially chosen, along with certain others like her, for radical new treatment. If we agreed, in six to ten weeks she'd be collected from the mental institute and taken in a community transport bus to one of the new Sonderbehandlungen – special handling centres – either in Saxony or in Brandenburg, near Berlin. There, at great expense to the state, she would be given the extra attention her condition required to make her better. It said it was the Reich's intention to get as many ill people healthy again and out of care as soon as possible.

Hilde says it is the answer to our prayers. Papa is overwhelmed. He says that at last Mama will get treatment and come home. I don't know if you can treat what Mama has. I am surprised the Reich is wasting money on new treatment for the likes of her.

November 18th, 1940

I saw Liesl today. I immediately felt sick. She was in front of me in the bread queue. Because of the cuts the village baker can't afford to use the bakery to bake. Instead he uses the medieval communal stone oven at the back of the square. We hand in our ration coupons one day and collect the bread the next. This is where everyone meets and gossips about the war – whose son has died, whose brother is still alive; who's had a letter, who has not; who's lost the most weight because of the rations, which tubby person is still eating more than her, or his, fair share.

Liesl stood that way she does, slightly lopsided, with her right arm stretched across the front of her waist, her hand hugging her left side. She was overdressed for a visit to the village square – most people traipse over in their house coat and old house slippers, saving their best for when the war is over.

A glossy black belt pulled her slinky cream dress into a knot at her middle. Her blond hair was clipped in a bob. She seemed thinner than before. Her left foot tapped the ground impatiently. She talked with the woman in front of her. She said, 'All I'm saying is that it's not fair. All those snotty women who don't work can come and get their rations whenever they like. They're first at the butcher's, first at the dairy, first in the bread queue. Whereas us workers, not only do we have to do a hard day's work before we get here, but then when we do finally get served there's nothing left. Bloody greedy upper-class bints have taken it all! Let them come home to half a sausage and chicory coffee after a day's work. Then on top of that, that 'useless eater' of a granny of mine doesn't know what rationing means and keeps eating my rations. My food! I'm telling you as soon as this war is over I am out of here – O.U.T!' She collected her loaves and strode off without even seeing me.

Berlin, December 1st, 1940
Dear Toni,
Georg is divorcing me. I am bewildered. When he left the flat this

*morning he said he wasn't coming back. As simple as that. He
accused me of being an 'ethnic dud'. Please do not tell Mama or
Papa or Hilde, you know their views on divorce. At least, don't
tell them yet.*

*I don't understand how he could do this. He says he's
sorry but as I can't provide him with a child it's his duty to find
someone who will. According to Himmler, 'Only one who leaves a
child behind can die in equanimity.'*

*I feel so let down! He knows I want children as desperately
as him! But I thought there was more to our relationship than
producing babies for the Reich. I love him. I can't imagine loving
anyone else. I thought he loved me. I am at a loss.*
Maria

December 13th, 1940

Women have been asked to volunteer to help with the war effort
by joining the signal auxiliaries. I have decided to sign up. The
Signal Corps training school is in Giessen. It is miles away. Near
Frankfurt am Mein. If I successfully complete the course I
won't need to come back to Lähn ever.

Papa was furious with me when I told him what I was doing.
He said I was abandoning them in their hour of need. What
need? The café is dead and Hilde is around to help anyway. Papa
wanted me to visit Mama before I left. He said I may not have
another chance to see her for a long time. He'd received another
letter from the General Foundation for Welfare and Institutional
Care. In a few weeks Mama will be taken for 'assessment' to a
transit centre at Lowenberg Hospital. From there she will be
sent to the special treatment centre. Unfortunately, he said,
visitors weren't allowed at the centres, something to do with
war time rules and regulations. I said I was sorry but I would

have no time to visit her before I left.

Berlin, Jan 5th, 1941
Dear Toni,
Georg has come back! He brought me a slice of cheese cake from the Konditorei. It was all wrapped up in a lovely silver box and tied with a pretty pink ribbon. It smelled so fresh and creamy and delicious. I knew he still loved me.

He says he wants to stay married to me but as 'I can't donate a child to the Führer' we must be divorced – since the new law of 1938 it's very quick nowadays.

He says he can't stay but he'll come and visit often. He says he can't live without me.

It was awful when he had to go. I begged him but he wouldn't stay. He promised to come again. It is so lonely here by myself.
Maria

February 21st, 1941

Papa asked me to visit his sister, my aunty Johanna, on my way to Giessen, where I had been invited to attend a training course before being accepted into the Signal Corps. Johanna lives in Hadamar, which is only about twenty-five miles from Giessen. Papa has not seen her for years, not since his and Mama's wedding. He said as I would be passing so close, it would be impolite not to visit.

I arrived in Hadamar by train from Berlin, where I'd overnighted in the Evangelical hostel. It was a fresh, spring afternoon. I was pleased to be away from Lähn – at last – and happy to be on the verge of doing something to serve our Führer Hitler and

Germany. Johanna met me at the station – she looked as different from Papa as you could imagine. Whereas Papa is tall and slim and handsome, Johanna is short and round and ugly.

She wore a navy blue woollen suit and a pointy, blue felt hat. A magnificent mink stole draped her stumpy shoulders. She immediately took me to a pretty little Konditorei in the middle of a cherry-tree-lined street at the edge of town. She insisted on sitting at an outside table, probably because she wanted to show off her stole rather than so that I could enjoy the delightful sight of the abundant pink cherry blossoms.

Johanna had hardly given our order when she began a tirade of abuse against Papa. She said he was a weak buffoon, a dreamer, a spineless loser. On and on she went. Then she started on Mama: she called her an upper-class indulged poodle; a pampered princess, vain, arrogant, lazy, selfish. No wonder Papa hadn't seen her for years. I did point out that Mama had been a hardworking doctor but Johanna only laughed and said becoming a doctor had just been a tactic by Mama to make Papa feel inferior.

It seemed nothing would stop her bilious attack. Then, as if on cue, from out of the café hared two young kids, a boy and girl of about eight and nine. They ran straight past Johanna, clipped the little foldaway chair she was perched on and sent her – and her hat and stole – sprawling all over the ground. Before she'd a chance to get up, the children were gone, chasing after the buses, which had just accelerated past the café.

I quickly went to assist Johanna. 'Brats! Hooligans!' she screamed after the children, who were still running after the buses as they headed up the hill. It was then I noticed the bus passenger windows were covered in white paper. No one could see in and no one inside could see out. The boy shouted: 'It's the murder buses!' The girl yelled, 'They're taking the loonies to be gassed! They're taking the loonies to be gassed!' The boy called out, 'They'll be baking them in the oven soon!'

Two waitresses took Johanna into the café to help tidy her up. An older woman at the table next to us shook her head sympathetically in Johanna's direction and said, 'Kids these days, eh!' But as soon as she was inside, the woman turned back to her elderly neighbour, nodded up towards the buses and said, 'If I get ill, whatever you do, don't send me to a state hospital. After the feeble-minded have been finished off, us old useless eaters will be next!'

The brown buses had now pulled up on the top of the hill at the entrance to a towering gothic building separated from the road by a brick wall and a fringe of scrawny chestnut trees. A monumental chimney stack protruded from the building's high roof. Two men in white coats hopped out of each bus. They were followed by a string of befuddled looking people wearing loose-fitting, washed-out summer clothes and no hats or scarves despite the spring chill.

Once off the buses, the passengers huddled together on the pavement and the white-coated men tried to herd them towards the building. It wasn't easy. An older man with a long straggly white beard kept slapping the sides of his head and trying to walk off in the wrong direction. Another younger man was so lame that every step he took made him wobble sideways. A pretty girl, with a round face and thick crunchy corkscrew brown hair, suddenly sat down on the pavement and wailed helplessly.

Eventually, by cajoling and shoving them the white-coated men managed to push the group through a security gate, past the gloomy chestnuts and into the grounds of the building. It was obviously a mental institution of some sort. The children following the bus had disappeared. I thought their taunts had been unkind.

The next day I left early, even though it meant I had an hour's wait for my bus in the morning chill. Johanna's accident in the café had only temporarily halted her tirade against Papa and Mama. I'd spent the rest of my stay having to listen to her poison. It transpired Papa had been Oma and Opa's favourite. I'd left her as soon a I could.

While I waited at the bus stop, clouds of charcoal smoke belched out of the chimney of the mental institution on the hill. The smoke puffed upwards then collapsed downwards, spreading a tidal wave of gritty fog over the centre of town. This was immediately followed by a putrid stench. It was so foul I had to cover my nose with my handkerchief.

A lady joined me at the bus stop. She was older, well dressed, in a dark green woollen coat, black headscarf and black leather gloves. We politely acknowledged each other with a nod. More and more smoke spewed out of the towering stack and smothered Hadamar in a blanket of soot. Gradually half a dozen flecks of what looked like ash fluttered from out of the murky clouds and floated onto the ground. At this point the lady beside me leaned over, gently picked up the flecks of dirt from where they had landed on the ground and placed them in a little cloth drawstring bag. I couldn't believe what I had just seen. And then for no reason, other than I was curious, I asked her what she'd picked up.

She looked at me oddly and said, 'You're not from here?'

'Lähn, in Lower Silesia.' I explained.

'You're far from home,' she said.

'I suppose.'

She frowned and took the little bag out of her coat pocket. Carefully, she teased open the drawstring and shook one of the pieces of ash she had just picked up on her leather glove. 'Know what this is?'

I looked at the wisp of charcoal material. 'It looks like hair,' I said with a shrug, unsure of what she intended.

She smiled, 'Right first time. It is hair.'

'Oh?' I said, not knowing what else to say.

She eased the strands back into the bag and put it in her pocket. 'Did you see the buses yesterday?' she said. 'They came in the afternoon.'

'I saw two buses,' I said, thinking that maybe she was a bit peculiar.

'We can get nine or ten in a week.'

I still didn't know what to say, so I simply nodded.

'The hair belonged to one of the poor souls they brought in on those buses.'

I laughed before I could stop myself. This was ridiculous. 'You can't know that that bit of fluff came from someone who came off those buses.'

'Yes, I can,' she said, quite adamantly.

'Even if someone got a hair cut as soon as she or he walked in the door, how on earth could the discarded hair end up on the street in front of us today? For all you know, it could be dog hairs.' The woman was clearly mad.

'Tell me something,' she said, smiling, 'If you knew someone who was close to you, who you loved – say, a brother or sister or mother – and they were suffering from some kind of really bad illness, what would you do about it?'

I had no idea what she was talking about. 'I'd go to the doctor and get them medical treatment.'

She smiled, 'Exactly. But, what if you did that and the doctor told you that this same person you love can't be treated. That this same person will be sick for the rest of her life and that she'll suffer for the rest of her life. What do you do then?'

'Well, I think they can treat most things now, so the question's not valid.' This was getting too bizarre for me. I thought it would be better to go away and come back later. 'If you'll excuse me.'

She grabbed my arm. 'You've seen the film, haven't you?'

'What are you doing?' I said, quickly pulling my arm free of her.

'Excuse me,' she immediately released her grip. 'I get carried away sometimes. Do forgive me.'

'Look,' I felt sorry for her for some reason. She seemed a pleasant enough person, 'I think maybe you're a little confused.'

'My sister works there,' she nodded in the direction of the hospital. 'That's how I know what happens. Sometimes they euthanise so many at once they're forced to put two bodies in the crematorium oven at the one time. But the ovens just aren't built to take that sort of punishment. The chimney gets clogged, the furnace doesn't work properly, that's how you get hairs floating about in the air and that awful, awful smell.'

I stared at her in total disbelief. 'You're saying the people who arrived on the bus yesterday have been killed?'

'Oh no, not killed,' she said, giving each of her gloves a little tug at the wrist, 'euthanised. They can get through over a hundred bodies in a day. My sister says their poor lives are a burden. My sister says the good doctors put the poor souls out of their suffering. My sister says they give these lives unworthy of life a "mercy-death".'

'Listen,' I said as firmly as I dared, looking around for someone else but it was still early and the street was deserted. 'I'm really sorry, but what you're suggesting, it can't be true.'

'But it is. They do it with gas. They used to give them injections. That was okay for the kids but adults need much bigger doses and such large quantities of those kind of drugs are really expensive, especially with a war on. So now they gas them with carbon monoxide.'

I shook my head. 'It's not possible.'

She cleared her throat, 'They say they don't know, but I think they must know. What do you think?'

'I'm sorry, I think you're muddled –'

'My sister says they don't know. She says on arrival they're made to strip for a medical examination. The physician sees them but instead of examining them he randomly assigns each of them a terminal disease taken from a list of 60. He then marks each person with a different coloured band-aid depending on which category of patient he or she is. There are three categories: either "put down", or "put down and remove brain for research", or "put down and break out gold teeth".'

My head began to throb. 'I don't believe you.' I wished, not for the first time since I'd arrived, I'd never set foot in Hadamar.

'My sister says after the pretend examination they're taken to have a shower. But what they don't know is that the shower cubicles have all been converted to be airtight and instead of water, gas comes out of the shower head. So the patients, still all naked, potter in one by one to do their ablutions and whoosh, carbon monoxide floods the room and no more suffering. But you'd think, if you were last in the queue, you would suspect, wouldn't you? You would notice no one coming back out of the shower, wouldn't you? My sister says, no. They don't know a thing because they're all drugged to make it easier on them, and they're more manageable then too. When they've euthanised 10,000 people they're going to have a little party to celebrate having helped the Reich save millions of Marks a year.'

Now I began to get really angry. She was talking complete rubbish and insulting the Reich on top of it. 'Your sister shouldn't say such things. She'll get into trouble.' A large inky fleck fluttered from out of the sky and landed on my coat sleeve. I didn't know whether to flick it away or give it to her or what.

'Imagine having a sister who does that?' said the lady, suddenly downhearted.

'Look, if it were true, there would be an outcry from the relatives. What sort of person would stand by and let something as horrible as you're suggesting happen to a family member?'

She sighs, 'But the relatives don't know, do they? They think their sick loved one has been taken away for special treatment, that's what the letter they get from the General Foundation for Welfare and Institutional Care says.'

I had heard that name before but I couldn't remember where. 'You're talking nonsense! This government has restored the family to its rightful place!'

'The relatives suspect nothing. But no sooner has the patient been taken away in the community transport buses than another letter arrives. It says their relative has tragically died, stating one of the sixty fatal diseases as cause. Of course, occasionally there are mistakes. One family were told their schizophrenic daughter had died of a burst appendix but the girl's appendix had been removed years earlier.

I was becoming exasperated. 'Our Führer wouldn't let this happen!'

'You think?' she said, sounding almost surprised. 'Have you seen the film?'

'You keep asking about the film?'

'Erb Krank – Hereditary ill? You must have seen it. It was a huge box office success. You know the one, about all the loonies in the asylums costing the Reich so much money?'

'I saw it, but I don't see –'

'There was another one called Opfer der Vergangenheit – Victims of the Past. If I remember correctly Victims of the Past is Herr Hitler's favourite film of all time. That movie has sound, of course, maybe that's why he prefers it. What they can do these days! It's wonderful!'

'What have they got to do with anything!' She was confusing me and making me so angry.

'You know, I can understand the idea of a mercy death, I can. Some of these poor people are so distressed maybe death is a mercy, but what I can't understand is why treat the remains with such disrespect?'

I sighed. She simply refused to listen to me.

'My sister says that after the bodies have been cremated, they sweep up the ashes into a big rubbish bin. From here the ash is indiscriminately scooped into random urns and sent out willy-nilly to the mourning loved ones. One family got their father's remains back with a hair pin in among the ashes.' She paused to clear her throat, there were tears in her eyes. 'How can you grieve knowing the body of your loved one is scattered over the rooftops of Hadamar's shops and offices? That's why I collect the bits whenever I see them. Later I'll take them to the church yard, at least there the ground is consecrated.'

All of a sudden I began to feel uncomfortable.

She sniffed. 'It's not my sister's fault. She's only doing her job. By the time they reach the Special Handling centres it's too late. The only way you can save someone is not to let them get sent to the Special Handling units in the first place.'

'Special Handling units?' I felt my stomach twist into a solid knot. That was the place Mama was being sent to for her special new treatment. Now I remembered where I'd heard of the General Foundation for Welfare and Institutional Care. They were the people who had sent Hilde and Papa the letter about Mama.

She nodded in the direction of the hospital and its reeking chimney stack. 'There are maybe a dozen special clinics around the country. Think there are a couple not too far from you, one in Saxony and another in Brandenburg. Some used to be straightforward hospitals. They were converted as soon as the war started. All doing the same thing. Carrying out mercy killings to save the almighty Third Reich a few pennies.' Just then the bus pulled up in front of us. 'Just pray,' she said climbing on board the vehicle, 'to our Lord God that no one you love gets sick, especially not sick here,' she pointed to her forehead. A tear trickled down her cheek. 'And especially pray to our Lord God that if they do, you don't ever get a letter from the General Foundation for Welfare and Institutional Care offering special treatment to make them better.'

Papa and Hilde were surprised to see me back. They didn't want to believe the story about the Special Handling centres. It was too fantastic. I said they could believe what they wanted, but I was going to go to the hospital and bring Mama home, even if I had to carry her out on my back. Whatever our differences in the past, there was no way I was ever going to let Mama end up being killed like an extra in some horror film.

Eventually, the three of us went to bring Mama home. However, when we got to the psychiatric hospital the matron told us that Mama had been taken to the transit centre in Löwenberg general hospital that morning. As the nurse understood it, Mama would stay at Löwenberg for 24 hours for tests, and then from there she would finally be taken to the Special Handling Clinic in Brandenburg. The nurse said we were very lucky that Mama had been selected for such special treatment.

Berlin, February 22nd, 1941
Dear Toni,
You should have told me sooner about the problems at home!
I understand you thought I was upset after my divorce but I
will never be so upset that I won't want to know about what is
happening to my family. Please don't keep things from me in the
future.
This news about a 'community transport wagon' and
'radical new treatment' is very alarming. Very alarming indeed!
You must impress upon Papa the importance of getting Mama
released from the hospital as soon as possible.
Georg used to talk about a new secret Nazi campaign
to rid Germany of 'life unworthy of life', called Aktion T4. The
headquarters for the campaign is here in Berlin at 4 Tiergarten
Strasse. It is truly horrific. Supposedly patients who are

The Blue Suitcase

considered according to 'the best available human judgment'
to have irreversible hereditary genetic disorders can be given
a 'mercy death'. In reality it means anyone with any genetic
disorder, from being born with six toes or a harelip to having
cystic fibrosis is being killed.

Other groups deemed 'unworthy of life' are those in care
with acute or chronic long-term mental health problems. This
includes people suffering from illnesses such as Alzheimer's or
schizophrenia or depression. In fact anyone suffering from any
severe psychosis of any sort whatsoever is at risk of being got rid
of. Mama is in danger! She must be taken out of care!

Georg said the special Aktion T4 medical team identify the
unfortunate individuals who are deemed 'unworthy' by writing
to hospitals and mental care units and asking for a list of those
mentally and physically disabled 'ill' patients whose prognosis
for recovery is not good. The medical teams don't know what the
lists are for. Some think the lists are used to identify those who
are too disabled to sign up for war duty, so they place their very
ill patients on the list hoping that they won't be sent to the front.
Others use the list as an opportunity to free the hospital of the
upkeep of caring for long-term costly patients.

The families of the chosen 'relative' receive a letter which
says that, at great expense to the Reich, their 'relative' has been
chosen for exclusive treatment. The family are told the 'relative'
will be collected on a specific date in a special community
transport wagon and taken to a special Reich facility for
treatment. But once they are 'rounded up' they are never seen
again!

You must get Mama out of the hospital now!
Maria

Hilde said my plan would never work. She said it was madness and we would both get arrested. In the end, though, she agreed to help. We'd hoped to enlist Dr Albers, but his papers had arrived and he was tending soldiers at the front.

We left immediately. Our bus got us into Löwenberg at midday. We went straight to the hospital. Three special brown buses, with white paper covering the passenger windows, were parked at the back of the building. Hilde gasped. They were just as the ones I'd seen in Hadamar. If the buses were there that meant Mama should still be inside the hospital. We didn't have a second to lose. We hurried through a side door and went straight to the nearest visitor toilets. Once inside the toilets we locked the door behind us and unpacked our things.

Quickly, I put one of Mama's old doctor's coats over my clothes and slung one of her old stethoscopes round my neck. Next I pinned her doctor's name pin on my lapel. Hilde dressed herself in a similar doctor's coat. When we were both ready I handed her one of Papa's old clipboards from his civil servant days. Suddenly Hilda looked pale. She said her legs had gone all wobbly. She said she couldn't do it. I told her to take a deep breath. She did. 'It's all a matter of confidence.' She took another breath. 'No hesitation,' I said and handed her the clipboard. She took it. Together we took one last deep breath, unlocked the toilet door and marched to the main reception area. I demanded directions to where the female patients for Special Handling were waiting. Without questioning us, the receptionist directed us straight to the ward.

The twenty-four bed female ward was littered with confused women. A quick glance around indicated no one in authority in sight. The women wore their day clothes and either sat on beds or walked aimlessly while giggling inanely or crying softly in between dribbling.

Hilde gave me a nudge and pointed to an emaciated middle-aged woman, with a sagging face and thinning white hair, which was cut in an abrupt short style. Mama was even thinner than before. She sat upright on the edge of a hard-backed hospital chair. Her expression was one of fear. She didn't acknowledge either Hilde or myself when we approached. Hilde took her hand and whispered, 'It's me?' Just then a nurse swooped in through the double doors of the ward. It was now or never. I quickly clapped my hands above my head and shouted, 'Everyone here! Over here!' A few of the women turned to look. 'The bus for the picnic is here!' Some faces brightened. 'Quick! Quick! Make a line behind the lady doctor!' I pointed to Hilde. 'The sooner we move, the quicker we will be on the bus!'

The nurse hurried up to me. 'Doctor, what's going on?' she looked almost as confused as the women patients.

'We are taking them to Special Handling, of course!' I clapped again and called out to the women. 'Quick! One by one here in a queue! Behind my assistant!'

'Frau Doctor,' the nurse looked in panic at the queue of women slowly following Hilde out of the ward, 'I was told they weren't leaving till this evening.'

'We're leaving early. We're giving them a picnic on the way.'

'A picnic?' she looked horrified.

'Are you questioning a direct order from a Reich doctor?' I demanded.

'No, not at all, I thought they weren't being moved until later because of – '

'Your name, nurse?' I interrupted.

She composed herself and said, 'Shall I get the men from the men's ward?'

'No. We'll come back for the men once the women are settled in the bus. Get me a list of the special patients. I'll check the names with our list.'

'Immediately, doctor.' The girl busied off to a desk in the centre of the ward and shuffled about with some papers there. Meanwhile, Hilde continued to lead the meandering column of slightly excited women – headed by Mama – out of the ward door and down the corridor. I quickly followed them. 'Hurry! Hurry!' I yelled, 'The picnic bus waits for no woman!'

The nurse came running after me and handed me the list. I nodded back to the ward and said, 'One of the ladies has had an accident by her bed. It has not been cleaned up.' The nurse bowed slightly and quickly disappeared back into the ward.

As we hastily hurried the women down the corridor, I continued to shout, 'Let's not keep the good bus driver waiting! Quick! Quick!' The women grew more and more excited but still no one stopped us. By the time we passed reception and reached the main entrance I could hardly breathe.

We manoeuvred the women out of the front door and into the centre of the landscaped grounds. After quickly checking no one had followed us, I put my hands back above my head, clapped loudly once more and shouted 'Halt!' The women slowly struggled to a stop. 'The bus is going to be late. We have to wait. Please feel free to wander all around the hospital gardens while you are waiting. We'll come back for you when the bus is here.' No one moved. 'Ladies! It's a pleasant afternoon, enjoy the daffodils and cowslips and primulas and if you keep walking you won't get too cold.' Slowly, some of the women started to drift off, some simply sat down where they were.

I turned to Hilde, she had Mama's hand in hers. She looked as if she was about to burst into tears. 'We're nearly there,' I whispered. She shook her head. 'I can't do this,' she said. 'I want to but I know I can't.' 'Yes, you can!' I urged. 'The gate is just twenty yards away.' Hilde stifled a sob. I took Mama's other hand. 'Don't look back.' I turned towards the gate of the hospital. Hilde faced the gate, gulped and nodded. Together we led Mama down the path and closer and closer to the exit. As soon as we were out the gate, we wriggled out of our doctor's coats and shoved them, minus Mama's pin, along with the stethoscope and Hilde's clipboard, under a bush.

Once out of the hospital we went swiftly to the bus station and collected our carpet bag from the left luggage office where we'd left it earlier. We took Mama into the public toilet. Here we dressed her in her stockings and boots, eased her into her coat and placed a hat on her head and leather gloves on her hands. We then got on the bus for Lähn and made our way to the back, sitting Mama between us. Eventually, after what seemed hours of waiting, the bus moved off. I heard a noise. It was Hilde. She was crying very quietly. 'We've done it,' I whispered. 'I know,' she said. We were home by eight.

1941–1947

December 14th, 1941

We are at war with America now. All women between 18 and 40 have been called up for Dienst Verpflichtung – obligatory war service. We will not be fighting but helping in other ways. It was on the Reich Radio and my war service papers say I am to go to Breslau and I am so pleased. At last no more endless hours of knitting scarves, or gathering fruit, or tedious, mind-numbing childminding in the women's group. And I am lucky because I am going somewhere I know and like.

Some of the other girls in my women's group are being sent to industrial centres in Upper Silesia. They're nervous about leaving. Hilde said Hitler is sending countryside girls to the towns and town girls to the countryside because he wants to isolate us. She said he's using classic divide and rule tactics to keep us vulnerable. In that way we are less likely to rebel or be influenced by rebels. She hates Hitler. She says the Aktion T4 plan was his idea.

No one has ever contacted us from the General Foundation for Welfare and Institutional Care but even so we never discuss the circumstances of Mama's return with anyone else. Hilde still feels bad that we weren't able to help the other women. I tell her we had no choice, we had to get Mama away from that place as quickly as possible. She knows I am right. I understand why she feels bad though, because I do too, but I don't want to believe Hitler knew about the mercy killings, I just don't.

Hilde has been granted permission to stay and help Papa look after Mama. I know they will take good care of her. I tell Hilde and Papa I'll soon be back but Hilde says there's not much chance of that now the Russians have joined the fight against Germany.

January 15th, 1942

I am 21 years old and back in Breslau. I am working for the war by being a conductress on a tram. I imagined I'd been doing something more exciting but it's not such boring work and I even have a kind of uniform. It's a very smart grey tunic, just like the Wehrmacht's.

We meet every morning at the tram depot at six and are given our route timetables. Some of the girls have come from as far away as Cologne and Hamburg. We are all happy to help the war effort and it is good to be back in Breslau. The city buildings are bedecked in magnificent flags and banners and SS officers sweep up and down Schweidnitzer Strasse, always in a hurry, always on the move for the Reich.

I work twelve hours a day and get one break. It can be quite cold, so when it's not busy I jump up and down and clap my hands to keep warm. We are all given lunch, which is usually bread and cheese and an apple. It's dark by the time I get home and I am filthy from handling the money and covered in smears of ink, which rubs off from the tickets and spreads all over my hands and clothes. I'll need to use my wages to buy extra warm clothes and soap cleaning powder.

In some ways it's as if I never left Breslau, though there is one big change, now you need a pass for everything: to get into town, to get out of town, to go to work, to come back, to be off work (luckily I'm never sick), to go home. Even riding a bicycle isn't allowed unless you have a permit, but I don't need a bike as I walk everywhere so it's not a problem. And there are so many rules to remember. The main one is not to let Jews or Poles sit on the tram and it's not as if they can pretend they don't know the rule because all the trams carry big posters on them saying 'Für Polen and Juden sitzen verboten!' – 'Jews and Poles are forbidden to sit!' And to make it easy for us Germans to know who is who, by law, Jewish people must now wear a yellow Star of David on their jacket or sleeve and the conscripted Poles and Eastern workers must wear a big yellow 'O' or 'East'.

By law, we must also report any German we see talking to a

Jew or Pole or Czech or anyone from the East. We must also report any Jew or conscripted worker we see going into the botanical gardens, or using the swimming baths, or riding a bicycle, or using a radio, or visiting the zoo. All these things are forbidden to them. They're not Reich citizens, but foreign nationals. So far, I haven't had to report anyone but I will if I have to. The fact is there aren't that many foreign nationals about. There's the old Jewish man who sweeps the streets but I don't count him.

Lähn, February 12th, 1942

Dear Toni,

How lovely it is to hear your stories of your exciting life in Breslau. You wouldn't think there was a war on. In fact nothing much seems to have changed in Breslau since you and Maria were at the Sports Festival. It's almost as if Breslau is in a permanent party mood. This is good to know. But, oh, Toni, what temptation too! All those handsome soldiers everywhere. All of them lonely and far from home. My dear sister, I pray for you every day and ask God to keep you from temptation – no matter how willing the spirit is, the flesh can be weak. Remember, my dear, it is better to take refuge in the Lord than to trust in man. It disturbs me that you don't go to mass any more, you would find such reward there.

Unfortunately, there is still no 'party' where our dear Mama is concerned. The lack of news from the front and Hansi, as well as your departure, has made her rather agitated again. I tell her she needs to be joyful in hope and faithful in prayer but she doesn't listen. Still, I am so glad you are settling back into Breslau.

And one last very practical thing. Papa needs pyjamas.
His present ones are in a terrible state and it's impossible to find
any clothes whatsoever here in Lähn. Even the seamstress in the
square has closed shop. I know pyjamas may seem irrelevant
in the cause for German victory but Papa cannot go about the
house naked. He still has his full 80 points on his clothes ration
card and I believe pyjamas are 30.

Also I need a new bra. I believe that is also 40 points.
Please can you look out for one. And I know everyone says
suspenders are impossible to find no matter what price you are
willing to pay, but if you do come across any I would be really
grateful for them.

Stay well. We miss you and pray for you every day
Hildegarde

Berlin, November 8th, 1943
Dear Toni,
We have suffered the most terrible bombardment these last
few weeks. It's been dreadful. Do not come and visit. It is too
dangerous. No one knows what is happening. The enemy can
strike at any time. Thousands have been killed and thousands
more have been made homeless and almost a quarter of the
buildings in Berlin seem to have been destroyed either by the
bombs or the firestorms that followed the bombings. At least we
have our air raid shelters. Do not come, though. Stay in Breslau,
where it is still safe.

Still no news from Hubert or Hansi? It's almost too much
to hope they could still be alive. I gave up expecting to hear from
Hilde, really she is simply not reliable. I don't know why she won't

write.

As for Georg, I have not seen him recently but I know I am in his thoughts.

Maria

Lähn, February 12th, 1944

Dear Toni,

While Papa was working in the town hall – they've asked him to help out – Mama had a turn, here in the house. Hansi was still here on leave and I asked him to help me with her, but he refused. He said it upset him too much to see all that education and training lost along with her mind. He seems not to realise we are equally upset. Does he think we are heartless? Poor Mama. She is better again now, but for how long?

Of course, I am sorry to hear that things in Breslau are beginning to show such signs of disintegration – war brothels, really? How disgusting for you. And Eastern workers everywhere! How ironic. Only a few years ago Hitler said Germany was Pole free and now he's bringing them back to help us.

And, yes, I can believe the increased number of refugees. We even get them here now. Poor things, hungry and homeless because of the war. And, yes, they are all from Inner Germany. I too have heard that they call Silesia the 'air raid bunker' of Germany.

And the 'Allies' really drop more bombs in one month that we do in a whole year? Georg really said that to Maria? He'd better be careful. Suggesting the Wehrmacht isn't invincible is treason. Even here in our little backwater we can get into *trouble for saying the wrong thing at the wrong time. Just the other day Frau Nicolin, you know the woman who is half-Polish, said something about how no one knows how the war will end (which is of course what we are all thinking nowadays) and it was passed on. We don't know by whom. The next day an SS officer came from Hirschberg and took her away on a charge of being a 'grumbler' and 'defeatist'. She was only narrowly saved from being sent to a concentration camp because she spoke good German and her employer vouched for her!*

We still have no news of Hubert. What of Maria? Surely she still cannot be without child? They will have to pay back that loan. Imagine that.

Thinking of you in my prayers and thoughts,
Hildegarde

Berlin, February 28th, 1944
Dear Toni,
The bombing is getting worse. Berlin is such a mess. The sky is always grey now. There is dust and grime everywhere. Thousands lie buried under countless tons of brick and mortar and twisted steel that was once department stores and factories and schools and offices. Whole tram routes have been cancelled because it is too dangerous to go along the streets in case a building collapses on top of them.

We go everywhere on foot – only the mighty Wehrmacht have motorised transport. And our rations are so meagre and food so scarce that everyone is continuously hungry, unless of course you are in the SS, they can have everything.

Looting is rife even though it's the death sentence if you are caught, but people are starving, what are they supposed to do? If only the bombing would let up. They say all the big towns in Germany are under similar attack. It's the noise I can't stand. I'm glad I don't have children because I'd be too worried for their safety if I did.

Georg has remarried.

Maria

March 3rd, 1944

There are forced Jewish and Eastern labourers everywhere. It's ever since 1942 when all the factories were moved from central Germany here to Breslau, in the middle of the air raid shelter of Germany. They say more weapons and war machinery are made in Breslau now than in the whole of Germany and that's why we need the forced labourers – to work in the armaments factories. My tram goes out to the east, towards Markstädt, where the giant new Krupp Berthawerk armaments factory is. The engineers are all German but the factory floor is manned by foreign forced workers.

On the early morning tram run I see hundreds and hundreds of them being marched towards the factory. They say most of them are from the big camp at Fünfteichen, but some are drafted in from camps and hostels in Breslau itself. It's these workers that seem to be able to wander the city freely when they are not working. They hang around the horrible brothels which are everywhere – some of these places actually have signs outside them saying 'For Foreign Labourers Only.'

Lähn, May 16th, 1944

Dear Toni,

I am so worried about Mama and feel so helpless. I try my

hardest but I am just a little pencil in the hand of God. Papa too is doing his best for Mama but only our Lord God the Almighty knows if our efforts will be good enough. Stay safe. I will pray for us all,

Hildegarde

August 5th, 1944

I saw Goatee Hanke today – our governor. He strode past with his entourage, heaven help anyone who gets in the way. He's thin and mean and so not my idea of a German at all. He swept into the Konditorei and then after a few minutes swept out again with a dainty little chocolate box dangling by a golden ribbon from his pinky.

We are constantly told to work harder and harder, to renounce luxury and pleasure, while he seems to indulge his every whim. Some call him a Nazi 'Golden Pheasant' – they'd better be careful the Gestapo don't hear them say that, it could be construed as grumbling or defeatism. The slightest thing can get you arrested and executed these days. They say hundreds have been guillotined in Kletschkau for 'sabotage'. It's hard to believe they were all saboteurs.

August 15th, 1944

Dearest Antonia,

Thank you for your letter and the scarf, which I wear night and day. It's madness at the front. The earth quakes with the destructive force of warfare. Swathes of countryside are levelled. Towns and villages are razed. Whole communities are wiped out. Nothing is left alive after the fighting. We fire at an average of one round every fifteen seconds and still they come after us. Still we don't surrender. I am only alive because of my colleagues, the

*'Looted Teuton' – the Poles who are forced to fight with us. They
are some of the bravest soldiers I have met. I'll never sing another
rude song about dirty Polish villages and Hitler's Lebensraum
again.*

from Hubert

September 1st, 1944

Führer Hitler has declared Breslau to be a fortress town.
Platoons of soldiers are due to arrive to defend us. Everyone is
concerned that this means the Russians are close. However, the
Silesian Daily News says the Russians are still miles away in
Poland and on the brink of collapse. But Hanke has ordered all
men aged between sixteen and sixty to sign up to the Volksstürm
– the German People Storm Defence Force. He says this new
force will help defend our glorious Breslau, that we will be an
example to all of Germany. He says, 'When the people stand up,
the storm will erupt!' But if the Russians are so far away, why do
we need them? And if they are closer than we think, how will a
few scrawny Hitler Youth boys, invalids and decrepit pensioners
be able to help? Meanwhile, as a precaution, they have started
building 'bunkers' along the banks of the Oder. And all the
while hundreds of German refugees continue to flood into
Breslau, escaping the Russians in the north east and the
bombings in the west.

Berlin, October 3rd, 1944

Dear Toni,

*It's good to hear Hubert got the scarf you knitted. He's lucky, we
can't even get wool here and anything that even vaguely looks as
if it could keep you warm has been commandeered to stop our
soldiers freezing at the Eastern Front.*

But I am really sorry the bombing has started in Breslau. This is bad news. But I am sure if Hanke has ordered the building of air raid shelters they will be built before yesterday, no one denies him, do they!

Here people are genuinely starving. There is simply not enough food. Rations are next to useless. It is freezing and there is no fuel. To keep warm, people go to the parks during the night and chop down the trees for firewood. The Gestapo can do nothing. We have had enough. There is outright defiance. We are so fed-up with all the disease and dirt and misery.
Maria

Lähn, October 26th, 1944
Dear Toni,
Mama's appetite has suddenly increased, which is good news, but unfortunately rationing has got worse so there isn't a lot of extra food around. And wood is so scarce we only cook once a day.

Of course, there's no coal as it's all been taken for the mighty Wehrmacht! I don't know what we will do this winter for heating, it's cold enough now! And they say it is going to be another particularly bad winter too. We'll just have to do what we did last year and keep our outdoor coats on indoors. I'll insist that boots come off this year, though, it was impossible to keep the floor clean last winter. We'll have to wear our winter socks on top of our woollen stockings.

As for bathing, it's a quick splash in icy water over the sink. And absolutely everything now has to be recycled since the Total War, nothing at all can be wasted or thrown out – not that

anyone has been wasting anything for a very long time. There are
no scraps for the refugees now.

So Maria is divorced but still regularly sees Georg, who has
married again? Can that be true? Has she no shame? Does his
new wife know? Oh, and can I remind you about the suspenders
again, I am absolutely desperate.
God bless.
Hilde

November 12th, 1944

My duties have been changed. I now work at the Link-Hoffman
works in the western suburbs. They say they are making rockets
there as well as their usual tanks and trucks. I work far from the
main factory area, cleaning and cooking in the kitchens. My
transport picks me up in the pitch black at 5.30. I have to walk
two kilometres to meet the transport. It wouldn't be that bad if
it wasn't for the cold. I wear as many clothes as I possibly can
without restricting my movement – two pairs of socks under
my work boots, Papa's pyjamas, the second pair I was due to
send him, under my own trousers, and the works trousers on
top. Two vests, two jumpers. And still I am cold.

Almost all the men on the main factory floor are forced labour
from one of the camps. I don't know which one, there are so
many. They arrive at the works at the same time as me, but they
arrive by foot, hundreds and hundreds of them. Their camp
issue clothes are meagre and their clogs clump ominously
against the ground as they march into their own entrance and
into the bowels of the factory. After twelve hours of working at
grinders and mills and lathes, and swathed in oil and sweat and
dirt and grime, they are marched back to the camp. It must be a
very long day for them but we are in a crisis and everyone has to
make an effort for the war.

The majority of the women working in the kitchens – like the men at the factory – are forced labour and come from one of the city camps. And like the men, they have either P or the yellow star stitched on to their sleeves. Beneath their rags they look very thin. We German women are absolutely forbidden to talk to the foreign women, which is not difficult because we are usually kept apart. Just once I came across them.

I had finished some lunch of noodle soup and bread and was hurrying back to the kitchens across the open yard, where the toilet block is. A scrawny line of foreign women were waiting to use the cubicles. They had only the meanest of scarves over their heads to protect them from the icy wind.

The woman in charge of them was wrapped in a leather coat and wore lace-up ankle boots and thick warm gloves and a big fur hat. She shouted for them to hurry, that she didn't intend to catch a cold on account of any miserable Jew or Polak. The foreign women shuffled more quickly. They were nearly finished, just one woman was still using one of the cubicles. The leather women suddenly threw the toilet door open, grabbed the poor woman still sitting inside and hurled her into the yard. 'Quickly, you lazy slag!' The poor girl wasn't even allowed time to dress herself properly or wipe the soiled mess off her clothes. Then this one in charge saw me. 'What are you looking at?' she demanded. I didn't know what to say. 'You want to come and join them, eh?' I quickly looked down and hurried on. I don't know why she has to be so horrible to them.

December 25th, 1944

Since the September air raids of last year the Russian bombers have not come back and as a consequence we cannot move in Breslau for refugees. The population is over one million now – that's double what it used to be.

They say many are coming from the Warthe region and the German General Government Administrative district of

Poland. They are fleeing the Russians, who they say have crossed the Silesian border and are marching towards the Oder. But this must be propaganda lies. The Russians can't be so close. They can't be. Meanwhile, the refugees who flood here from Inner Germany think they are dreaming when they see our trams and buses all working, our brightly lit shops still open for business, albeit with limited supplies. They gasp at the sight of children ice-skating gaily across the frozen moat and having snowball fights and laughing. Where they have come from their homes have been flattened, there is no food and typhoid and tetanus are rife.

January 1945, Berlin
Dear Toni,
Are you sure? Hilde is both married and pregnant? Are you sure?
Of course I am happy for her, but I don't believe it's possible to
fall in love with someone you only know through a few letters.
And then to get married – to someone you haven't even met – by
post! It's ridiculous. War or no war!

Really, if she wanted to get pregnant that badly she didn't
have to go to all that trouble. She could have stopped any soldier
and they would have obliged. Here in Berlin it is nothing to be
pregnant out of wedlock, women are called Rekrutenmaschinen
– recruiting machines – or even Gebärmaschinen – birthing
machines. When it comes to making babies for the Reich, being
married doesn't come into it. However, clearly in Lähn things
are a bit more old-fashioned and having that certificate to say
you are a couple is obviously important. And no church wedding
either, although these days no one has a church wedding, do
they?

I am happy for her, I really am, yes! The father is an

officer, you said? If this is true, she will get support from the Lebensborn Unit. If I were lucky enough to fall pregnant, I would do everything in my power to make sure the baby had as many advantages as possible – the Lebensborn Unit have all the modern equipment to bring a healthy baby into life.

It must have been a huge shock for Papa! Little St Therese married and pregnant, and you say he and Mama knew nothing about it, that she organised it all through the League of Large Family Letter Centre?

How ironic: she is married by proxy and sleeps with her husband, who she had never met before, just the one time when he is on leave and becomes pregnant. Meanwhile, I am divorced from the only man I have ever loved because no matter how many times I tried, I could not get with child.

Happy New Year.

Maria

Potato shortage imminent

January 1945 - Berlin Radio has warned the German population of an imminent potato shortage and is demanding that every citizen play a role in preventing unnecessary wastage of potatoes.

The broadcast claims that a summer drought is responsible for the shortage.

It warns that anybody seen feeding livestock with potatoes fit for human consumption is commiting an unforgivable crime against the German population.

The German government has promised greater supplies of alternative foodstuffs to make up for this temporary shortage.

January 3rd, 1945

Rumours say the Russians are marching closer to Breslau day by day, but our Silesian Daily News says they are miles away in Poland. We are told not to worry. We are told even if we did have to evacuate, the appropriate instructions would be given in good time. I hate the scare mongers, they are playing into the Reds' hands. Why can't they see that? They make it difficult not to feel a little bit afraid. But the sight of our boys running around in their snow camouflage and field greys is reassuring. If the worst comes to the worst, at least these new garrisons camped around the city will save us.

January 18th, 1945

The Russians are back in their planes and bombing us. They are blowing up our railways. The explosions are frightening. Our boys will stop them though with their anti-aircraft missiles. I know they will.

January 20th, 1945

This morning my transport didn't show. I didn't know what to do. After an hour of waiting in the bitter frosty dark, I decided to go home and back to bed. I woke up to a terrible racket from outside. Someone was shouting. It was just after 10 am:

Achtung! Achtung! Citizens of Breslau! This is an obligatory order from Gauleiter Hanke. Breslau is to be evacuated. There is no reason for alarm. Women and children will leave first. Small hand luggage is to be taken with you. Women with small children, bring milk; the Nazi Welfare Organisation will set up cooking points with paraffin stoves so you can warm up the milk. We repeat, Breslau is to be evacuated. Achtung! Achtung!

I jumped out of bed and looked out the window. The announcement was being sent from the city loudhailing system that had been set up in the city streets for the 1938 Sportsfest and never taken down. One thousand loudspeakers blared over and over again:

We repeat, Breslau is to be evacuated. Achtung! Achtung!

We were to leave? Surely this couldn't be happening. It was freezing. I hurriedly got dressed, putting on as many layers as possible. I put a half loaf of old bread and two apples into my knapsack and packed a few clothes and my jotters and writing bits and pieces into my case – Hubert's old blue case – and left.

This is an obligatory order! Don't panic! Women and children, take only what you can carry! Transport is waiting for you! Leave Breslau immediately!

Outside the streets were jammed. Panicking women laden down with bags and suitcases dragged bewildered children. Everyone was shouting hysterically. 'The Russians are coming! The Russians are coming!' Some people had chairs tied to their backs. Others pulled handcarts or prams full of bed linen, pots and pans. Some dragged sledges across the snow-covered street. Elderly men and women were helped along by children as young as four and five. The sick and injured hobbled awkwardly, aided by panicking loved ones.

This is an obligatory order! Don't panic! Women and children, take only what you can carry! Leave Breslau immediately!

I couldn't think. 'The Russians are coming! The Russians are coming!' What direction were we supposed to go in? A shout. 'Lorries are leaving from Salt Square.' Everyone in the street turned as one. I joined them. We hurried to the square. There were lorries but they were already packed to bursting with people, hanging on desperately to every inch of the vehicle. There were seventeen lorries. I counted every one of them. No one else could have physically got on any of them, even if the soldiers barring our way would have let us. The loudhailers boomed:

This is an obligatory order from your Gauleiter Hanke! All woman and children and sick people have to leave Breslau immediately. Take only what you can carry! This is an order! Leave immediately! Take only what you can carry! Leave immediately! Leave immediately! This is an order!

'Buses! Buses are leaving from the Market Square on the Ring!' Another rumour. The ever-burgeoning throng turned and shuffled towards the Ring. There were motor buses. Tens of motor buses. Again we were too late. Inside people stood squashed face to face. Again, huddles of soldiers stopped us getting close. The buses moved off one by one, churning up snowy sludge in their wake.

Leave immediately! Leave immediately! This is an order! Leave immediately! This is an order!

A yell. 'The train stations! There are still trains!' And we all, as one, turned. Some headed west to the Freiburger Station, the rest of us struggled down Schweidnitzer Street towards the main train station.

Leave immediately! Leave immediately! This is an order! Leave immediately! This is an order!

At the entrance to the station the crowds were even denser. I pushed inside. It was heaving. There was only one train to be seen. It was guarded by tens of belligerent soldiers in their field grey uniforms. Crowds of distraught people begged them to be let on it. The soldiers held them back. Behind the soldiers the platform was littered with the mangled bodies of the walking war wounded. Uniforms in bloody tatters. Prim nurses swooped between them. They carried blankets and drips and clean sheets.

One of the few trains that hadn't been bombed by the Russians was being kept for the mighty Wehrmacht. Barely audible above the mounting panic and distress came more announcements from the train station's own loudhailer: 'Four-year-old Erna has lost her mother, can her mother come and get her from the station masters office! Can little Pieter's mother please come to the office. Pieter is waiting for her! Maria is here with her little sister, they have lost their oma and opa. Please come and get them! Tante Dora is looking for her niece Eva. Eva come to the station master's office! Come now!' Then above all the clamour the one train roared into life.

A desperate surge of people threw themselves against the soldiers. The soldiers pushed them back. Behind the guards the prim nurses huddled the wounded on board. The crowd pushed again. It was bedlam. A child lost the grip of her mother's hand; an elderly lady was swallowed into the pushing bodies; an elderly man wept as his arms were twisted behind his back; a heavily pregnant woman screamed. Shots were fired. No one cared. The crowd thrashed and clawed its way forward. More shots. Then someone noticed the train had left. The crowd collapsed.

This is a new order! Women and children and the sick who can walk are ordered to leave Breslau by foot! Leave now!

Leave Breslau by foot! Go in the direction of Opperau-Kanth! Vehicles will meet you! Women and children, you are commanded to leave by foot! Leave now!

All around me distressed faces wailed. 'How can we walk in this cold?' 'Where is Kanth?' 'Why are there no trains?' 'When is the next train?' 'My cousin is sick.' 'I can't find my little Anna, have you seen my little Anna?' 'They expect us to walk?' 'What about buses?' 'Kanth is over 20 kilometres away!' 'I'm waiting.' 'What about food?' 'That bastard Hanke!' 'It's not so far.' 'Try the station master's office.' 'No, I'm sorry, I've not seen Anna.' Suddenly I couldn't breathe. Darting pains shot across my chest. I sucked in gulps of air but I still couldn't breathe. More and more people thrust into the station. Black spots flashed in front of my eyes. My legs began to crumple. I put my hand against a station pillar to steady myself. What was happening to me? I desperately tried to breathe. My chest ached! I had to get outside. I tried again – long, slow breaths. The searing pain in my chest eased. I staggered out of the station. I sat down on a bench. Fear fluttered over every surface of my skin. I took some more breaths.

Take only what you can carry! Walk in the direction of Kanth! Your country depends on you! This is an order! You must leave for your own safety!

I wanted to stay on the bench. I didn't want to leave but I had to. Everyone knows the Russians are butchers. When I thought I could walk, I stood up. A group of people left the station and headed for Tauentzien Street. I followed them. It started to snow again. The wind whistled through my thin layers. I tied my two cloth scarves tighter around my head, if only I had kept just one of the woollen scarves I had knitted. I kept walking. By the time we reached the outskirts of Breslau there were hundreds of us traipsing in the cold and snow. Someone said we would find sheds on the way with rations in them, maybe.

The further away we tramped from Breslau, the more choked the country road became – all of Silesia seemed to be fleeing the Soviets in one long grim column. All the while we walked, tiny slate specks hummed high overhead. Russian planes. Very quickly my feet became numb. Ice crystals formed around my nose. Those who had wrapped blankets around their bodies struggled to walk. But they were not as slow as the women and the children dragging handcarts.

Some people pushed tiny prams, which stuck in the sleet and ice, others dragged sledges, which were better able to cope with the snow. Occasionally a car slid past us. Some families even had ponies and carts, the poor beasts sometimes had to pull two or three wagons strapped together. An odd person here and there pushed a bicycle through the sludge and sleet but most people simply walked. Someone said it was colder than minus sixteen degrees Centigrade. When the snow let up, the sky filled with leaflets from the Soviets: *Germans! Surrender now! Nothing will happen to you! Surrender now!*

The first casualty was an elderly, overweight lady. She tripped and hurt her ankle. Three little children helped her sit on a snow-covered log. Bedraggled lines of people walked past her. Heads down. I asked if she needed assistance. She shook her head. The children gripped her hands. I left them there sitting on the damp log, a cloud of wet snow billowing around them.

The next casualty was a toddler, maybe only two or three years old. We'd been walking for some time now. A woman ahead somewhere cried out, 'My baby's milk is frozen in the bottle! Where are the cooking points? Where?' Someone else sobbed,

'Where's the transport they promised?' At that moment the toddler simply collapsed to the ground. Either from the cold or the lack of food or shock. The mother fell to the ground beside the little girl. Very quickly it became clear the girl was dead. The woman wailed inconsolably. Two women tried to comfort her but she wouldn't stop sobbing. No one knew what to do. It was too cold to stand still. We had to carry on. The two women tried again to help the mother, but she yelled at them to leave her alone and began grubbing about in the snow with her bare hands. People next to me whispered, 'She's digging a grave! She's digging a grave!' Anyone who tried to help was pushed away. Eventually we had to walk on, it was too cold to stop. It looked as if she was going to stay there with her daughter.

The snow was so heavy at times I couldn't see my hands in front of my face. My lips were numb. I tried to keep my head down to protect my cheeks and chin against the icy sleet. All I wanted to do was get away. Then the person in front of me turned round. I almost walked into her. She blocked my way. A heavy woollen shawl covered three quarters of her face. The top of a tiny baby's head, swaddled in a blanket sling, popped out of the top of her thick overcoat. A toddler clung to her gloved hand and sobbed, and two slightly older boys of about five and six, barely able to stagger, hung on to either end of her coat. She carried a brown suitcase in her free hand.

The column of refugees coming up behind us parted around our obstruction and carried on. Her face – what I could see of it – was gaunt and raw from the cold. She looked the same age as me. She simply said, 'I'm going back.' I said, 'The Russians are coming.' 'I don't care,' she said. I said, 'But there'll be help in Kanth.' She said, 'I can't do it.' I thought she was mad and moved to the side to let her past. Just then the tiny head of her baby flopped to one side and hung awkwardly over the edge of the top of her coat. Its little eyes were closed and its miniature face was a grim blue-grey colour. I experienced a terrible chill, worse than anything the weather could cause. The tiny child was dead. 'Your baby?' I said in shock. She said, 'I'm not leaving him.'

I didn't want to go back, I didn't even know her but I couldn't let her carry the burden of her dead child all alone. I took the case from her hand – it was heavy. Together, we shuffled to the side of the oncoming lanes of refugees and started trudging back. No one noticed or cared we were going the wrong way.

The snow eased again but the icy wind became even stronger. In white fields we saw frozen cows, legs akimbo. Under a giant, leafless chestnut tree we saw a lone shivering boy with a huge suitcase. He refused to walk back with us because his mama had told him to wait. The wind changed directions and pushed in our faces. My stomach gnawed at my insides. I wanted my bread but my fingers were too numb to take my bag off my back and get it.

We continued to walk. I tried not to imagine what it was like to watch helplessly while your baby died in your arms from the cold and hunger. A lorry pulled up beside us. Was it going to give us a lift? We hurried towards it. Some of the other refugees did the same.

Three soldiers appeared from out of the back. They threatened us with guns and told us to keep away. One soldier stayed on the truck while the other two hopped out. They hurried to a snow covered mound at the side of the road, positioned themselves at either end of it and lifted it up. It was clearly heavy, they struggled to carry it. The third soldier jumped out of the vehicle to help them. Together they manhandled the ice mound on to the back of the truck. Someone said, 'It's the Suchkommandos, they're taking away the dead.'

When we reached the outskirts of Breslau, dusk was falling and the Suchkommando lorry had already gone back and forwards twice. As we approached the centre the crowds got denser and the shouts and wails and sirens grew louder and louder.

Attention! Attention! Leave now! Leave now!

We pushed against the stream of people coming towards us. Posters everywhere told us to 'Leave now!' The young mother said, 'I'm going to try for a train.' 'But your baby?' I said. She shook her head firmly, 'I'm not leaving him behind.' Then she took her case back and slowly headed into the throng of the station, her children stumbling behind her. 'Would Pieter and Dieter come to the station master's office, your mother is waiting for you. Would the mother of Ingrid come and take her...'

I tramped along the icy streets to my flat on Kaiser Strasse. A middle-aged woman dressed in a navy blue felt suit sat on the pavement with her legs outstretched, one of her shoes was missing. She sobbed. I knew I should help but there was nothing I could do. Ahead a group of people had gathered around a patch of red mess smeared into the grey slush. As I approached I heard someone say, 'That's where the girl from the bread shop miscarried.' I walked up Taschen Street and crossed the icy moat, no one was skating on it today. Liebich Höhe on my right was in total darkness. The silhouette of the domed building on the hill made me shiver. When I was younger I'd always imagined my lover would take me there to propose and we'd dance the night away at the wonderful Liebich Dance Palace below. The next day we'd continue the celebration by hiring a rowing boat and he'd row me up and down the moat while we drank champagne from fluted glasses and picnicked on food from a straw basket. We'd wave to people walking along the city promenade and we'd love our lives.

I hurried up to Kloster Strasse. It was so dark now it was almost impossible to see. I heard the gentle peel of St Mauritius.

It was a welcome relief from the chaotic yelling and frantic orders of the loudhailers which had finally stopped. I'd always liked St Mauritius, it was such a pretty building with its onion-shaped little steeple. Soft mumbling from behind its heavy wooden door suggested there were people inside. Father Paul Piekert, the parish priest, seemed not to be leaving. They say he openly criticises the Nazis and isn't afraid of the Gestapo or the guillotine or the hangman's noose. Mama would like him.

My apartment block was just across the Kaiser Bridge, off Kaiser Street. I walked faster. In the gloom every shadow threatened to be a murderer or rapist. I reached the bridge and looked over the wall. I could just see the ink black Oder splish–splash against the bank beneath me. It smelled of bulrushes and cold damp. Only five minutes to go.

The apartment block was silent. I shared the flat with three other girls also doing their 'war duty' in Breslau. We hardly saw each other as we all worked at different times and in different places. Was I the only one not to have fled? My little room was freezing. Completely exhausted I lay down on my bed. A scuffling noise below me made me jump. Had the looting started already? I strained to hear some more. Nothing. I dragged myself out of my bed and quietly set a chair up against the handle of my room door. If someone broke in, they'd wake me up and at least I'd have a chance to defend myself. I'd get some sleep then tomorrow I would leave. I thought I wouldn't sleep but I did.

January 21st, 1945

The announcements from the loudhailers started up again first thing this morning. All civil servants not eligible for the Volkssturm were ordered to leave with the women and children. But the only way to leave is by foot, and the weather is even worse. Ilse Braun, the sister of Eva Braun, who everyone knows is Herr Hitler's mistress, got the last place on the last train to leave the city. She, along with Cardinal Bertram, managed to escape. How fortunate for them.

They say today alone the Suchkommandos collected 400 bodies from one small stretch of the Kanth road. The city parks are being used as burial grounds because all the graveyards are full. Worse still, there is a pile of little corpses in the New Market that the authorities seem to have forgotten about. It's too horrible. I know I must leave. I don't want to be taken by the Russians, but I am so tired. I will leave tomorrow, maybe the weather will have eased by then.

January 22nd, 1945

In the Schlesische Tageszeitung, the Silesian daily newspaper, our goatee-face governor called all remaining men in the city to defend the suburbs. *Men of Breslau, you are ordered to join the outer defence of our Fortress Breslau. The fortress will be defended to the end.* This is the same newspaper that only a few days ago said the Russians were still miles away in Poland.

They have begun emptying some of the hospitals, the university offices, the law courts, even the big civil service building on Lessingsplatz. The contents of the buildings are being transferred by lorries to safe towns and cities far away from the Russians. They are even evacuating some of the big forced labour camps in the outer suburbs. Meanwhile, everyone else has to make their own miserable way out of Breslau by foot. It seems tax documents, bedpans, library books, archaeological artefacts, and even forced labourers are more important to the Reich than its citizens. I am still too tired. I'll leave tomorrow.

January 23rd, 1945

Our beautiful parks are stuffed with the frozen bodies of the citizens who failed to survive the ice cold death-march to Kanth, but still people are leaving. I should leave too. I know I should. They say the Russians have secured two bridgeheads across the

Oder at Steinau and Brieg, that they have taken Militisch and are camped out on the Trebnitz hills, that's less than 50 kilometres away. I know I should go but I can't face the walk. And surely our front swine will stop them.

January 24th, 1945

All remaining citizens unfit for military service have been told to leave. I want to go but as soon as I think of that black caravan of death inching its way into the blinding white snow my lungs contract and I can't breathe. But there was no bombing today so maybe the Russians are leaving us alone.

Berlin, February 2nd, 1945
Dear Toni,
The bombing here is endless, the Americans attack during
the day and the British throughout the night. There is not a
street or lane that isn't damaged and gaping holes where whole
communities once lived. A window which isn't broken is unheard
of, the few buildings that exist are crumbling. The working tram
lines that remain are blasted out of shape daily, still the buckled
metal is battered back into shape and off we go again, as if
everything was normal.

The city is shrouded in soot and acrid ash, it's as if we are
in permanent dusk. And now when the bombing starts I don't
even bother with the shelters.

The shelters are so crowded it's unbearable. We have to
crouch, one person huddled almost on top of the next, for hours
on end and the stench of sour body odour and excrement is
obscene. In the underground tunnel I used to go to you ran a
greater risk of starving of oxygen than being hit by a bomb. We

took to lighting candles and placing them on the ground to check if the air was still good. If the candle went out, we'd know it's time to move the children up higher and for us to stand up.

Last week a tragedy occurred. In the miserable darkness of the shelter it was almost impossible to see. Our tiny candle barely cast a shadow over the dank tunnel wall. We sat in our gloomy despair and waited as usual. Occasionally, there was the odd comment, the odd sobbing, the odd grunt from strangers fumbling in the dark in desperate loneliness, but mostly we sat in silence as the noise of the bombs overhead blocked out all proper conversation.

Eventually, the candle went out as it always does. Wearily we all pushed ourselves up a bit. The candle was placed on a chair – left for this purpose and lit again. And we waited again. And waited, all of us squashed together in sweaty despair, not knowing if we'd be buried alive there or if we'd see the light of day or ever smell fresh air again. Then the candle went out again. This time the candle was placed on a high ledge. We all stood upright now. It was then that this couple started to get all agitated. Their child was missing.

The father thought the mother had her, the mother thought the father had her. Neither of them had her. It was chaos for a few minutes while everyone stumbled about looking for her. And then she was found. A quiet little heap, all curled up on the ground, as if dozing. She must have dropped off to sleep and so not realised when the candle had gone out. You would have thought the parents would go mad, but they simply lifted her up and went outside. One man blamed the Hungarian plumber who we'd let in, saying he had breathed in the oxygen that should

have been the girl's. Some others agreed. But it was too late. He is
never going to be let in again.

　　And we don't say Heil Hitler any more, he is hated
outright, we say Bleib übrig – be left over and stay alive!
So, Toni, dear, stay alive!

January 28th, 1945

They say the Ivans have actually reached the city suburbs, that our lads are holding them there in arm-to-arm combat. It doesn't seem possible. How can they be so close? And their planes have attacked again. We citizens of Breslau who are left , and there are thousands of us still here, are so scared we spend half our time hiding in our cellars.

Of course, most of the time the attacks are aimed at strategic targets like the armament factories and railway stations, but they also indiscriminately attack the city.

Yesterday the old cemetery was bombed, destroying tombs and scattering the ancient bones of those buried years ago all over the streets.

The fiercest fighting is in the western suburbs around Gandau airstrip. At night the sky is lit up with red explosions from Russian anti-aircraft fire as they shoot at our planes as they take off under cover of darkness.

Most of the time our boys fly to safety but occasionally we see the deadly fireballs reach their target and watch in horror and dismay as one of our planes bursts into flames and plummets to the ground.

They say Gandau airstrip must be protected at all costs. If we become surrounded, the airstrip will be the only way to get anything in and out of the city. No one wants to believe the Russians will surround us but if they are already in the southern suburbs, it could happen. And then where shall we go for safety?

If this side of the Oder isn't safe and the other side isn't safe, then what do we do? It's too awful to contemplate. This is not something we can say out loud, though. Even now in these terrible times you cannot appear to criticise the Reich and you especially cannot criticise our governor, Goatee-Hanke, it is punishable by death.

January 29th, 1945

We woke up to discover huge red placards all over the city, telling us that our deputy mayor, Dr Spielhagen, had been executed as according to martial law at six o' clock this morning. He had been shot by firing squad in front of the Frederick II monument on the Ring by order of the Nazi party district leader, Hanke, as Reich defence commissary.

The placards said that Dr Spielhagen had intended to leave his post without permission and was seeking employment elsewhere. Everyone was shocked at the news. Everyone knew that all Spielhagen had wanted to do was take his family out of Breslau to safety – which is what we all want to do. Some said Hanke had ordered his body to be slung into the River Oder from the Lessing Bridge.

The final words on the placard said, 'Those who are afraid to die an honourable death will die in ignominy!'

January 30th, 1945

There are soldiers everywhere – working, defending, rushing backwards and forwards. They have set up flak and artillery batteries in our beautiful Botanical Gardens, just north of Sand Island, as well as in the middle of the New Market and the garden of the Archbishop's Palace. There are also machine gun nests in some church steeples and they say the bridges over the Oder have been wired with explosives. No one wants to think of what the significance of these actions might be. There are also new first aid posts being set up all over the city because the working hospitals cannot cope.

January 30th, 1945

People continue to leave despite the bitter cold. Some always come back. I can't face the trip. I can't.

February 1st, 1945

Hanke has had Dr Sommer, the head of the Department of Agriculture of Breslau, executed by firing squad for cowardice. Everyone is talking about it. First Spielhagen, now Sommer. Who next?

February 2nd, 1945

Five young lads have been shot! Three fourteen-year-olds and two sixteen-year-olds. They had burgled a neglected barge and found a few cigarettes and a bit of alcohol. Some people in the ration queue today were talking about it. They were only youths, for heaven's sakes! How is killing them helping to defeat the Reds?

Everyone knows someone who's been executed for equally innocuous reasons – a soldier who was not on properly authorised leave; a brother for taking the abandoned belongings of an evacuee; a forced labourer who wasn't in his camp when he should have been; a sister who was accused of helping a deserter.

Some said the executed ones were the lucky ones because they couldn't feel pain any more, unlike those poor people still being held in Kletschkau prison for being 'defeatist' or 'alarmist' or 'shirking'! At night their tortured screams can be heard streets away. Then the worst thing happened, while we were standing in the ration queue whispering about the 'executions', the Kettenspürhunde, our Military Police, and their beastly dogs, swooped on us.

We all froze. Had they heard our 'grumblings'? They said they were looking for a deserter. No one knew who they were talking about. All the while they quizzed us their chained beasts snarled and slavered at our heels. Eventually they left us.

These execution squads roam around the city, all strapped up to the nines with their shields and guns and hounds of the Baskervilles, hunting down looters and deserters. They attack first and don't ask questions. You must never get in their way. No one knows who are worse, them or the Gestapo – at least the Gestapo don't have dogs.

February 3rd, 1945

Every single, vaguely able-bodied person, including the hundreds and hundreds of foreign prisoners still in the forced labour camp on Clausewitz Street, which is one of the few camps not to have been evacuated, has been conscripted into work brigades. If we don't follow our orders, we will be arrested for "shirking". But of course we will follow orders, all of us want to help stop the Russians!

I am on brick duties, along with half a dozen other women and a handful of conscripted 'foreign' workers. We collect bricks from those houses that have been demolished by the Russian bombs. It's dangerous. Any minute a wall can collapse on us, but we are not shirkers. No one wants to let the Russians in.

We take the bricks to the work patrols, who are building barricades on the edge of the city centre. Along with our bricks, they use gravestones and girders. We are glad they are building strong barricades but none of us want to believe the Russians will get this close.

February 4th, 1945

The Russians bombed us all night. This was the worst yet, a continuous barrage of thunderous fearful explosions. It went on and on. I sat huddled in the underground cellar of the apartment building, listening to the fervent prayers and stifled sobs of the people I share it with. In the end I put my fingers in my ears to try to block out the sobbing and the terrifying whistling sound of the missiles as they hurtled down towards us. If I was going to be blown to smithereens, I didn't want to know.

We crept out of our cellar at daybreak to a cloud of dust and debris. We were glad to have survived but then as the day progressed the sad news came of the deaths. Scores and scores of our fellow Breslau citizens had been massacred. And then we started to get the news of the horrific fate of our German brothers and sisters in East Prussia, now in the hands of the Russians.

They say the men have been massacred and not a single German woman has been spared and that the Reds now refer to the rape of a German woman as 'ausprobiert' – as in 'tried and tested', and the murder of a German woman as 'das Geschäft erledigt' or 'finished with the business'.

February 12th, 1945

Everyone is on edge and scared – scared to say what they think, and scared of what might come. Those not killed by the bombing are collapsing in the street from stress and anxiety.

Then there are the suicides. An old woman in the bread queue said she'd returned from church to find her daughter hanging by her neck. She'd climbed up on to the kitchen table, slung a belt round a butcher's hook in the ceiling, buckled the belt into a noose, put her head in and jumped off the table. Another woman cut her wrists, after she'd smothered her three children with a cushion. They say there have been sixty suicides in the last four weeks. When will it all end?

February 13th, 1945

Spitzbart Hanke – the Golden Pheasant – swooped past me today in a big black car. He wears his shiny black leather coat with a mountain of war medals strapped to his chest and orders us to endure. The hypocrite.

They say his bunker in the university library basement is decorated in absolute luxury – all silk rugs and velvet curtains and Old Masters. They say he and all the other Golden Pheasants screw their mistresses at night and in the morning have hot croissants, dripping in butter and blackberry jam, and fresh coffee, no doubt from Colombia. No German special blend chicory coffee for them. How can they behave like that?

Today we looked for bricks by the university.

February 14th, 1945

Russians tanks are in South Park, only a few kilometres down from my old home in Kaiser Wilhelm Street! Everyone is in a panic!

They thought the Reds would strike the northern suburbs first, so all the citizens in the northern suburbs were made to move to the empty southern ones. But the Reds surprised everyone. Somehow, though, the SS commandeered a couple of trams and had the drivers take them as close to South Park as they could. They managed to pick up all the fleeing citizens.

The sight of the trams bringing everyone into the centre seemed surreal, it was as if everything was back to normal. But life is anything but normal, when we are not being bombed, we are being hounded by the Gestapo for shirking or the Reds are dropping their propaganda leaflets on us, informing us of the dire fate that has befallen our families now in their hands. I don't want to believe we cannot survive this. We must endure.

Berlin, February 14th, 1945
Dear Toni,
They've started locking the toilets because so many people have started to commit suicide in them – despite the disgusting state of the places. It's too awful. Now when I hear the sirens I stay in my flat. I can't face the despair of the air raid shelters any longer.

Only if the bombing is really, really loud do I go down to my cellar – not the air raid cellar, or the underground, just my own cellar at the bottom of our apartment block. There are a few of us there, who can't stand the confinement and stench of the bunkers any longer.

As for Georg, I know he is still here in Berlin. I actually bumped into him and he ignored me. All that talk of love! How could he?

Maria

February 15th, 1945

We are besieged! We are besieged! The Russians have completely surrounded us! They have got as close as Hindensburgplatz in the south of the city, a stone's throw from our old Kaiser Wilhelm Street, and just four kilometres from the centre.

We can hear the gunfire from the suburbs in the city centre all the time. RAT-A-TAT-TAT. They say Fortress Posen has fallen. RAT-A-TAT-TAT. We are completely besieged. No one wants to believe it. We must endure!

February 16th, 1945

Today we dug up paving stones to be taken to the work-commandos on the frontline. They use them to barricade the windows in the empty buildings where our lads are hiding – they leave just enough of an opening for the machine guns to fire from.

February 20th, 1945

We have new orders from Goatee-Hanke. We have to go to the university library and take all the books that have not been taken to safety and bring them to be used to reinforce the fortifications.

When there are no more books to be found, we have to bring

anything, bricks, plaster, rubble, furniture, scrap metal. At one point we were even ordered to help move tram cars: along with a dozen soldiers grappling with ropes and levers, we were made to push and shove and haul the warped iron hulks of two tram cars until they finally sat side by side across the Schweidnitzer Street junction. We civilians didn't have gloves or tools to help us, we just used our bare hands, which were torn to bloody shreds.

These inner fortifications continue to alarm us civilians. Surely the Russians won't get this close.

March 5th, 1945

We have a new commander-in-charge of the fortress, a General Niehoff. He has replaced General von Ahlfen. They say Hanke thought von Ahlfen too defeatist. People say Niehoff is very brave. They say he landed last night in the dark at Gandau. They say it is the third time he tried to get here. The previous two times the Reds' anti-aircraft fire was too strong.

They say last night, his pilot took the plane as high up in the sky as he could and then killed the engines. The plane fell silently, swirling round and round in the dark, and then just as it was about to hit the tops of the trees of the airstrip, the pilot switched the engine on and landed the plane in the dark. Even so, the Russians managed to spot them and General Niehoff had to crawl away to safety on his hands and knees.

They say if anyone can get us help, he can, and if anyone can keep the airport open, it is him. Today he visited the citizens of Breslau by going from cellar to cellar – we citizens have made holes between the cellars so we can move between them when the gunfire above is so bad that we can't get out. And he visited the lads at the frontline in the suburbs.

He says he will not let the Russians in. He says he will get help. His command headquarters are in the damp and dingy ice-storage cellar at Liebich Höhe.

March 6th, 1945

We are all so scared. Every day we hear the crack of machine gunfire and the roar of tank fire grow louder and louder, meaning the Reds are getting closer and closer. There are stories of Ivans surprising people in their homes just as they are sitting down to dinner.

Our general says we must endure! His latest move is to make 'dead areas', to help our boys with their arm-to-arm combat in the suburbs. Brandkommandos – the Burn and Slash Units – are blowing up buildings at strategic points in the suburbs, clearing the area and leaving dead areas, giving our boys a clear line of fire at the enemy.

Before the buildings are blown up, Entrümpelungs-kommandos, or the Clearance Squads, empty them. Without even bothering to try let the owners of the houses know what they are doing – many are still here in the cellars – the squads throw the contents of the houses into the street, and set the stuff on fire.

Nothing is exempt, not furniture, crockery, pictures, letters, religious items, sentimental mementoes, photos. They even empty churches. They say making dead areas is a clever move on our part, but those who have had all their possessions destroyed are in despair. They say they have lost everything.

March 8th, 1945

They say our lads at the frontline are mounting torpedoes on to trolleys. The boys shove the contraption into the Ivans as it's about to fire. They say it is a success. If it doesn't stop the Ivans advancing, we are done for.

March 9th, 1945

They say our lads are using 'wonder weapons', which are remote-controlled miniature tanks, to stop the Reds getting any further forward. They say the mini-tanks get right into the enemy area and detonate explosions. Surely, such modern technology will help us.

March 11th, 1945

They say the Reds have reached Höfchenplatz. That is so close to where I used to live. They say the fighting is going on room by room, apartment by apartment, block by block. We all hope they can hold them and we can last out. The air raids continue. There are more and more dead.

March 12th, 1945

No one knows if we will receive help or how long we can last. Some people are listening to Radio Russia. They say our lads are being shot in their hundreds of thousands. The Russians say our fright will eat our souls. They shouldn't listen to the radio. We must survive.

March 14th, 1945

On every house door there is the slogan 'Every house a fortress', but most of us are living in the cellars at the bottom of the houses.

March 15th

I passed the wine bar that Maria took me to before. There were people in it drinking, not wine though, beer. It was as if all the shooting from the suburbs and bombing and the dead bodies everywhere was an everyday occurrence.

March 16th, 1945

All running water, sewage and gas supplies have been bombed. We have to get water from the wells.

March 17th, 1945

They say it is becoming harder and harder to get supplies in and those needing emergency medical attention out.

March 22nd, 1945

Everyone is whispering about it. A sixteen-year-old German girl, Cilli, who had been cruelly captured by the Reds and then recaptured by our lads during a counterattack, was executed. The Gestapo said because she had survived being with the Reds she must be a Soviet spy. It is horrifying.

They also shot another sixteen-year-old boy for desertion. A young lad called Horst. He was only in the Reserves. They say when his section came under attack from the Soviets he panicked and ran away. They were just boys.

March 23rd, 1945

They say the Russians have almost captured Gandau airport in the north. If we lose the airport we will be completely cut off. It will be a disaster as we will not be able to get anything, or anyone, in or out. So General Niehoff has ordered a new runway to be built in the centre of town, far away from the Russian attacks in the suburbs. It will mean vital supplies can be brought in and the sick and the wounded can be taken off to safety and care.

He designated the area north of the Kaiser bridge, from Kaiser Street to the Scheitniger Star, as suitable. The beautiful townhouses and tree-edged-squares and the churches and university buildings were reduced to rubble in one afternoon.

Everyone is very sad about the loss of our lovely buildings but it had to be done. And now we leftover civilians, including old men and women, children – feral orphans as young as ten – and foreign forced labourers are clearing rubble mountains, telegraph poles, tramlines, iron girders and anything else that might obstruct a plane from landing on or taking off from Kaiser Street. And I have been made homeless and have to find an empty cellar to stay.

March 25th, 1945

We have no tools to clear the rubble so we have to use our bare hands. We work in shifts, throughout the day and night. As if that is not bad enough, almost as soon as we start the work, Russian planes sniff us out and attack us. Now we work with our eyes and ears strained at all times.

The distant droning of the Soviet aircraft sounds like the buzzing of an inconsequential fly at first. Then it gets louder. We run for cover but there is no cover because everything has been flattened. First come the Schwarzer Tods, the Black Deaths. They are deadly enough, but they are followed by the Nähmaschinen, the Sewing Machines. Their awful hum, hum, humming engine noise sounds like a sewing machine. It is followed by a worse noise, silence. The pilots cut their engines and attack by stealth. We fear the Sewing Machines the most.

As we flee, the planes drop incendiaries and fragmentation bombs and spit machine gun fire at us. When they finally leave the runway is smeared with the blood and guts of writhing mangled bodies, the remains of those not fast enough. We are forced to continue to work while our fellow citizens go ripe under our noses.

The stretcher bearers come, eventually, but always too late. We may as well be digging our own graves.

They say our lads are using a type of wonder weapon, Piss-beutels or piss bags. Bags of yellow-green liquid are chucked into the Reds' bunkers and cellars. They say when the bag bursts the chemical given off from the liquid destroys the lungs when breathed in.

Please, God, stop the Reds getting any closer! It is already Hell on earth. The noise, the stench of warm blood, of sweat and faeces, of putrid flesh is revolting. My fingers and lips bleed all the time now.

There are more and more deaths from the constant attacks,

from typhoid, from dysentery, from exhaustion, from hunger. No one complains. No one dares.

One of the workers in my detail is called Kowalenko. He has Ost sewn on to his sleeve. He smiled at me today.

We saw a Versorgungsbombe – a supply parachute – dangling from the Kaiser Bridge. The red silk parachute with its white strings looked like a bright red splash of blood. Some soldiers came and cut it down. It has ammunition in it.

Lähn, March, 1945
Dearest Toni,
At last we have had a letter from Maria. She said she got back to Berlin safely but only just. As her train approached the outskirts of Dresden, it became apparent the city was being firebombed.

The passengers were told to get off the train and flee. They ran into a barn for cover. In her panic, Maria left her suitcase on the platform. It had Papa's money inside, he had given her some of his savings to look after for him. For the next twenty-four hours she watched as Dresden was attacked again and again. When the bombing finally stopped she went back to the station. Incredibly, her suitcase was still there, in the middle of the platform, exactly where she had left it. In the distance all of Dresden was in flames, just like in the story in the Bible. All the trains were cancelled, so she hitchhiked on a lorry with another girl.

The lorry took them all the way to Berlin. She says Berlin is a mess. Everyone is talking about defeat. No one knows where Herr Hitler is or cares. I feel sorry for Maria. I think she is jealous of my pregnancy and when she was here she told me she was very lonely in Berlin. She wanted to stay with us but Papa told her it was

better to leave. He said she would be safer in Berlin and at least she
had work and rations there.

However, Papa now feels bad because he heard on the radio
that the Russians have crossed the Silesian border – even Papa
listens to the BBC World Service now. The BBC say Berlin will be
captured any day. They say the Russians and Americans are in
a race to get there first. They also say Breslau is under siege. But
you are in Breslau. It's so confusing. Do you think it can be true? Is
Breslau under siege?
God Bless
Hilde

March 31st, 1945

Yesterday evening, just after dark, while we were still working on the runway we heard the distance rattle of Soviet sniper attack and our counterattack in the western suburbs. Then once again the gunshot sound was masked by another sound, from overhead. The droning grew louder and louder – it wasn't the hum from just one or two planes, it was the angry buzz of a whole swarm of them! We fled to our underground cellars and got there just as the unmistakable sound of hurtling missiles exploded overhead, followed immediately by the deafening sound of murderous strafing.

All night bombs and gunfire thudded around us. The wooden supports of our large apartment block shuddered again and again. We were twenty in this little place, squashed together in the dank sweaty tomb, trembling and trying not to cry. One man kept repeating 'Holy Mary, Mother of God! Holy Mary, Mother of God!' and eventually a woman shouted at him to shut up.

The only light came from a thin candle, which kept going out from the air pressure change caused by the exploding bombs. The air was foul with the smell of body sweat and fear and as the night wore on the chamber filled with chalk and mortar and plaster dust, which wafted in through the cellar ventilating bricks. If we weren't crushed under the weight of the building when it collapsed we'd probably be suffocated.

There was a lull in the attack. Someone opened the cellar door and a wave of frosty grey morning light pushed inside. The women next to me quietly wished everyone a Happy Easter – it was Easter Sunday – and offered around a tin with home-made crumble and poppy seed cake in it. One by one we nibbled on the cake, I can't even remember what it tasted like.

Gradually, we crept outside. A wild wind whipped our clothes. We gulped in what should have been fresh air but instead tasted of carbide and dust and blood. Across the river enormous flames engulfed whole buildings, entire blocks were towering furnaces. Further up on our side of the river, the twin spires on Cathedral Island were alight. Sand Island was also ablaze.

The fierce wind grew stronger, it drove the consuming flames into a frenzy. Clouds of black-grey smoke puffed into the air, smudging the collapsing skyline. To the left I thought I could just see the spire of Mauritius Church collapse, sending red and yellow sparks dancing into the clouds. A few more people joined us on the street. No one knew what to say. Some older people started to cry. Then we heard the awful telltale sub, sub, subbing sound. The Soviet planes were coming back.

We started to run. The droning got louder. Then the strafing began. RAT-A-TAT-TAT. It came from behind us. We covered our heads with our arms and darted away from the bullets. RAT-A-TAT-TAT. Shells exploded on the ground in front of us. We ran to the left. RAT-A-TAT-TAT. Dust, rubble, stones, bullets flew in all directions. We zigzagged right. Left. More gun shot. It was as if they were playing with us.

We reached the cellar. We dived inside. We pressed ourselves against its dirty walls. A thud, a shudder, a terrific roar. For a moment I couldn't hear. White distemper creaked in puffs from the corners of the cellar ceiling. The foundations around us trembled. A woman screamed hysterically. Someone tried to calm her. It seemed that the apartment block next to ours had collapsed.

April 2nd, 1945

The Sewing Machines and the Black Deaths attacked us all day, firing their missiles and incendiaries without relief but still we had to work on the Blutbahn – the 'bloody runway'. We were surrounded by smouldering rubble and rotting, putrid cadavers and a skyline that was constantly burning.

At lunchtime a church bell rang out from the city centre. We thought it was an Easter message, but someone said it was caused by the waves of heat from the burning buildings below.

They say the Red Army are in Gleiwitz. They say they are raping and butchering anything that moves. They say we have to hurry and finish the runway so we can all be airlifted if they come.

April 3rd, 1945

It was eerily quiet when we woke up today. Some of us were ordered to take advantage of the lull in the attack and scavenge for tools to help speed up the work on the runway. We were led across the river. The devastation was worse close up. The streets were a jumble of rubble and dust, every other building was in ruins: Mauritius Church was a pile of smouldering bricks, Ohlauer Street was burnt out, Feld Street was destroyed, the magnificent Art Nouveau Post Office building was in ruins, Bruder Street was burnt out and the moat and Liebich Höhe – our commander's headquarters – was smothered in ash.

In Tauentzien Street gaping black holes remained where there had once stood grand townhouses. The smell of death hung everywhere. It came from the rotting remains of mangled horses and the mutilated, bloody corpses of Breslau citizens, whose festering carcasses had still not been taken away.

Sewer pipes lay broken and jagged, weeping raw sewage ran into the street to mingle with the fizzing blood of the dead. Nurses and medical orderlies ran up and down searching for people in still smouldering buildings and tending to the wounded.

A group of soldiers appeared. They half-carried, half-dragged three badly bleeding men between them. We ran to help. Between all of us we brought the injured men to the big overground bunker on Striegauer Platz. It is an ugly, round, concrete and steel, six-storey structure with no windows. It was one of our original air raid shelters but it is now a military hospital.

We entered through two steel, fireproof doors into a wall of darkness and the stench of pus and blood and ether. Light from two feeble electric light bulbs revealed a narrow staircase. One of the soldiers led the way. We struggled up the staircase as it wound around the building.

Eventually, we stopped on a landing, which gave way to a dingy corridor. Concrete cells led off either side of it. In the cells, in the almost total darkness, lay two, three, maybe four dying and wounded soldiers. Their moaning and groaning was almost unbearable.

A nurse appeared and told us to leave our wounded soldiers on the corridor floor, which we did. Then we fled. By the time we'd reached the ground floor my eyes had grown accustomed to the dim light. I saw a stack of corpses by the stairs, each with a broken dog tag dangling from its purpling toes.

Outside we were told we still had to find tools, so we carried on. Civilians wandered the streets in a daze, while others covered the dead in curtains, sheets and even flags, anything was better than leaving the bodies uncovered.

Healthy soldiers and reservists bustled in all directions and dilapidated wagons swerved round corners and army lorries bumped over the debris, taking supplies to somewhere. At the sides of the pavements we saw makeshift grave after makeshift grave – the parks and graveyards had filled up a long time ago.

We marched on further south. Stopping every now and then to scour the few buildings left standing for whatever they could yield. We found some forks, two mangled trowels and a broken spade. We avoided the decimated Wertheim department store. It was too unsafe.

We searched the smouldering theatre on Springer Street and the half-flattened market hall next to it. Suddenly a whirring sound. A grenade! We dived for cover behind a garden wall on Schiller Street. Boom! The bodies of four people lay splattered all over the ground in front of us. Someone began to scream. We were told to continue.

We raked through decrepit workshops stinking of piss. RAT-A-TAT-TAT! Machine gunfire from out of nowhere!

We threw ourselves inside the nearest apartment building. RAT-A-TAT-TAT! The commando in charge of us told us to follow him. 'Go up! It's safer! Too vulnerable on the ground floor!'

We hurried after him. RAT-A-TAT-TAT. He led the way two steps at a time. I passed glistening rats droppings, human excrement, crumbling plaster, a blood-stained man's waistcoat, a porcelain teacup with a triangular chip missing from the rim, a picture frame, glass shattered, no picture.

'Hurry! Hurry!' he yelled. We reached the fourth floor. RAT-A-TAT-TAT. The walls were pockmarked with bullet holes. Plaster dust, shards of glass and rubble covered the floor. Battered window frames, hanging off the wall, revealed gaping holes to the outside, which allowed grimy daylight to flood in.

We flattened ourselves against the nearest wall and listened. Silence. The machine gun fire had stopped. As quietly as I could I forced myself to breathe – in, out, in, out. My hands were shaking. My forehead was washed in sweat even though I was cold. We were two women and eight men, and only two of the men had guns.

Finally, the commando in charge of us slid down the wall and flopped down on the mucky rubble-strewn floor. He spat wearily. It seems we were closer to the battle front than he thought. We waited and waited. No one spoke. Then, suddenly, the commando got up and disappeared through an opening into the next room. He returned after a few moments and beckoned us to follow him.

We crept after him, keeping low through the doorway. In the middle of more broken windows, more daylight, more rat droppings, more sour-rancid smells, under a pile of plaster dust and broken white crockery stood a baby grand piano. A three-legged wooden stool waited by the piano.

He sat on the stool and immediately looked ridiculous as his legs were so long his knees jutted up into the piano keyboard. He removed his helmet and set it, along with his gun, on the floor at his side. He then opened the lid of the piano, some rubble and grime splattered to the floor, and started to play. Magical musical notes filled the room. It was a Strauss waltz.

I couldn't remember when I had last heard music. It was so beautiful I wanted to cry. He eventually stopped. Before we could say anything loud clapping exploded from below us. 'Zugabe! Zugabe!' It was the Russians. 'Encore! Encore!' The Russian soldiers were directly beneath us! Our pianist waved his fingers over the piano keys once more and began playing a polka. Huge cheers rang out from below. One of us laughed. We all laughed. Then we listened.

I thought of Mama and Papa, of Hubert and Hansi, of Hilde with her baby on the way and Maria with no baby on the way, and I thought I could smell the scent of sweet honeysuckle. He played another Solka and then a waltz. The Russians clapped. We clapped. *Zugabe! Encore!* Then above the clapping, we heard a familiar hum, hum, humming. The Soviet planes were back.

The clapping below stopped. Our soldier untangled his gangly legs from underneath the piano and stood up. For a second I thought he was going to salute the instrument. Instead, he slowly closed the lid, picked up his helmet and his gun.

Movement from below us suggested the Russians were leaving. The drone of the planes grew more menacing. We needed to find a cellar-bunker to hide in before it was too late.

April 5th, 1945

Goatee-Hanke inspected our runway today. He said Gandau airfield had been taken by the Russians and we must work even harder to finish the runway. He flounced in front of us, daring us to complain about the constant attacks, the mounting numbers of dead. Everyone hates him. Some of us were put on 'fire alert'.

April 6th, 1945

More air raids but still we have to work on that bloody, bloody Blutbahn. My fingers are covered in thousands of little cuts, full of dirt and tiny pieces of wire and grit, and I am starving. We are all starving as our rations are simply not enough. One small tiny chimera in a black day, I saw Kowalenko again. He was right next to me. His knuckles were also bleeding. He smiled.

April 7th, 1945

The death toll is mounting horrifically. We have to run and hide in our cellars all the time. Some say more than 90 Soviet planes were in action today. They say the Russians in the suburbs are using megaphones to call on our soldiers to surrender.

April 8th, 1945

There were so many air attacks today we didn't dare leave our bunker-cellars. Commandant Niehoff has abandoned his headquarters at Liebich Höhe and joined Goatee-Hanke in his university library basement. They say more than 180 Soviet aircraft flew over us today. When we finally could come out of the cellars mutilated corpses littered the streets.

April 10th, 1945

Somehow in between all the attacks on the runway one of our planes landed on it and took away twenty-two of the wounded. They say this is the beginning of our evacuation at last. They say we will all be airlifted to safety. Can this be true?

Berlin, April 11th, 1945
Dear Toni,
I got a letter from Papa. Hildegarde is well. She is back home from hospital and recuperating. The doctor says she will make a full recovery but is unlikely to be able to conceive again.

The baby was a girl. Hilde has called her Cecilia after Mama. Poor Hilde. I thought she was very foolish to do what she did but this is so tragic. I never could have imagined this. They made a grave for her by the peach tree. What sad times we live in.

The miscarriage was caused by an undetected venereal disease, gonorrhoea, which she says she must have caught from her SS letter-writing husband. Poor Hildegarde. The nurse in the hospital said that venereal disease has increased fourfold in the last ten years because of Hitler's talk of "procreation" as if it's recreation.

I remember Georg saying Himmler said that every man who leaves a child behind can die in equanimity. What sort of attitude is that? The family, which is supposed to be so sacred, has been playing second fiddle to Hitler's baby making fervour.

Here the bombing is as bad as ever. Huge missiles
sing through the air, they explode on contact and send up an
enormous pall of black smoke and a fountain of debris which
make the terrific explosions of before seem nothing. But by far
the worst are the little phosphorus bombs they send in after the
big ones. The little firebombs fly into the unprotected buildings
and set light to everything – houses, hospitals, canning factories,
nurseries, homes, paint factories, water treatment plants, gas
works. The air is filled with poisonous fumes and nothing is left.
Nothing is left standing.
Stay alive.
Maria

April 11th, 1945

I was given a copy of the anti-Nazi Freiheitskämpfer, the
Freedom Fighter newspaper. You can be shot if caught reading
it. It says Niehoff is a buffoon who 'Fiddles while Breslau burns'
and that we citizens of Breslau mean nothing to the Nazi party.
They terrorise and bully us and don't care if we live or die. How
did it come to this?

April 18th, 1945

His name was on the noticeboard. The first one in the list of
executions. Of course there would be more than one Kowalenko
in Breslau. Hanged by the neck for 'shirking' his duty. I had to
go to Gallows Row. I had never been there before, but I needed
to see, just in case it wasn't my Kowalenko. So I went.

I don't know how I didn't faint or throw up. There were four of
them. Three men and one woman.

He was the second from the right. They dangled from the
branches of the trees, yards above the rubble and simmering

ash from the previous day's firebombing. All crooked. Lifeless.

His trousers were too short. He had no socks or shoes on. Surely they hadn't hanged him with no shoes on, or had they already been stolen? His skin was waxy white. I wanted to touch his foot. I was close enough to. I wanted him to know he wasn't alone. But my fingers began to tremble as soon as I made to move my hand. I couldn't do it.

I hate this life. It's not worth living. But I don't want to give it up.

April 20th, 1945

They say General Niehoff had chocolates sent to the soldiers on the frontline to celebrate Herr Hitler's birthday. They say they were especially flown in, that they somehow managed to land on the other airfield to the north. I can't believe it. We are starving. They also say Hanke is drafting women to frontline combat service.

April 28th, 1945

The bombing is continuous. It is impossible to work on the runway. We spend all our time in the cellars, coming out only to gasp some fresh air and for our toilet. They say although the airfield at Gandau has been finally taken, planes are landing on the Friesenwiese and Oferwiese meadows.

There is still hope, maybe we can still be evacuated. But some people have had enough. Yesterday in the northern suburbs of Carlowitz, Zimpel and Bischohfswalde, just over two kilometres north of our runway, there was a full-scale revolt.

More than 1500 hundred people, almost all women, waved white flags and besieged the party offices and stoned military command posts, demanding an end to the fighting. More than a hundred of them were arrested. Seventeen were executed. If only we knew when help will come.

April 30th, 1945

They say the Russians are as close as Streigauer Platz and Tschepiner Platz in the west by the Linke-Hofman factory where I worked. That is just over a kilometre from the Market Square on the Ring. In the south they are in control of Kaiser Wilhelm Street right up to the theatre. Meanwhile, there is no sign of an evacuation. What is going to happen to us? Why won't our commander do something to get us out? How much longer can we last?

May 1st, 1945

It was on the radio. Everyone is talking about it. Hitler committed suicide!

May 2nd, 1945

Berlin has surrendered to the Russians. Niehoff and Hanke continue to say we will not capitulate.

May 3rd, 1945

Hamburg has surrendered to the British. Everyone is saying we will be next.

May 4th, 1945

All day the Russians have been hailing us through giant loudspeakers, threatening to raze Breslau, and all of us in it, if we don't surrender immediately. No one knows what our generals are doing. Some SS officers locked themselves in the Jahrhunderthalle, one of the few buildings to have survived the bombing, others have committed suicide.

They say there have been more civilian demonstrations in Zimpel. They say those few religious leaders remaining in Breslau, led by Father Ernst Hornig, have demanded an immediate end to the fighting. They were sent away. Hanke says we will never capitulate. It is bedlam.

May 5th, 1945

No one knows what is happening. There is no shouting from the giant loudhailers today, no shooting from the frontline suburbs. It is peculiarly quiet. Everyone is panicking. Is this the calm before the storm? No one knows what to do.

May 6th, 1945

It has been another eerily silent day. They say there were Russian soldiers bathing in the Oder and Hanke sneaked off last night. The bastard commandeered a pilot and a Fiesler Storch light aircraft and flew away, taking off from our bloody runway!

May 7th, 1945

This morning four of us women crept out of our cellar and made our way to the main square. On our way there we saw some of our men gathered outside the Market Hall. Their weapons were on the ground beside them. They looked exhausted. So, it was over. It was actually over.

Shortly afterwards we watched some Soviets round them up and march them out of town. We think they are being taken to Russia. Oh, our poor lads! Someone said Niehoff had signed our surrender last night and is a prisoner of war. We have been left alone with the Russian soldiers.

The looting started even before the line of our men had disappeared. Gangs of marauding Ivans began to run from street to street, chasing petrified Germans out of their homes.

They plundered everything: food, alcohol, curtains, clothes, pictures, bedding, window frames, wheelbarrows, bicycles, wardrobes, tables, chairs. We even saw two Russians lug a piano into the street and then pour petrol over the rooms they'd just ransacked and set the building alight. It was monstrous.

Those that weren't looting stood around shouting, drinking, smoking, leaning on their fixed bayonets, celebrating.

We women tried not to panic and hurried to go back to our

cellar. A Soviet officer appeared from nowhere. He stopped us. In excellent German he said he needed women to help cook and clean for his men. He gave his word whoever came would be well treated and in return for our help we would receive food and a little cash. We didn't know if we could trust him, but he seemed honourable and we needed to eat so we all four agreed to help.

He took us to the cellars underneath the café opposite Haus Barasch. As soon as we entered the dimly lit cavern, we knew we'd made a mistake.

The six or so men there were clearly drunk. They shouted 'Davai suda!' 'Women come!' in a rude way and encircled us before we had a chance to leave. One shoved me on to a wooden bed and fell on top of me. He fumbled at my breasts. I screamed. I tried to push him off. He just laughed. His breath stunk of sour yeast and rotten eggs. Then as suddenly as he'd fallen on top of me, he slumped to one side, comatose.

For a second I didn't know what to do. The other soldiers had cornered the women in the back of the cellar. They forced glasses of vodka into their trembling hands and ordered them to drink. Quietly, I pushed the Ivan's disgusting body off mine and slipped out of the exit and ran.

I am going home. I know all the back roads and shortcuts. I only have my small blue suitcase so I can travel light. I will keep my head down and take the country road to Hirschberg and home.

There are thousands of us. Women and men, brothers and sisters, aunts and uncles, grandparents, boys and girls. Everyone carrying or pushing something: a pram, a handcart, a bicycle, a bag, a suitcase, a holdall, a bread basket. Some people are almost too laden down to move. Others march resolutely. Almost all of us are wrapped in sores and festering wounds. One long miserable line, as far away from the Russians as possible. There are others, though, going in the opposite direction. Why are they going the wrong way?

We smell him before we see him. A bloated, putrid blackening heap of abandoned flesh. A boy, perhaps six years old. Maybe as young as four. A woman with a bruised face wants to bury him, but the body is too decomposed. We agree to come back later to give him a decent burial.

There are fourteen in our group today. Yesterday there were six. The numbers keep changing – when we stop to rest new people join us while others leave. Some recognise friends or neighbours; others have reached their village. Some even turn round and go back. We stop when it is dark. We sleep wherever we can. In a ditch. Under a hedge. Anywhere.

Dawn arrives. Cold. Hungry. I can't get up. My bones ache. No matter how hard I try I can't move. I silently scold myself and will myself to get up. I don't know how the older people continue – especially those with illnesses. Somehow, eventually, I pull myself up. When we are all on our feet, clothes hard from being caked in dirt, we start to walk. Again. One swollen foot after the other.

There is one very small girl in our group with an old man, we think he is her grandfather. He is skin and bones and crippled with arthritis. He has to bend to keep her hand in his twisted hand. He hobbles along. Over his shoulder he carries a large bundle of their belongings, wrapped in a dirty floral curtain tied with a piece of thick rope. In her free hand the little girl drags a chipped white enamel kettle by a piece of string. As she walks the kettle thunks against the ground: thunk, thunk, thunk. It sounds like a death-knell.

At dawn today a group of four of us women find ourselves in Landeshut. I tell them I am only a day's walk or so from my home and they are happy for me. The town is full of Polish soldiers. We tell them we are looking for food and water in Landeshut. They say the town is now called Kamienna Gora and we are forbidden to speak German. We decide it is not a friendly place and try to leave but the Polish officers herd us together with some other women. There are around twenty of us. We all think we are going to be raped, maybe even killed, and are petrified.

The men force us out of town at gunpoint. They take us to a field and tell us to dig. They say we are digging a grave. We think the grave is for ourselves. Some women start to cry. The officers tell them to shut up. They say the grave is already taken – there are Polish people in it.

We don't want to dig but the men aim their guns at our heads. We drop to our knees. The black soil is wet as it has started to rain. I scrape the ground and the earth crumbles between my fingers. Some townsfolk come and shout at us in Polish. We don't have to know Polish to know they are being rude. Some throw stones. The officers chase them away.

I dig and dig and a dead animal smell begins to exude from the soil. A scream, the woman next to me has found a leg bone. Another woman uncovers a skull and cries out. We beg to be allowed to stop. The Polish officers insist we continue.

We dig deeper and deeper. Gradually we discover arms and legs held together with gelatinous black sinews; caved-in chests; putrid, festering liquid organs and gaunt heads covered in scraps of yellowed paper thin skin. At last the soil is removed. Hollow eyes and grimacing bare teeth taunt us. We are sitting inside a giant grave of thirty decomposed corpses.

We think our job is done. We are covered in sweat and earth and the sour, fatty, rancid gone-off meat smell is revolting. One or two woman are sick. I don't know why I am not. Probably because I am starving and I have nothing in my stomach to throw up.

We get up to climb out of the grave. We are told to stay. The commander says that before we can get out we have to pick a corpse and kiss him on the mouth. We protest. We sob. We scream and shout out but he insists. If we do not kiss the corpses we will not be allowed out of the grave. And then he laughs and the other men all laugh with him.

I start to shake and cannot stop. I know these poor things on the ground are someone's brother or uncle but I cannot bear to look at them. I cannot bear to be beside them. They stink. I stink. I want to run away. I am going to scream. I know I am and then I will be shot. The officers continue to laugh. Their guns point at us. Some of the women kneel. They wipe the debris from the mouths of the skeletons. I want to run but I too sit down next to a corpse. The skull is arched upwards as if lifting up to meet me halfway. His slimy, sticky-out, dirt covered teeth grin. Black slurry seeps from two muddy eye sockets and oozes into a hollow place where his nose should have been. I lean forward to touch him and now I vomit. I wretch again and again and nothing more comes. I think I would rather be dead than do this. There is a commotion. Some shouting. I look round. Red Army officers have arrived. Now I know I will be raped.

In perfect German the Red Army commander orders us to stop what we are doing. He demands an explanation from the Polish officer. The Polish officer smirks and, in German, says he is checking the bodies to see how they were killed. The Russian officer immediately halts the degradation. The Polish officer is furious. There is a ruckus but the Russian is clearly in charge. He tells us women to leave at once and not come back. We quickly scramble out of the grave. We are not raped.

May 20th, 1945

I am back.

I arrived in the afternoon. Lähn was very quiet. The red flag with the hammer and sickle flies over the town hall. Hilde cried when she saw me and went to give me an embrace. I was filthy. I pulled away. She ignored my protest. As she hugged me, I saw Mama hiding behind her. Her 'house dress' had food stains on it and her bare legs looked like bleached twiglets as they poked out of her house slippers. She clutched a handkerchief next to her mouth. Her hair was cut short and brushed back from her face. I smiled at her. She grimaced, turned and shuffled back into the house. Hilde said, 'She's developed a pain in her side. It makes walking difficult.'

Papa appeared. He gave me an awkward embrace and brought me inside. He said Maria was in Berlin. There was no news of Hansi or Hubert or the whereabouts of our cousins and the various aunts and uncles. The Russians were in charge. No one knew what was going to happen to us. He said we couldn't leave the village without permission and we couldn't stay unless we had been given it. He said I needed to go to the town hall immediately and sort out my papers.

The Russian official at the town hall gave me my permit and ration papers for bread, butter, milk and cheese. He spoke good German. He said if I had any problems to come to him, then told me to report back to the town hall the next morning for work duty.

On my return from the town hall Hilde made me a small dinner of fried potatoes from a meagre secret supply she had hidden in the cellar – along with some onions, sausage, beetroot, oats and apple compote. As soon as the first waxy white chunk of potato touched my lips, I thought I would be sick. Hilde told me to take my time. While I struggled to eat, she said it was good I was going to work because I'd get paid and although it wouldn't be a lot of money, we would need it: Papa's savings had been frozen and his pension stopped. They had no money at all.

After I ate what I could, Hilde prepared me a bath. The water shimmered in the enamel tub. It made me feel bad to think of my filthy body contaminating something so pure. It was warm. Hilde had used some of her valuable wood to boil some water to take the chill off the cold. She'd also saved a slither of Lily of the Valley soap for me. She said she would keep an eye out for the Russians, they wandered in and out of the houses whenever they felt like it. I told her I was sorry about the baby. She said she didn't want to speak about it.

After my bath I tried to get some sleep but it was no good, every time I closed my eyes violent flish-flashes, exploding shapes and colours, roaring sounds and whining whistling ricocheted around my head. For months now I was more awake when I closed my eyes than when they were open.

Eight of us stood together outside the town hall in front of the flapping red hammer and sickle. All of us under thirty. I recognised the two Marias, they'd been in the women's group I'd joined when I moved back to Lähn.

Maria R said she'd spent most of the war in France as a clerk in the army. She lived with her mother. Her brothers had all been killed in action and her father had committed suicide and her aunts and sisters had already left for Berlin.

Maria N said all Germans were going to be forced to leave but as her family were half-Polish, they had been told they would probably be allowed to stay. She said she didn't want to stay, when her time came to go she was going as far away as possible from here. Too many horrible things had happened. Only two days ago she'd been given permission – along with three others – to go to one of the outlying farms to get milk. While waiting for the farmer's wife to fill their containers, they'd heard this awful screaming and shouting coming from one of the outhouses. They'd rushed to see what was going on. A Russian soldier was dragging a young girl of maybe only thirteen into one of the farm buildings.

The girl sobbed and begged to be let free but he simply threw her inside the outhouse and slammed the barn doors behind him. Even from where they stood they could hear the thumps and punches of his blows as he pummelled her over and over again. Her agonised screams made no difference. Gradually her tortured shouts became whimpers and then eventually even the whimpering stopped. Then there was silence.

Eventually, the barn door opened. The listening women quickly hid, they didn't want to be the next. When they were sure he had gone, they crept back to the outhouse. The little girl lay just inside the door on the straw floor. She was naked and covered in blood and pus. Her body was battered out of shape. She was dead.

May 11th, 1945

At exactly eight by the town hall clock the Russian commander-in-charge, a weary looking man in a grubby uniform, appeared from our ex-mayor's house – someone said our mayor had been sent to a salt mine in Siberia.

The commander told us in broken German that every day from now on, between eight and four, except Sundays, it was our job to clean up after the Russian soldiers temporarily billeted around the village.

We were all horrified at the thought of being in such close proximity to such beasts. The commander dismissed any fears, saying his soldiers would treat us with the utmost respect. None of us believed him. The Commander then ordered two girls to go to the primary school and three girls to go to the German

House, the biggest hotel in Lähn. The two Marias were to go to the technical school and I was sent home, because as from today nine soldiers were staying at the café Concordia. I must have looked surprised. The commander said, 'What? You thought you would be able to keep that great big house for yourselves?'

When I got back to Concordia the Ivans were already there, clomping about making scuff marks all over our polished floorboards with their dirty great big boots. I hated them, they were the enemy and they were in our house, but Hilde said we couldn't think like that any more. We quickly packed our belongings into the small hand cart – we could only take what we would carry.

We'd been allocated the seamstress's house – a two bedroomed flat overlooking the square. All the cupboards and drawers were still full of her sewing things. Hilde said we were lucky, some families had been given little more than cattle sheds to live in. She said she would make us some new clothes with the material left behind. As soon as we'd unpacked I had to go back and clean up after the soldiers.

May 14th, 1945

The pain in Mama's side was worse. She couldn't get out of bed today and she had a fever. I went to the officer at the town hall to ask for help. He said that what medical help there was, was for Russian and Poles and certainly not to be wasted on Germans. I was so angry and frustrated.

Hilde and I continuously washed Mama down with a tepid cloth. Her temperature finally decreased. For how long we don't know.

May 17th, 1945

I have a 'stalker'. Every day when I finish cleaning up after our Russian 'lodgers', this one soldier follows me home. He stays three or four yards behind me and never speaks. When I go to the bread oven he is there; when I go for a walk around the village with Hilde he is there; when I accompany her to church, he is there. He is not like the other soldiers, he doesn't sneer at me or make rude gestures. He never tries to brush against me while I am cleaning or try to follow me anywhere private. I don't know what he wants. Hilde says I must keep away from him.

May 18th, 1945

There is still no definite news of what is to become of us Germans. We are not allowed newspapers and all radios have been confiscated. Rumours say all of Silesia belongs to Poland and there are fifteen million German refugees fleeing westwards.

Berlin, June 17th, 1945
Dear Mama and Papa,
Berlin is a heap of gaunt, burned-out, flame-seared buildings and rubble mountains. The pungent stench of death hangs everywhere. Frankfurter Allee has not one single building left standing. And for some reason I am alive.

It seems Berlin is not the only city to have been decimated. Dresden was totally erased after the very attack I witnessed and Cologne is a gigantic wasteland.

In one attack against Hamburg flames rolled a mile into the sky and roasted alive hundreds of thousands of civilians in street temperatures of a thousand degrees. Frankfurt-on-Main has been reduced to a mass of rubble and all the cities and industrial areas in the Ruhr and Saar regions have been laid waste.

I am alive but I don't feel lucky.

Maria

June 23rd, 1945

First thing this morning I was ordered to the town hall. There were a few others already waiting. None of us knew why we were there.

Eventually, our Russian commander appeared from his new house and told us that just yesterday two children playing in the neighbouring village had stepped on a mine and been blown up. He didn't want this to happen here. So, from now on we were responsible for detecting mines. We protested. He said we could always work in the salt mines if we preferred.

We were six girls and four young men. We'd been picked because we were young and fit. We were each given a two meter long stick with a reinforced metal point and taken to the outskirts of the village for 'training'.

For two hours we practised poking our sticks in the ground until we touched a hard object, which had been hidden earlier by our 'trainer'. We were then shown how to ever-so-carefully uncover the object and move it to a safe place for 'defusing' – trained soldiers would do the defusing.

A crowd of older people gathered to watch us. As soon as they realised what we were doing they became angry. They shouted that the work was too dangerous for untrained people.

One woman wailed that she didn't want her only son, who had been spared at the front, to be blown up at home. Their protests made no difference.

At the end of the two hours, our Soviet trainer, accompanied by two guards and a first aider, led us into a field. He ordered us to fan out in an even line and start prodding.

I was placed next to one of the men. At first I didn't recognise him, then he said, 'Hello, Toni.' It was Rolf. He was older, of course, and more thick set, but it was definitely him. I felt bile rise in the back of my throat. He asked where I'd been during the war. I ignored him. After all this time how could being in his presence still make me feel so terrible?

He talked to me as if nothing had happened between us. His raspy voice sapped my strength. He said during the war he'd been posted in the middle of darkest Norway, where some decrepit Norwegian had sneaked up behind him and walloped him over the head with a big stick. He'd woken up in hospital with a head injury and his discharge papers. I prodded and prodded in front of me, trying to focus on finding mines. I had been so stupid to have ever trusted them. As if reading my mind, Rolf said, 'Look, Toni, I'm sorry about before. Liesl was jealous of you, she poisoned me against you. I was stupid.'

I said nothing.

He said, 'Her grandmother died. Liesl sold the house. She's in Hirschberg now.'

I continued to ignore him.

'Well, that's all I wanted to say. Sorry.'

I'll never forgive him, or her.

It seemed to take us hours to sweep the field. No one found anything. We were given a five minute break. Rolf came to sit beside me but I moved away from him. While we rested, a farmer led a huge throbbing bull into the field we had just cleared. Within seconds there was a huge explosion! BOOM!

For a second I couldn't hear or think. Then I saw the animal's steaming purple insides splattered all over the green summer grass. The farmer began hurling abuse at us for killing his bull. Everyone started talking at once. 'We'd just cleared that field!' 'How could we have missed the mine?' 'That bull could have been one of us!'

Some villagers appeared and demanded to know what the explosion was about. For a while it was chaos but eventually the villagers were made to leave, the farmer was made to leave and we were made to carry on.

Rolf ended up next to me again. I developed a bitter headache. He wouldn't stop talking. He said he'd heard my mother was sick. He said he wanted to help. I continued to ignore him. The heat was stifling. Glistening sweaty beads slipped down my bare arm, over my hand, on to my clammy fingers and my dirty wooden prodder. I worried that one of those minute drops would splash on to the grass and trigger an explosion even though I knew it really couldn't.

At noon we stopped for a break and were given bread and cheese by our guards and then we carried on. Only when it began to get dark were we allowed to stop. By then my head throbbed so violently I thought I would throw up. We got home after eight. The curfew had started.

When I told Hilde and Papa about the mine seeking duty, they were furious – and worried for me. I am worried for me. I didn't say anything about Rolf.

June 24th, 1945

It is Sunday. Mama is sick again. We must get help but we don't know where from. Papa said there was a rumour about a German doctor in the next village. He said he was going to try to get a message to him to come and check Mama. But before we could talk further we were summoned to the town hall. Again! Only Hilde was allowed to stay to look after Mama.

From the town hall we were sent to the German House Hotel – although it has a new name now. When we got there we were made to watch a film about atrocities that occurred against mankind in Dachau and Auschwitz. It was horrible. Afterwards some of the girls cried. Some said it was propaganda, but I knew it could be true – for the Reich all people had become objects, to be bullied and terrorised and killed however they saw fit.

When the film was over, the men were told to leave. Rolf was with them. He waved but I looked away. As soon as the men were gone someone pulled back the curtains and the summer sun flooded the room. Next the film paraphernalia was removed and the chairs we'd been sitting on were rearranged to form two rows, one at either side of the big dining room. Finally, a queue of Ivans trooped in, cap in hand, looking almost shy. My stalker was among them.

The soldiers sat on one side of the hall and we girls were told to sit at the other. Four other soldiers went to the far corner of the room and started to unpack an accordion, two violins and a set of drums. We waited in silence, unsure of what was going to happen next.

Within a very short time the four soldiers were all set and the drummer beat a one, two, three on the side of the drum. The accordion player nodded and along with the violinists started playing a cheeky Russian-cum-gypsy-type Cossack dance.

The Ivans immediately cheered, some even got up and started stamping and stomping and twirling and dancing. The music played on and on. I watched amazed. Then the music changed to a polka and the soldiers, all sweaty and hot and bothered, started to come across. Surely we weren't expected to dance? Not after watching that film? Not with them?

My stalker appeared in front of me. He held out his hand, clearly inviting me up. I didn't want to get up. Then he leaned forward and in broken German said, 'You have something I want. I can pay.'

Berlin, July 1st, 1945
Dear Mama and Papa and Toni and Hilde,
Hubert is here with me. He is safe. He has been demobbed.
Fortunately, I live in the British zone of Berlin – Berlin has been
carved up between the Russians, the Americans, the British and

the French. If the flat had been in the Russian zone, Hubert would have been taken to a Russian or eastern slave camp.

Here he is allowed to work, although, of course, there is no work. However, I am very lucky, I still have a job at the bank. It seems while we are starving and penniless, the American GI soldiers who seem to be all over the British zone as well as their own zone have plenty of everything, especially money. If it were not for my paltry income we would have starved to death. As it is we are only just managing to stay alive.

The rations are negligible. The shelves in the shops are empty. We live from day to day. The streets are not safe. There are looters everywhere and people wander about aimlessly, seemingly hallucinating, as if drunk, but there is no alcohol. There is nothing. People are emaciated. Their clothes hang loose on their bodies, the lower extremities are like the bones of a skeleton, their hands shake as though with palsy, the muscles of the arms are withered, the skin lies in folds and is without elasticity, the joints stick out as though broken.

The weight of the women of average height and build has fallen to below 50 kilos. The number of stillborn children is approaching the number of those born alive, and even if they come into the world of normal weight, they start immediately to lose weight and die shortly.

Very often the mothers cannot stand the loss of blood in childbirth and perish. They say infant mortality has reached a horrifying 90 per cent. Some people are so hungry they are even eating the grass that is growing through the cracks of the pavements. At the same time they say the United Nations Relief and Rehabilitation Administration (UNRRA) are supplying the

Norwegians, Belgians, Dutch, Greeks, Poles and French with billions of dollars worth of goods which they, in turn, sell to those with the money to buy, thus bringing to themselves handsome revenues in lieu of taxes. But here, in Germany, where there is widespread hunger and poverty, UNRRA is specifically forbidden to function. No Central Red Cross is permitted to function here because we are the enemy. Meanwhile, thousands upon thousands of relief packages sent to Germany from overseas friends are being stockpiled in warehouses.

 UNRRA say that while, of course, there are many, many innocent people in Germany who had little to do with the Nazi terror, the administrative burden of trying to find these people and treat them differently from the rest is almost insuperable. They say any effort to help those in the war-stricken areas are directly aimed at taking care of those who fought the Germans. They say eventually we, the enemy, will be given some attention. We will all be dead by then.

Maria

July 2nd, 1945

Vlasov – that is the name of my stalker – wants Papa's wristwatch. He said where he comes from a watch is a sign of affluence and breeding and very sought after. Papa's watch is one of the most handsome wristwatches Vlasov has ever seen.

He said he would give Papa whatever he wanted for it and that we should sell it before someone just comes and takes it. He said he will send the watch to his mother back home, who is very poor. He sent her his wages so she could buy food but when she tried to use the paper Reichs and Rentenmarks they were refused, no one values them there. The sale of the watch would give her enough money to buy a cow.

Dear Mama and Papa and Toni and Hilde,
Hubert and I were at the station today looking for food. A
refugee train came in. It was like a macabre Noah's ark. Every
car was jammed with German families carrying all their earthly
belongings in sacks, bags and tin trunks. The bedraggled people
dragged themselves and their luggage from the carriages. I
heard someone say they had been travelling for eleven days from
Poland without food or water or a place to do their toilet.

91 corpses were pulled from the train. Relatives shrieked
and sobbed as the bodies were loaded into American trucks
and taken away from them. Hubert heard that the dead would
be buried in a pit near one of the concentration camps outside
Berlin.

We saw four screaming women bound together with
rope. The German Red Cross girl said that the soldiers had done
that to prevent the women from clawing other passengers – the
mothers were so undernourished that they'd not been able to feed
their infants and had gone insane watching their babies slowly
die before their eyes. Another woman, in tears, was stopped as
she tried to hurry away. When she was searched they found a
small bundle hidden under her coat. It was a little body. The
Red Cross girl said the soldiers search all the weeping women for
bundles, to make sure they are not carrying infant corpses with
them.

It is truly awful here.
Maria

July 5th, 1945

Mama is a little better. Vlasov gave Papa 10,000 RMs for his watch. We can't believe our luck.

July 9th, 1945

At work today we passed an upsidedown cart at the side of the road, wheels spinning upwards, hay scattered across our path. It clearly had gone over a mine. Its yoke lay empty. We thought, at least the animal that had been pulling it had been spared. We couldn't see the farmer who owned it, we assumed he'd gone for help. Our trainer ordered us to upright the cart.

All of us, including the soldiers, gripped the cart and heaved. When we uprighted the cart we discovered the stinking, mangled bodies of the farmer and his son underneath. It was awful. Work was cancelled. The soldiers and the men carried the bloody bodies between them and we all went back to Lähn.

As we approached the square, people came from all directions to see what was going on. Papa was with them. At the sight of the dead bodies some people began to sob, others yelled curses, some became hysterical.

The men set the bodies down on the stone ground in the middle of the square. Very quickly chaos erupted. The commotion drew the Russian commander out of his house. On seeing the two corpses he took off his coat and covered the bodies. Next he made a speech about what people should do if a similar accident happens in the future. Then he said all work duties were cancelled until after the deceased had been buried and ordered the soldiers to take the corpses to the hospital. Finally we were dismissed.

As Papa and I turned to leave, Rolf appeared. Before I could stop him, he'd introduced himself to Papa as a 'good' friend from school and fellow 'mine sweeper'. After they shook hands, Rolf inquired after Mama, suggesting in doing so that I had been the one who had told him she was ill. I couldn't look at Rolf. Papa explained Mama's situation and Rolf expressed sympathy. He said his own grandfather up at the farm was also sick but they were lucky, a Polish nurse came to treat the old man twice a week. Rolf's grandfather was Polish so entitled to the treatment. Papa said he was very fortunate. Rolf agreed but said at least Mama still had her family with her. Rolf's family had all fled months ago. If Rolf had not stayed behind his sick grandfather would have been left all alone. I took that moment to leave. When Papa finally came home, he told me how much Rolf's sense of familial duty had impressed him. I said I didn't like Rolf. Papa said he thought him a very trustworthy German.

July 16th, 1945

Mama had a high temperature again today, even higher than the last time. Somehow Papa got word to the German doctor in the next village and he came to visit Mama – as a 'key worker' the doctor has been given permission to work and stay in his own house, at least until he's not needed any more.

The doctor told us he was only allowed to treat Russians and Poles, but he gave Mama a quick examination anyway. After checking her over, he said Mama should be in hospital, but as it was only for the Russian soldiers or Poles, we would have to do the best we can for her at home. He said she needed penicillin, but there wasn't any. Papa is distraught.

July 19th, 1945

Hilde and I spent all last night and today taking it in turns to bathe Mama with a tepid cloth to try to lower her fever. It seems to have made a little difference. Meanwhile, Papa was in an odd mood, and still is.

July 22nd, 1945

Mama is the same, but all weekend Papa continued to behave very oddly. One minute cheerful and excited, the next anxious and bewildered. He never even went to church yesterday. Hilde said it's the strain of worrying about Mama. It seems more than that to me.

July 24th, 1945

Today Papa was the most agitated I had ever seen. By midday he hadn't even shaved, something he'd never done before. Hilde and I made him sit down and refused to let him leave until he told us what was upsetting him.

Finally Papa explained he was worried about Rolf. It seemed Rolf had told Papa he knew where he could some penicillin for Mama, but it would be expensive. Papa hadn't hesitated. He'd given Rolf all his money, including Vlasov's cash. However, since then he'd not been around. Papa was convinced Rolf had been arrested for dealing on the black market and it was his fault.

I groaned. Why, oh why, hadn't Papa discussed this with me first? I was sure Rolf wasn't reliable. Papa was cross with me for saying such a thing. He was adamant Rolf could be trusted.

Maybe Papa is right. Maybe Rolf has changed. Anyway, we'll soon know. Mine clearing duty is back on. I will see Rolf tomorrow and ask him about the penicillin. And if, for some reason he doesn't turn up for work, I'll go to the family farm and ask him what's going on.

July 25th, 1945

The absolutely worst possible thing happened, the whole village was ordered to assemble in the market square at 9 am. Even Mama had to come. As we gathered, I looked out for Rolf but couldn't see him anywhere.

When it looked as if the village were all there – except for Rolf, where was he? – our Russian commander-in-charge demanded silence. This morning he had an escort of half a dozen soldiers, which was unusual. They fanned out behind him in a half-circle, their rifles slightly raised, as if expecting trouble.

The commander said we had to leave the village. This

announcement stunned us. We had to go to the woods and stay there until we were told to come back. There was an outcry. 'We're not leaving!' 'Never!' 'You can't get rid of us like that!' We had all heard the stories of mass murders in secluded woods. 'If you're going to kill us, kill us in our homes at least!' The commander held up his arms for us to keep calm. The shouting continued. 'Cowards!' 'We're not leaving!' 'We're not leaving!' The soldiers around us became restless. They raised their guns. No one noticed or cared.

'Bitte, you are all being very very foolish,' the commander shouted. 'Please, you are all worrying unnecessarily. Please, I give my word that nothing will happen to you.' Gradually we calmed down and the soldiers let their guns fall back to their sides. The commander said, 'We are simply going to carry out some necessary repairs on the buildings and generally check the village is in order.'

Mama became extremely agitated, she didn't understand what all the noise was about. She tugged at my arm. She wanted to go back to the house. The commander finally said, 'You have no choice. Bitte! Go now. Please, pack only what is absolutely essential and return as soon as possible. If you are not back within half an hour there will be reprisals.'

We grabbed what we could carry and were back in the square within ten minutes. We were all anxious. Mama was particularly distressed. She kept waving her arms about and repeatedly asked to go home. It took Papa and Hilde all their effort to keep her calm. I remonstrated with the soldiers, who had started rounding us out of the house almost as soon as we'd got there. They had the good grace to look ashamed.

When everyone had reassembled the Russian ordered us to march to the wood by Karlsdorf. Again there was an uproar. 'You can't expect old folk to walk in this heat!' 'No way!' 'What – no transport?' 'That's four kilometres!' 'How long are we to stay? 'The Red Cross will have something to say about this!' The commander took out his gun and fired a shot in the air. That shut us up. 'Under no circumstances,' he barked, 'must you leave the wood until someone comes and gives you permission to return. Be warned, disobedience will be punishable by death.' There was silence. Then he ordered his soldiers to escort us out of our own village and take us to the woods.

We were a raggedy, higgledy-piggledy thread of just over 100 people, a large proportion of whom were infirm, older people, including Mama, who needed help. On top of that, everyone was agitated and stressed. It took a long time to walk the four kilometres to the wood. The soldiers gently pushed and prompted us but we wouldn't be hurried. All the while we walked, I noticed Rolf wasn't with us. I couldn't understand where he was, there had been no 'transports' in the last week, so he hadn't been 'expelled'.

Eventually we made it to the wood and our escorts left us in the middle of a shaded clearing by a stream. It was cool and there was room for everyone to gather. The Russian soldiers said we had to stay there until they returned to get us. 'Just like Hansel and Gretel,' someone murmured.

Gradually, as everyone found a comfortable patch of ground to spread out on, the moans and groans died down. By nightfall the group was more or less resigned to having to wait, but I wasn't. I couldn't. Mama's breathing was shallow. The walk had brought her fever back. Where was Rolf? What if he had got penicillin for Mama? If he hadn't, with the money he'd give back we could ask someone else to.

A couple of hours after nightfall I couldn't wait any longer. I had to go back to the village and find Rolf. Hilde was horrified when I told her. She reminded me of the commander's threat to kill anyone who left the wood. I said I didn't care about the death threats. If they'd wanted to shoot us they would have done so by now. I had to find Rolf, just in case he could help, or at the very least to get our money back off him. Hilde didn't want me to leave. As we argued, Hans, the retired primary teacher, joined us. He said he'd heard me saying I was going to Lähn and would come with me. He said he thought something odd was going on. He wanted to see what the Russians were up to. Only then did Hilde agree to me leaving them.

In the clear moonlight we half-ran, half-walked back, sticking to the woods for cover.

Hans struggled to keep up. He was in his sixties, carrying too much weight and had a bad back, but he refused to abandon me. He said he had a daughter my age. She'd been visiting her aunt in Lamsdorf when the Russians had arrived. He'd not seen or heard from her since.

By the time we reached the village square he was sweating profusely and desperately needed a drink. The only sign of life, apart from our own precarious breathing, was the chirruping of thousands of crickets. The Russians seemed to have gone.

We crept past the communal oven and along the bridle path towards the technical college where most of the Russians had been housed. Hans wanted to check they had really left. A scuffling noise behind us made us freeze. We anxiously glanced about. Nothing. Then there it was again. A noise like metal against metal. We were next to the primary school. Hans still had the key to the building. He quickly unlocked the door and we threw ourselves inside.

Once we were sure no one was coming after us, we inched up to the nearest window and peeked out. A column of about a dozen people plodded past the school. They pulled handcarts laden with bags and boxes. They chatted quietly to each other. Hans said they were speaking Polish and he knew a little Polish. Then he went out.

In the semi-dark I watched Hans approach a man at the end column. He wheeled a pushbike with a large box strapped on the saddle. They talked for what seemed like hours but it was probably only minutes and then Hans was back. He said the people were Polish. That there was nothing left where they had come from: between them, the German and the Soviet military had destroyed all their crops, slaughtered all their cattle, taken all food supplies for themselves and razed their houses. They'd been told Silesia was part of Poland now, that it was a land of plenty with big houses furnished to the hilt, just waiting for Polish people to move into.

They'd walked for miles and miles. Starving. Dragging and pushing their things till they got blisters. But so far everywhere they'd been the Russians had been before them and taken everything of value – in some towns they'd even taken floorboards, doors, door-posts, washbasins, electric plugs and switches, all sent to Mother Russia. In another town he'd seen a pile of confiscated wirelesses and typewriters stacked in the open, destroyed by rain and the elements. Lähn didn't seem a bad village but they were going to carry on, hold out for a more prosperous place to live. But there were more Poles coming behind them, hundreds and thousands. Some would stay. They had nowhere else to go.

The news confirmed all the rumours. Silesia belonged to Poland. My home didn't exist any more.

When we were sure the line of Poles had gone, I asked Hans if he would come with me to Rolf's farm. He was surprised I knew Rolf. I wasn't sure if I should tell him about the arrangement Papa had made with Rolf, it was difficult to know who to trust. In the end I did.

Hans sighed when he heard my story. He said Rolf been seen sneaking out of Lähn late at night a couple of days ago. As for the farm, no one had lived there for years. Rolf had been living with some mates in Liesl's grandmother's old house. Worse than that, before he left, he'd been mouthing off to his cronies how he'd come into money and was getting out before he got blown up on mine duty.

I wanted to scream. I felt as if Rolf had kicked me in the head

– for a second time. Hans said he was sorry. If it was any consolation the Marks would be worthless in 'Poland', but maybe if Rolf got to Germany he'd get something for them. I groaned into my hands. Poor Papa. If only he hadn't trusted Rolf. As for Mama, I couldn't bear to think what was going to happen without help.

If I ever see Rolf again I will kill him.

We arrived back in the wood just before daybreak. Hilde cried when I told her about Rolf. Papa was grim. Shortly after dawn we told the others the Russian soldiers had gone. They didn't believe us at first. Eventually, after a lot of discussion, Hans persuaded everyone to return. The only good news is that we have moved back into Concordia.

Berlin, August 1st, 1945
Dear Mama and Papa,
We have had news of Hansi. It is unbelievable. This complete stranger turned up at the flat and said he had been in a camp in Russia with him – of all the camps in Russia and all the millions of soldiers, he happened to be with Hansi. We are so lucky!

He was a healthy-looking lad of just seventeen, but it turned out he had terminal cancer and this was why he had been allowed to leave the camp. He said it is very difficult to get information in or out of the camps. Only prisoners in special favour, which is almost no one, are allowed to send a postcard to their loved ones. This is why Hans Joachim has not been in touch. Even prisoners leaving the camp for Germany are not allowed to take letters for comrades – all prisoners released are searched and if they are found smuggling mail for comrades they are beaten up and the mail is destroyed.

*However, this young lad has an incredible memory.
When he knew he was to be freed he memorised the names and
addresses of relatives to whom he could report for his fellow
prisoners. Incredibly, he memorised eighty names and addresses
in Berlin of the relatives of his prisoner friends. Of course, he
found the buildings at most of the addresses in rubble, with the
whereabouts of the former occupants unknown, but nevertheless
he continued to visit all of the eighty addresses given to him by
his comrades and finally found us, living in this damp, half-
destroyed hovel, which we share with rats and lice.*

*We made him stay and shared our precious chicory
coffee. He told us the daily diet in Russian slave camps is soup
and lectures on the glories of Communism and the evils of
western democracy. Oh, poor Hansi! The slightest disobedience
is penalised by such heavy work that a third of the culprits die
within three weeks from exhaustion. At least a tenth of the slaves
who arrived with them had died by the time he left. Only the
very strong survive – or the very lucky.*

*He said if Hansi was lucky he would eventually be released
into the Western Zone in Berlin and be safe. Unlucky Germans
are the ones who are released as unfit for further forced labour
and returned to the Russian zone and then happen to recuperate.
If this happens they are rearrested and sent back for more labour.
Moreover, able-bodied Germans who are released by the British
or Americans to return to their former homes in the new Russian
zones are arrested by the Russians and sent to the Soviet Union
for enslavement, on the pretext that they have been rendered
politically unreliable through exposure to British or American*

influences. If Hansi survives, he should be sent to us here.

This young man further said that when they were caught they had to march twenty-two miles a day. Those physically handicapped went in handcarts or carts pulled by spare beasts. Rather than be turned over to the Russians, some had committed suicide or tried to incapacitate themselves by slashing their bodies with knives, razors or bits of glass.

He also said the soldiers were marched toward huge depots near Leningrad, Moscow, Minsk, Stalingrad, Kiev, Kharkov and Sevastopol. He and Hansi ended up in Minsk, where they were told they had to rebuild the Russian towns and villages they had destroyed. They would not return home until the work was completed. The conditions are very bad in every camp but some are worse than others. They'd heard stories of camps where prisoners had been forced to lick up infectious faeces from the underwear of their fellow prisoners suffering from dysentery, and in other places inmates were forced to lick the bespattered brains of their fellow prisoners who had been beaten to death.

It is a miracle that he is even still alive. We will pray he is both strong and lucky.
Maria

August 3rd, 1945

We have a Polish mayor, a Polish vicar, a Polish doctor and more and more of the businesses have been taken over by Poles – there is a Polish baker, a Polish butcher, a Polish teacher. The bank manager is Polish and so is the hairdresser. The village is not called Lähn anymore but Wlen.

All we talk about is getting Mama well enough to travel for

when we are expelled. None of us knows when that will be.

We are forbidden to speak German in public and German children must speak Polish while at school – because of course, the curriculum and teaching is in Polish. It is forbidden for Germans to own a radio; it is forbidden for Germans to read a newspaper; it is forbidden for Germans to travel at night, or be out after eight o'clock in the evening, or ride a bike, or buy fruit, or get the free typhoid and tetanus injections that are being given to all the Poles because of the epidemics – we Germans must pay if we want to stay healthy because public healthcare is forbidden to Germans. There are ration cards for the Poles, but there are no ration cards for us Germans, unless we work.

For everything we do we need permission from our Polish mayor. He alone will expel us when he is ready. He says we will not be able to leave until the Bober railway bridge is repaired. So from now on all young and able people, which includes me, are on bridge repair duty. There are very few tools and it is backbreaking work. Some of us are also still occasionally sent on mine duty, although we find fewer and fewer mines and we are sent further and further away. The other day we went as far as Marzdorf. We didn't find anything but the farmers were very kind and gave us some food for trying, which I brought home for Mama.

Very fortunately, Papa's savings have been unfrozen but the exchange rate for zlotys is awful – two Reichsmark for one zloty. And now the latest news is that we have to pay thirty zloty per room monthly rent to stay in our own home. There are ten rooms in Concordia and I only get ten zlotys a day so we simply won't be able to afford to stay in our own home.

Papa now has a job too. He wanted to stay at home with Mama but every 'able' German aged between 14 and 60 must take a job. Papa explained to the Mayor, Papa can also speak Polish, which I didn't know, that he used to be a senior civil servant and could do administrative work. The mayor laughed at him and said he could work either as a cleaner or a porter. He now works as a porter in the hospital. He also gets paid ten zloty a day. Hilde is allowed to stay at home and care for Mama but neither of them get rations. Papa finds his job very demeaning but he says nothing.

September 25th, 1945

We were fortunate having our house all to ourselves for so long. We now have a Polish lodger. We have no choice but share our house with him, we can't afford not to. He has commandeered the three biggest rooms and brought his own cooker with him and installed it in the middle of our best guest room. He also has a pig. Fortunately, he's keeping that outside in the back. Maria said in Berlin some Poles keep their pigs in their living rooms.

Our lodger brought three women with him, his bride-to-be and his two sisters. Within a week of him being here he announced his marriage. The day of the wedding they had a little celebration in the house – our house – and we four were invited.

First, the two sisters walked into our dining room wearing our clothes. The cheek! Not that the clothes were that wonderful because the Russian soldiers have taken everything of true value and sent it home to their womenfolk, but they were the only nice outfits Hilde and I had left: my blue dress, Hilde's green skirt, my cream silk blouse, my only good shoes and Hilde's hat. To add insult to injury, the bride appeared next wearing Mama's wedding dress, the one Maria wore on her wedding day and Mama had been keeping for me and Hilde. The stupid girl was bursting out if it, but she didn't care. She looked gross. I was furious. They had simply ransacked the house and taken what they wanted. Magnanimously, we were given permission to drink coffee from our own cups and eat cake off our own good porcelain plates. How dare they!

I avoided our lodger and his hideous, smug sisters at all times. But then one day the 'fat bride' stopped me on our stairs. Her German was very poor but she knew enough to explain that she had noticed how swollen and bruised my hands were from the digging on bridge duty. She said she'd found me a job with a Polish lady living by the square, who needed help with her three children. Her husband was a Polish officer in the army and he was missing. She wasn't coping very well. She said it was well paid work and would be much lighter work than the bridge work. At first I thought I'd refuse but it was a good offer so I accepted.

It was very difficult to understand my new boss. At first I hated her, even more than the fat bride and her ridiculous sisters. She continuously criticised everything I did and never stopped telling me of the hundreds of thousands of cruelties that had been perpetrated against her by the Germans – and the Russians – during the war. Then one day she found out how ill Mama was. She immediately asked her friend to visit Mama. Her friend is a Polish nurse called Mariela, who is wonderful. She helps Hilde bathe Mama and brings us food and medicine – paid for by my boss – to help make Mama better. She even treated my hands, which were still infected and swollen from working on the bridge.

Berlin, September 28th, 1945
Dear Mama and Papa,
If there is a good thing to be said about living in the Western
Zone it is that we are not in the Russian zone, the bad thing is

the GIs. They assume every German woman is immoral and it is their privilege to force their attentions on us and insult us with indecent proposals. Yesterday some GI cretin slowed his jeep down as he passed me and patted me on the posterior! It is outrageous. None of the other occupation forces do this. It has become so bad that the wives of the men of the occupation forces have to wear special badges on their arms to distinguish them from German women and so protect them against indecent advances by the American men.

The GIs call seeking the attention of German women as going frattin. It is, of course, forbidden, but they simply do as they please. And, sadly, there are some German women who encourage their behaviour. When there is so little to inspire hope, it is no wonder.

Hubert, who has at last found work in the hospital canteen, says the nurses say thirty-five per cent of the civilian venereal disease victims are girls under twenty. It is no surprise. Unattached, they wander about and offer themselves, for food or bed. Very simply they have one thing left to sell, and they sell it. It may be worse than starvation, but it will put off dying for months – or even years. You could say the rape that happened at the end of the war is a thing of the past, because now a bit of food, a bar of chocolate, or a bar of soap makes it unnecessary.

The German woman has lost her perennial fight for decency because the indecent alone survive. Those who can establish contacts with members of the armed forces can get anything, from soap to shoes.
I have not had to sink that low, yet.
Maria

September 30th, 1945

Mariela said Mama was worse than usual. She called in a new German doctor, who had just arrived in the village. He was very grave and said he needed to perform an emergency operation for a prolapsed uterus. He needed an instrument from a colleague in Löwenberg. Mariela said she'd help him with the operation and I said I'd get the instrument.

Our Polish bride-lodger let me borrow her bike and I cycled all the way to Löwenberg, got the instrument and cycled back. The whole time I was away I was frantic that I would be caught and arrested for cycling without permission and not be able to return, or that Mama would die while I was away. But when I got back – it took me four hours – I wasn't too late. The German doctor did what he had to do and Mariela and Hilde helped. The operation happened in the nick of time, within a few days the German doctor was evacuated.

Berlin, October 3rd, 1945

Dear Mama and Papa,

I have just finished selling the last of my decent clothes on the black market and made some new ones from our only curtains and bed sheets. Hubert and myself now have nothing left to sell to supplement our starvation rations: we have sold my wedding ring and my watch, Hubert's watch, boots, laces and socks and hankies, sheets, our other pair of shoes, my spring dress, underwear, more socks, Hubert's jacket, copper wire from the telephone line, the kettle – we heat water, when we can, in an old tin.

I don't know what we will do when winter comes. The flat is exposed and unsafe and impossible to heat even if we had fuel to heat it. That is why the only thing I have not sold is my fox fur.

It is the only thing that will keep me warm when the time comes. Hubert has his heavy jacket.

When I am at work, Hubert defends our little flat and protects our meagre possessions from looters. My coat would fetch a lot of money on the black market.
Maria

November 15th, 1945

I have no job. My Polish boss lady, Mrs Bonschowaska, has moved with her family to another village. I will miss her. At least Mariela is still here. Bored, I wandered into the next village and got caught trying to buy apples from a farmer. The Polish police held me until nightfall and then told me not to try buy fruit again. I would have got into even bigger trouble if I had been caught stealing fruit, which I had been doing earlier.

I am so fed-up never knowing when we are to leave or what is going on in the world – if it wasn't for Maria's letters, we wouldn't have a clue what is happening outside of Lähn, or Wlen, which I am constantly told it is now called. Anyway, I have decided to go and see if Görlitz really is the new border between Germany and Poland. Some of the other Germans in Lähn have give me a little money to help pay for the trip as they are also eager for news.

I got a pass to go to Löwenberg no problem. It was cold but not freezing when I arrived. The council office was closed so I had to stay overnight in the Christian hospice. The next day the weather was worse but the council granted me my pass to walk to Görlitz so I carried on. It took one day to reach Lauben, where I stayed overnight in the evangelical vicarage. It was full of refugees waiting for their transport. It was much cleaner than the hospice in Löwenberg and the vicar's wife gave me an apple and bread for breakfast.

It was late in the afternoon when I reached Görlitz. Hundreds of people were gathered in the centre of town. As I approached I realised the people were queuing to cross the Old Town bridge. Four border guards let some people across, but most like me, were told to go home and wait for the official 'refugee' transport to take us to Germany. It was madness. I could clearly see across the river to the other side of the town. People were going about their afternoon business as if everything was normal. It was not even fifty yards away. It was such a shock to have it confirmed that the other side of the river was Germany but this side wasn't. A sudden scream made the crowd jump. It came from the riverbank. We rushed to look.

A large barge floated down the river towards us. In it, huddled together on a giant bed of straw, were scores of children ranging in ages from about two to fourteen. Even in the purpling half-light their hollow, vacant eyes, their swollen bellies, their bloated knees and puffy feet were clear to see – the familiar grisly signs of starvation.

Everyone started to shout at once. 'Are they alive?' 'Where have they come from?' 'They're breathing!' A handful of men slithered down the bank of the river in an attempt to reach them. 'Pass me a stick!' 'Throw me rope!' 'We must get them before they go over the weir!' A shot rang out loud and clear above our heads. Everyone froze.

One of the four border guards stood on the wall of the bridge. His gun was pointed at the men on the bank. 'Get away from the river's edge!' The men looked stunned. The guard said again, 'Move away!' All the while the barge drifted closer and closer towards the bridge and the weir beyond. The men on the bank shook their heads and reluctantly stepped away from the water's edge. Someone shouted, 'Look! They're floating over to the other side!' The lap-lapping water of the River Neisse shunted the barge to the far bank, where some men and women were scrambling down the bank. A rowing boat was pushed into the cold water. Anxious splashing. Desperate shouts. In the rapidly fading light the barge and all the children were hauled to the shore.

'At least they're in Germany,' I said to no one in particular. The woman next to me said, 'Yes, but the Russians are in charge over there now. It's not what it used to be like. Whatever happens, you don't want to be sent there when you get expelled.'

When I finally left the bridge and set out for Maria R's aunt's house, my home in Görlitz for the night, it had started to rain. The occasional feeble orange street lamp stopped me from getting completely lost. It was then, as I hurried in the wet and dark, that I saw Rolf. The bastard thief. His coat collar was turned up against the wet and cold and his winter cap was pulled low over his face. I'd recognise him anywhere.

He raced along the opposite side of the road and ducked down a side lane. I went to follow him when two Polish police ran up behind me. They demanded to know if I had seen someone matching Rolf's description. I showed them exactly where he'd gone. I never saw any of them again.

I stayed with Maria R's aunt overnight. It was so cold in her house we couldn't sleep, so we sat up all night talking. She said only a few months ago you could have walked over the bridge without any problem. She didn't understand why we couldn't now. Her old mother lived over the other side, she couldn't even visit her. The poor old woman was all alone. In peacetime her daughters used to swim across the river to visit her – a man tried to swim across only last week and they shot him.

When I finally got back to Lähn. Mama and Papa and Hilde were relieved to see me. I told everyone what I had seen.

Christmas was quiet.

January 3rd, 1946

January brought letters from Germany, full of bad news:

In the east, armed Czech women attacked Aunt Ulla, who was expecting. They repeatedly hit her womb with truncheons until she miscarried.

Mama's brother Julius was attacked on the streets in Luchtensee and killed.

Aunt Liesbeth was evacuated to Denmark with her children and locked in a train wagon for 56 hours, without food or water, forced to sit in their own toilet. In their wagon alone five people died – an older couple, a young man and two children from different families. Their bodies were left in the wagon for the whole trip. Slowing going ripe. Some poor children were so hungry they tried to eat bits of coal found in the carriage. There were no windows, only a slit at the top of the wagon walls, which let in a fraction of light and air. Only when they crossed the border into Denmark did they get help.

Uncle Karly was abducted in the Caucasus and taken to a labour camp where he died.

Cousin Trude died while fleeing Landeshut and was buried at the side of the road, no one knows where.

Some good news: a Polish lady teacher has moved into Mama's writing room and is making good use of Mama's piano. Meanwhile, we have started to occupy ourselves by knitting, even Mama knits, which is wonderful as it suggests she is much better.

We are knitting cardigans for our Polish ladies in exchange for butter. Papa is also industrious, he is helping our Polish newly-wed, who appears to be some sort of accountant and Papa is helping him with his bookkeeping. For this Papa earns us potatoes and milk and some rapeseed oil, courtesy of the Pole's customers.

June 24th, 1946

Mama is dead. I wasn't prepared. I thought she was getting better.

It was sunny this morning so Papa decided it was a good day to walk to Löwenberg to have a talk with the officials there. He wanted to ask for permission to apply for work in an administrative post. He isn't very happy being a porter and we also need more money – our rent has gone up and the utility bills are four times that of the Poles, and we need money for Mama's medicine now that Mrs B isn't here to pay for it. I agreed to go with him – for something to do and to keep him company. We were given permission to be away for two days.

When we finally got there it was afternoon – Löwenberg is fifteen miles away. The area officials were very unfriendly. They told Papa he was a good-for-nothing Kraut, who was lucky to have a job! They said if Papa complained one more time he would lose his job and his house. It was a very unpleasant experience. We stayed overnight in the hostel and left at first light to walk back in silence. When we reached Concordia it was midday. Mama was in bed. Hilde was sitting with her.

All the colour had gone from Mama's face and she looked very frail. We thought she was sleeping but she must have been awake because she opened her eyes and said quietly 'Any luck?' to Papa. He shook his head. She gave him a small smile and then closed her eyes. By the evening she was restless and her breathing became very shallow.

Despite the curfew Papa fetched nurse Mariela, who brought another Polish nurse with her, Martina. She was also very sweet. They said Mama had an infection. She sent us out of Mama's bedroom while they gave Mama a little wash and changed her nighty. When we came back into her room Mama's pillows were all plumped up. A small sidelight kept the room from being in darkness. Mama's head rested gently in the middle of the pillows. Her eyes were closed. She looked very small.

The three of us sat around her bed and chatted quietly. We talked about the mean men in Löwenberg, about Papa's garden and about who would be next in the village to be 'expelled'. Papa was at the top of the bed. He held Mama's small hand in his long fingers. Hilde and I were at the bottom.

Suddenly nurse Mariela, who was standing behind us with Martina, leaned over and tapped Hilde on the shoulder and said, 'I think it's time.' Hilde sobbed and looked at Mama. Papa gripped Mama's hand more tightly. Tears had formed in his eyes. I didn't understand. 'Time for what?' I said. Hilde had taken Mama's other hand. 'What is it?' I whispered, trying not to speak too loudly to avoid disturbing Mama. Hilde said between soft sobs, 'It's Mama.' I still didn't know what she meant. Hilde said, 'Oh, Toni, she's passed away.' I hadn't even realised. I hadn't even realised. How could I have not realised?

We had the burial in the cemetery on the hill. The blackcurrants were ripe all around us. The Polish priest was there and Hans, the ex-school teacher. Mariela and Martina came, and our Polish guests. There was no one left in the village who knew Mama – even the two Marias have been evacuated. Mama was only 58. Maria and Hubert weren't even allowed to come and they're only in Berlin. Hubert was so upset. Hansi is still in Russia.

This is the worst thing that has ever happened to me in my life.

Berlin, September 14th, 1946
Dear Papa,
Hansi is back. He is actually here. We'd heard a few crippled

and ailing Germans were being returned from the Russian slave camps to Berlin. It was the morning of September 10th. We went to meet a 20-car trainload of returning forced labourers. German Red Cross girls were also there to welcome them.

Armed guards rode on top of the sealed wagons. As soon as the train stopped, they jumped down and opened the cars. Thin, scabby-faced men in rags, begging for water or hysterically calling for help to remove the dead, tumbled out of the containers. Scores and scores of men, almost incapable of walking, collapsed on to the platform, and still more came out of the cars.

Eventually we spotted Hansi. He was almost unrecognisable. He didn't seem to know who we were or where he was. He said he thought he'd been travelling from the East for almost a week. He'd had no food or water and had to sleep beside a dead man for the whole week. I didn't count them but Hubert said the Red Cross girls removed more than twenty-five corpses from the train.

Hansi said the Russian guards and doctors did nothing to care for the sick on the trip. After months of malnutrition in the Russian labour camps the train was too much for many of them. Then before we could get him off the platform he collapsed. The Red Cross girls helped us take him to the hospital. He has not regained consciousness. They say he will not last the week. He doesn't know that Mama is dead.
Maria and Hubert

October 26th, 1946

There are hardly any of us left now.

Someone, maybe one of the Russian soldiers, built a swing near the summer house. Now in the warm late summer evenings I sit and swing back and forth by myself. It is good that Papa likes gardening, we have an abundance of fruit now: rich black and yellow and red currants, peaches and apricots – father is especially proud of his apricots.

A carpet of violets spreads beneath the trees to the clematis, which covers the back wall in a shower of brilliant crimson suns. There's the late sweet peas, bursts of pastel pockets, and the lily-of-the valleys by the summerhouse, running out of control as always. And, of course, father's roses. They border the perimeter walls in beds of bright pinks and yellows. Only Papa can create such beautiful blooms. Mama loved his roses. The delicate fragrance of the yellow ones in the balmy summer air is delicious. It reminds of that evening when Hubert told me he was going to join the Hitler Youth.

I hope I will be able to sleep when I go to bed, but I know it is not likely. No matter how exhausted I am, I can never fall sleep.

June 12th, 1947

Our names have been called – myself, Papa and Hilde's. We are finally being expelled to West Germany. We can take up to thirty kilos of luggage. Thirty kilos isn't that much for a lifetime but we have nothing anyway. Papa doesn't want to abandon Mama's grave but we have no choice. Our Polish mayor said, 'If Gerhart Hauptman, the famous Nobel prize winner, had to leave, then you have to.'

When we left to get our transport at eight the sky was an endless blue and the garden was full of colour. A delicate orange scent wafted from all the blooms as we walked away from Concordia. A small, simple horse and cart waited for us at the square. Papa was unimpressed but I was glad it was so simple. An old woman from one of the outlying farms was also waiting to leave. Nurse

Mariela came to wave us off. When we left the village, Hilde cried. I looked back. The square was deserted apart from Mariela, who was also crying.

We were taken down to Hirschberg – now called Jelenia Gora – in a truck. It is an all Polish town, as if it had never been German. You could only hear Polish being spoken. The occasional person wore a white armband with the letter 'N' on it. Someone said 'N' was the first letter in the Polish word for German – or was it Russian, I can't remember now.

We stayed in a refugee hostel until our big transport was ready to take us to Germany. There were about three hundred of us in the hostel. The hostel was clean and everyone seemed friendly, though no one talked much. After two days in Hirschberg we had to submit our luggage for checking just in case we were smuggling gold or millions of zlotys out of the country – we were only permitted to take 500 zlotys with us. I had very little in my blue case. It wouldn't take them long to check it.

Once everyone's luggage was checked and cleared – no one was carrying contraband cash, as it happens – we were put on the lorries. The trip took four days. We were not allowed to stop in what is now called the Eastern Zone of Communist Germany but had to travel straight to Berlin. Here we were allowed off and went to live with Maria in West Berlin.

I couldn't believe the state of Berlin when we got there, it is still in ruins. Many of the buildings are rubble. Whole districts have no lighting. Shelves in the shops are bare. Money is in occupation marks or something called a scar mark or a Rentenmark. Our zlotys are worthless. Almost everyone is gaunt and ill looking. 'Forget safe little Lähn. This is the real world!' Maria said angrily when we showed our shock.

Maria's flat is very small. Maria keeps it exceptionally tidy and has very few things. She sold everything she had on the black market to buy food, everything she said but her fur coat which she needs in winter as it is so cold. We'd soon find out. Papa hoped to find administrative work, but Maria laughed in his face when he said this. 'There is no "administrative" work and even if there was, absolutely no one would be interested in employing some hick, has-been civil servant from the East like you!'

Every day for three weeks Papa put on his only suit, which is much too baggy for him. He placed his Homburg hat on his head and looked for work. But Maria is right. There is no work to be found. The hundreds of thousand of Berliners and all the millions of German refugees from the East already have whatever jobs there are to be had. In the end Hubert found Papa work as a porter at the hospital where he works.

Papa was reluctant to take the post, much to Maria's fury. She told him to be grateful for what he got. She said most refugees had to be content with clearing rubble 'and someone with your lily white fingers wouldn't last long doing that, would you!' Even worse, she said, many men of his age were left to wander the streets and scavenge. We don't know what to say to Maria when she talks like this. So we say nothing.

It is wonderful to see Hubert. He says no matter how bad it is here we are lucky we are in the British and American zone and not in the Russian zone.

It is four weeks since Papa started at the hospital. Maria's flat has one bedroom. We three girls share that, Hubert and Papa sleep in the living room. There is a tiny bathroom and a tiny kitchen, which you can't sit in. She calls it a 'galley' kitchen. We eat very sparingly. Maria says by the time the rent and electricity and basic food is paid for there is absolutely no money left.

Maria says we will have to go to a refugee camp if we can't find work. She says we are not trying to help and she can't afford to keep us. But we are trying. Every day we put cardboard in the inside of our shoes to stop the dirt getting in and trudge the streets. We can't even find work clearing rubble as all the other refugees do that and won't share the work with anyone else. Some people have money. Some people have cars. But most people have nothing.

Every day when I wake up and find myself in Maria's tiny bedroom, in her tiny sterile flat, I have morbid thoughts and feel like crying. But I don't. I make myself think of the quote from Thomas Mann – 'For the sake of goodness and love, man shall let death have no sovereignty over his thoughts.' I will not let death have sovereignty over my thoughts.

Papa came home from the hospital all excited. One of his porter colleagues has a rich brother living in Argentina. He is offering to pay good money for a woman to go over and do his cooking and cleaning. In return she will get food and board and a good wage. Papa said he thought Hilde would be excellent for such a job.

Hilde has agreed to go to Argentina. Papa made all the arrangements through the telephone at the Post Office. The Argentinian German has already wired her ticket. She said to Papa and Hubert she was happy to go but she said to me that she was not. 'Why didn't Papa ask you or Maria if you wanted to be this man's housekeeper? Papa thinks just because I looked after Mama I'm not capable of doing anything else.' I said she shouldn't go if she didn't want to. She said she has to go. 'I'm twenty nine going on thirty. I can't have children and I have no skills and no money and it's clear Maria is not going to let me stay any longer. She hates me.' I said that Maria didn't hate her. But she shook her head. 'Maybe it'll work out. Maybe I'll like

Argentina. Maybe the work will not be just cooking and cleaning. Maybe the man will be nice and we'll get on. Maybe we'll even get married.'

Hilde has gone. I miss her already. Maria tells me every day I am not looking hard enough for work. Hubert tells her to lay off, but she doesn't. She says I am a lazy parasite. Just lately I have started to want to cry at the slightest thing, not just when I wake up in the morning. I will not give in to it. I will not.

Papa came home all excited from the hospital and asked me if I wanted to be a nurse. I thought maybe they were looking for nursing assistants at the hospital. He explained: the United Nations are helping 'displaced people' find work. He said they are funding a training scheme for German women to become nurses. He said he thought I would make a good nurse. He said lodging and food and training are provided and employment was guaranteed when the training is over. All I had to do was apply. I asked him where the training was to take place. He said in Great Britain. The British had destroyed our cities and slaughtered our soldiers. He wants me to go there? He said he'd thought of me because of my English. I said I would do it.

Now that I am leaving, Maria is nice to me. She even gave me a share of her potato ration – to build up my strength for the trip. Last night before we went to sleep she talked for the first time of Hansi's death. There had been no money to bury him so the hospital had him cremated.

She said he'd regained consciousness for a few days and talked about the camp – not the Russian camp but the German concentration camp in Dachau. He'd told her he'd been made to wear a pink triangle on his sleeve. She asked me if I understood the significance of his wearing the pink triangle. I said I did.

I asked her about the sketch book with the pictures of Georg in it. I wanted to know why she'd had it as it clearly belonged to

Hansi. She said she'd found the drawing pad in Hansi's room during one of Mama's big clean-ups, just sitting there. She'd hidden it in her room to stop anyone else discovering it. Then somehow Hilde had found it and shown it to Mama and Papa. Maria knew the truth would have devastated them, that's why she'd said the sketch pad was hers. We stopped talking after that. I think Maria would have made a very good nun.

I am three years away from being thirty. I am going by boat to Liverpool in Great Britain. All I am taking with me is one small blue suitcase, which has almost nothing in it.

From Liverpool I am to go to a college in Wales, where I will undergo an intensive English language course. Then I am to be sent to Edinburgh in Scotland. There I will train at Leith Hospital to be a nurse.

Maria says Edinburgh is the capital of Scotland. There is a castle there and many fine buildings. She says I will like it. Papa says there are art galleries and museums and theatres. He says I will like it. Hubert says the British are the enemy. He doesn't want me to go and is furious with Papa for suggesting it. He says Scottish men wear dresses and it rains all the time in Scotland. He says I will hate it. I say I am going. Finally, Hubert says if I must go, whatever I do, I must not marry a Scottish man. I tell him not to worry, that will never happen.

Since the end of the war about 3,000,000 people, mostly women and children and over-aged men, have been killed in eastern Germany and south-eastern Europe; about 15,000,000 people have been deported or had to flee from their homesteads and are on the road. About 25 per cent of these people, over 3,000,000, have perished. About 4,000,000 men and women have been deported to eastern Europe and Russia as slaves.

Gruesome Harvest, Ralph Franklin Keeling,
Institute of American Economics, 1947

The most offensive infringement of the right based on historical evolution and of any human right generally is to deprive populations of their right to occupy the country where they live by forcing them to settle elsewhere.

Albert Schweitzer, from his speech when he accepted the Nobel Prize for Peace (Oslo, November 4th, 1954).

Glossary

Am Ring	Literally means 'at the ring'. The 'ring' itself is the main central marketplace in Breslau, which dates back to the Middle Ages.
Beamte	Government official or civil servant.
Bezirksamt	Office of the local city council/authority.
Black Reichswehr	From the Schwarze Reichswehr, literally meaning Black Imperial army and the name for the illegal paramilitary groups created by the Germans during the Weimar Republic – raised despite restrictions imposed by the Versailles Treaty.
Bleib übrig!	From 'übrigbleiben', literally meaning to be left over or to remain. In the novel it means 'Stay alive!' or 'Don't give up!'
Blitzkrieg	Lightning war – this was a type of attack used by the Germans in World War II based on speed and surprise.
Blutbahn	'Bloody runway' is the runway built in the centre of Breslau during the siege – the 'bloody' makes reference to the large number of people killed by enemy fire while working on it.
Blut und Ehre	'Blood and Honour' is the Hitler Youth motto.

Bolshevik	Marxist Communist or revolutionary.
Brandkommandos	Slash and burn squads.
Bubikopf	'Bob' haircut.
Bund Deutscher Mädel (BDM)	The League of German Girls – part of the Hitler Youth organisation.
Deutsches Reich/ Drittes Reich	German Reich/Third Reich – these are the common names for Germany between 1933 and 1945, while it was led by Adolf Hitler and the National Socialist German Worker's Party (NSDAP).
Dienst Verpflichtung	War service duty.
Dummkopf	German slang for idiot.
Erledigt das Geschäft	The phrase literally means 'finished with the business' or 'put to rest'. Here it is used in conjunction with 'ausprobiert' as in 'ausprobiert und erledigt das Geschäft', which translates as 'tried and tested' or 'done and dusted'.
FAMO	'Fahrzeug und Motorenbau GmbH' was the name of the main German manufacturer of tractors and tanks at the time (the name is derived from the first two letters of the two main words).
Fehme	A secret German nationalist organisation.
Feldpost	The German military mail service.
Führer	'Leader' – a title which Hitler took for himself as in 'Leader of the German Reich and People'.

Geheime Staatspolizei	The full name for the German Secret State Police or the Gestapo (Geheime Staatspolizei).
Adolf Hitler	Adolf Hitler was the absolute dictator of Germany from 1934 to 1945.
Heil Hitler	'Hail Hitler' – after 1935 it became customary when meeting someone in Nazi Germany to give the Hitler salute and say the words 'Heil Hitler'.
Herbert Norkus	Herbert Norkus was a Hitler Youth member who was murdered by German Communists. He became a model and martyr for the Hitler Youth and was widely used in Nazi propaganda.
Ivans	A nickname referring to the Russian Soldiers by Germans during WWII.
Jahrhunderthalle	The famous 100 year exhibition hall in Breslau.
Jid	Racist slang for Jewish person.
Kaufhaus/Haus	Department store/store, as in Kaufhaus Barasch and Kaufhaus Wertheim.
Kaiser	Emperor.
Ketten-Spurhunde	The nickname for the German Military police meaning 'chained dogs'.
Kleingarten	An allotment.
Kletschkau prison	The main prison in Breslau.
Kohlrabi	A type of German swede or turnip.
KPD	Kommunistische Partei Deutschlands – the German Communist Party.

Konditorei	A cake shop.
Königs-Wusterhausen	A city which lies south east of Berlin.
Krupp	A famous German manufacturer of steel and ammunition and armaments.
Lebensborn Project	'Lebensborn' is old German for 'the Fount of Life' – it was the name of a Nazi programme set up by SS leader Heinrich Himmler. On the surface it provided maternity homes and financial assistance to the wives of SS members and unmarried mothers. However, its overall purpose was to reverse the decline in the German population and increase the Germanic/Nordic population of Germany. To this end, the organisation carried out many secret and disturbing practices.
Luftfeld	Airfield – also sometimes used as the abbreviated form of Luftwaffe-Feld-Division ie: the German airforce.
Nähmaschine	The German nickname for the Polikarpov U2 or Po2, a general-purpose Soviet biplane and made a rattling noise similar to a sewing machine.
Nazi	A common English term, which is derived from the letters Na and Zi in NazionalsoZialist – the German name for a member of the National Socialist German Workers' Party under Adolf Hitler.

Nazi Germany	The common name for Germany between 1933 and 1945, while led by Adolf Hitler.
Nazi Party	The common name for the National Socialist German Worker's Party (Nationalsozialistische Deutsche Arbeiterpartei or NSDAP) led by Adolf Hitler between 1933 and 1945.
Oma /Opa	Nickname for grandmother and grandfather, as in grandma and grandpa/granny and grandad etc.
Ost	"East' was often used in reference to a forced labourer from one of the occupied Eastern territories.
Polak	Racist slang for a Polish person.
Rentenmark	A currency issued in 1923 to stop the hyperinflation of 1922 and 1923 in Germany. The last Rentenmark notes were valid until 1948.
Reich	An empire/nation/realm or 'imperial' or 'sovereign' as in sovereign empire.
Reichsmark	The Reichsmark became the new legal tender in 1924, equal in value to the Rentenmark. The Reichsmark (RM) was the currency in Germany from 1924 until June 20, 1948.
Reichstag	'Imperial Diet' – the parliament of Germany until 1945. The main chamber of the German parliament is now called the Bundestag ('Federal Diet'), but the

building in which it meets is still called the Reichstag.

Scheisse	Vulgar German slang for shit.
Schutzstaffel (SS)	'Shield Squadron' or Praetorian Guard' the SS grew from a small paramilitary unit to a powerful force that served Hitler. Its officers numbered almost a million (both on the front lines and as political police) and managed to exert as much political influence in the Third Reich as the Wehrmacht, Germany's regular armed forces.
Sieg Heil	'Hail Victory' was a common call at political rallies, where it was shouted in unison by thousands.
Sonderbehandlung	'Special treatment' – this has a negative connotation because it was used as a euphemistic camouflaging term for killing people in Nazi Germany.
Sturmabteilung (SA)	'Storm Detachment' but is usually translated as 'stormtroopers'. A paramilitary organization of the Nazi Party. SA men were often called Brownshirts because of the colour of their uniforms; this distinguished them from the Schutzstaffel (SS), who wore black and brown uniforms. The SA was very important to Adolf Hitler's rise to power, but was effectively superseded by the SS after the Night of the Long Knives (June/July 1934).

Schwarze Tod	'Black Death' was the nickname by Germans for the Soviet Il-2 Shturmovik, a low-altitude, heavily armed and armoured tankbuster aircraft.
Suchkommandos	Units deployed to search for the dead on the Kanth Death March.
Teur	Expensive.
Völkerscher Beobachter	'People's Observer' – the newspaper of the Nazi Party from 1920. For twenty-five years it formed part of the official public face of the Nazi party.
Volksstürm	'People's Storm' or 'People's Assault' was a German national militia-cum-homeguard founded on Adolf Hitler's orders on October 18, 1944, made up of conscripted males between the ages of 16 to 60 years not already serving in some military unit.
Wehrmacht	'Defence force' was the name for the armed forces of Germany from 1935 to 1945. It included the Heer (army), the Kriegsmarine (navy) and the Luftwaffe (air force).
Weimar Republic	The name given by historians to the parliamentary republic established in 1919 in Germany to replace the imperial form of government, and named after Weimar, the place where the constitutional assembly took place. Its official name was still Deutsches Reich (German Empire). 1933 is usually seen

	as the end of the Weimar Republic and the beginning of Hitler's Third Reich.
Weinstube	A wine bar.
Würstchen	A small German sausage.

Acknowledgments

I am indebted to the following authors and books: Norman Davies and Roger Moorehouse, *Microcosm, Portrait of a Central European City*; Sebastian Siebel-Achenbach, *Lower Silesia from Nazi Germany to Communist Poland, 1942-1949*; Alfred-Maurice de Zayas, *A Terrible Revenge, The Ethnic Cleansing of the East European Germans*; Beata Maciejewska, *Wroclaw – History of the City*; Dr Johannes Kaps, translated by Gladys H Hartinger, *Tragedy of Silesia 1945–1946 (A Documentary Account with a Special Survey of the Archdiocese of Breslau)*; Ralph Franklin Keeling (Institute of American Economics), *Gruesome Harvest – The Costly Attempt to Exterminate the People of Germany*; Fourth International (Vol.2 no 8), October 1941, *The Life of German Political Prisoners*; Antony Beevor, *Berlin, The Downfall, 1945*; Regina Mari Shelton, *To Lose A War, Memories of a German Girl*; Anthony McElligot, *The German Urban Experience, 1900-1945*.

Marianne Wheelaghan was born and brought up in Scotland. She left home at seventeen to travel, something she'd always wanted to do. After twenty years of being on the move, she returned to settle in her home town of Edinburgh. When she is not writing, she is running her online writing school. The Blue Suitcase is her first novel to be published by Pilrig Press.